DAUGHTER OF RA

BLOOD OF RA BOOK TWO

M. SASINOWSKI

KINGSMILL PRESS

ISBN 978-1-7324467-3-1

ISBN 978-1-7324467-2-4 (ebook)

This is a work of fiction. Names, characters, and incidents are the product of the author's imagination, except in the case of historical figures and events, which are used fictitiously.

For Vera

PART 1

VALEDICTION

RA, grant me strength…

My feet pound the marble as I charge the gilded stairs to the door of the sleeping chamber. My heart rings against my chest, echoing the clamor of the palace bells. The bitter scent of ash that hangs in the air sweetens the taste of bile in the back of my throat.

With a snarl, the man leaps forward, and his sword scythes with vicious intent. Weaponless and unable to parry, I dive under his blade. The man reels, surprised at missing his mark, but there is no hesitation in his next move.

He cuts down with his right. The blade scours only marble as I roll aside. His balance upset, he staggers for a heartbeat. It is all the time I need. My fist rams into his face, the brunt of my blow doubled by my fury and fear for my kin.

Blood erupts from his nose and he wavers, eyes glazed. He never recovers as I move in and thrust my fingers to his throat. He crumples, eyes bulging.

I snatch the sword from his limp grasp an instant before another blade lashes out. With a sharp clash, steel meets steel, and I deflect the savage slice. He turns full circle, leaps and strikes. I parry and counter to his head. When he lifts his blade to defend, I change the angle of my attack, dropping low. My weapon cuts through his thigh, cleaving bone. I reach the door at the end of the hall before he drops to the ground, screaming, clutching his useless limb.

I storm into the sleeping chamber. My breath catches in my throat at the sight. My wife, dagger in hand, besieged by three invaders. My rage swells at the crimson lines on her skin, her wounds numerous and deep. I roar and charge. All eyes lock onto mine, one pair swells with hope, the others flare with hatred. Two men turn to intercept.

We meet in full stride. The first to reach me is the first to die. He moves to defend, and our blades meet in a sharp clash. I spin my weapon and lock my grip, slicing the blade deep across his torso as we pass. He gasps, and the blood bursts out. The second man is on me in an instant, knuckles white on the hilt of his sword. With a growl he charges, cutting low with his left, then spinning about, his sword screaming to my neck. Our blades weave a dance of liquid fire in the glow of the torches, the clash of steel on steel ringing into the night. Then it is over. His hands grasp his throat, blood seeping between his fingers.

I spin to face the third man.

Time stops.

The attacker's blade sinks into the soft flesh beneath my beloved's breasts. He tears the sword free, and she slumps to her knees, clutching the ghastly wound.

My mind rejects my sight.

My soul shatters.

The howl of a wounded beast thunders through the chamber as I close the distance between us in a single leap. The murderer draws back, his sword raised, but his fate is sealed. I know not when I strike the killing blow. The blood flows freely, and the man writhes on the ground, clutching his gut, his sword in my hand.

I sink to my knees at my beloved's side.

Hathor... I mouth her name, the sight before me robbing me of my speech.

"Horus..." Her voice is thin. She coughs, and red spittle mars her lips.

"Be still... do not speak." My eyes are glued to her face. The radiance of her golden skin dims with every slowing beat of her heart. The delicate lines of her face are twisted with pain and fear.

My hand presses to her chest as her life weeps from her, warm and silky between my fingers. "The healers will be here soon." My voice sounds distant to my own ears.

"Horus," she says again. I know the words before she utters them. My eyes beg her to remain silent.

"They took him," she whispers, "they took Imset."

Her pleading eyes turn glassy, but before she leaves, a mother's final appeal.

"Find him... Bring back our son."

Our gazes meet in a last embrace, then she is gone.

My vision fades. The pounding in my ears surges like a wave.

I am Horus.

Son of Isis and Osiris.

I shall know no—

The sound of my son's name rips out of my throat, drowning the wailing of the alarms.

———

"IMSET!"

The scream passed through Alyssa's lips, its echoes erupting like cracks of thunder in her head.

Imset...

Her body shuddered as the rush of adrenaline receded. She swallowed, trying to flush down the taste of the ash and bile that lingered in her throat. The memories began to fade from her mind.

No.

Not memories.

She pressed her fists against her temples, willing her mind and body to reject the onslaught of the—

Dreams.

Just... dreams.

Her phone alarm rang again. She silenced it. Slowly, too slowly, the gilded marble columns of Horus's bed chamber transformed into the cluttered back seat of an SUV.

Alyssa rubbed her eyes, trying to focus on the narrow cobblestone street leading down to the pier. The sun had just crested the red-thatched roofs and the spires rising above Prague's old town, painting the west bank of the Vltava river a fiery orange.

She leaned her head into the seat and sucked in air, trying to calm herself. She focused on her breathing, forcing all other thoughts from her mind.

Her phone dinged with a text message.

HISTORICAL STACKS. 10 MINS.

Finally.

She reached for her tablet in the passenger seat and pulled up the schematic of the Prague National Library. She studied the image one more time, memorizing the building layout. *I sure hope the floor plan is right.* She craned her neck up to the small terrace directly above her. *Actually, I really hope I don't need to find out.*

Either way, soon she'd know whether the ten-hour drive following the latest clue will have been worth it, or whether it would turn into just another notch in the tally of dead leads about the Society, the secretive group of ultra-rich crackpots obsessed with the Hall of Records and the ancient crystal her father had found under the Sphinx. After four fruitless months in Zurich and over much of Europe, she had stumbled upon a three-decade-old thesis in Rotterdam written by a Czech historian who had agreed to meet her here. She wasn't holding out too much hope, but it was one of the few references she and Clay had been able to dig up that even hinted at the existence of the Society. Not to mention her first warm lead since starting this hunt.

Alyssa slipped on her sneakers and opened the door. She breathed deeply, savoring the crisp morning breeze against her skin and stretching the kinks from her neck before setting out along the deserted cobblestone street.

She turned left and trotted up the wide stairs to the main entrance of the library. A scattering of students lazed on the steps, Starbucks cups glued to their palms. No one seemed to pay her any attention as she made for the giant copper doors and entered.

Old world mixed with new in the great hall that served as the reception area. Ornate columns rose from a tiled chessboard floor up to the fifty-foot Gothic ceiling while huge high-definition monitors hung on wood paneled walls, cycling through images of paintings and multi-language informational blurbs. A bespectacled woman perched behind a tall counter, and a guard dressed in a blue uniform glanced up. Alyssa caught the guard's eye, and he offered a slight, unenthusiastic nod. The woman retreated to the computer screen, showing even less interest. Alyssa gave the guard a quick smile and ducked into the women's bathroom across from the reception desk.

The scent of bleach and citrus invaded her nostrils as she slipped into the handicapped stall. Cracked tiles lined the walls, and a dated porcelain sink and commode crowded the small space, but at least they looked freshly cleaned. *Nothing like morning hygiene in a public restroom.* She sighed as the thought of her oversized tub in Cairo knotted her chest. *Is a bathtub and a clean toilet too much to ask for someone who prevented a global disaster?* she thought, chuckling wryly.

It didn't take long after the near miss of the Horus epidemic for the Society to regroup. Despite attempts to contain the details about the ancient genes in Alyssa's blood and their role in developing the cure, the information got leaked to the news. Her father was furious since it had made her a prime target for any factions of the Society that still remained operational, turning her current pursuit into a dangerous game of cat and mouse. Kade insisted on her coming back home to Cairo, but what good would that do? Still… she missed her old man.

The knot in her chest squeezed tighter. Alyssa slumped over the sink and clenched the cool porcelain. She lifted her head and scrutinized her reflection. Her skin looked dreadful, and she needed a haircut. Badly. Her split ends had split ends on them. Crisscrossing most of Europe, bunking in an SUV for months, hadn't done either one any favors.

She studied her eyes. Perhaps it was only the way the fluorescent lights reflected in her irises, but their deep hazel seemed to have softened to a golden brown. The strange dreams… or memories… or visions… or whatever has been messing with her mind hadn't been the only unsettling things happening inside her. Since her exposure to Thoth's weapon in the Hall of Records, she'd been noticing… *developments*. Like being able to hear conversations from across the room, or making out the fine print in a newspaper at the far end of a bus. It was both thrilling and unsettling.

Kinda like starting puberty again at seventeen… and without having some girl on Quora to tell you you're not the only one… and that boys dig those changes.

Boys…

She smiled for the first time that day when she pictured Paul's playful grin. Thankfully, he had fully recovered from his injuries, and his second year at Oxford was in full swing. He had just declared his concentration. *Medical physics and molecular biochemistry.* She chuckled. *And here I thought archaeology was a mouthful.*

Between his study schedule and her travels, they hadn't

been able to see each other since Cairo, but they texted daily and talked as often as they could. Still... it didn't seem enough.

Alyssa shook off the thoughts and turned on the faucet. She splashed some cold water on her face then lifted her sweatshirt over her head and cleaned up as well as she could, birdbath-style, and brushed her teeth. She slipped the sweatshirt back on and brushed out her hair then pulled it into a ponytail. She capped off her morning hygiene by spritzing on a dash of perfume.

That's as good as it's gonna get.

She left the restroom and climbed a flight of stairs to the historical stacks section on the mezzanine level. Row after row of bookshelves heaved under the weight of the old volumes. She marveled at the knowledge housed inside this hall. Each of the shelves seemed to go on forever.

A short man stepped out from one of the narrow aisles. He was in his mid-fifties, dressed in blue slacks and a gray, button-down sweater worn thin at the elbows. He gazed kindly at Alyssa through a pair of black-rimmed glasses.

"Alyssa?" he asked when she approached him. It sounded like *Aleesa.*

"Dr. Danek," she replied and held out her hand.

"Please, call me Konrad," he said, his voice gentle despite the hard, rolled *r.* His handshake was warm and clammy. Alyssa forced herself not to flinch at the touch and managed to tug her lips into a smile. "Thank you for meeting me, Konrad."

"Ha, it is not often that I get email about thesis I wrote thirty years ago," he said and pointed to a chair at one of the long tables. "Sit, sit."

Alyssa sank into the chair and wiped her hand on her jeans.

He seemed nice enough, but the small hairs on her arms stirred and lifted whenever she caught his eyes.

"Your trip to Prague, it was good, yes?"

Ten-hour nonstop drive from Amsterdam, she thought. She simply nodded in response.

"You had chance to see our city?"

"I have not," she replied, folding her hands. "I came here just to meet with you."

"Yes, yes. Of course," he said and pulled up in a chair beside her. "You want to ask questions about Society and Eric Cayce?"

Alyssa blinked. *It's Edgar—not Eric—Cayce.* She opened her mouth, but the expression on his face stalled her. At first she thought she had only imagined it, but it was his scent that had caused her apprehension. He smelled of... anxiety... fear. Her keen hearing had picked up the strain in his voice, the subconscious tension to his words.

Konrad's gaze slid away from hers for a moment and rested on the door at the far end of the hall, just long enough for her to notice. Uneasiness washed over her, through her. She tensed up as if to stand, but he placed a clammy hand on her arm, his fingers tightening, urging her to stay.

"We have much to discuss," he said, his eyes moving to the wide stairs leading to the lobby. He gave the slightest shake of his head. Alyssa compelled herself to lean back, and he patted her arm.

"How much do you know about Cayce?" he asked.

"He was an American psychic." Alyssa forced the anxiety from her voice. "He was fascinated with the occult—and with Atlantis."

Konrad nodded approvingly. "In his early years, Cayce was greatly influenced by Helena Blavatsky, a Russian occultist. In 1877, she published book called *Isis Unveiled*."

"*Isis Unveiled*?"

"It was hailed a master key to mysteries of ancient and modern sciences, and theology. It included description of mythical continent of Lemuria, which, until the mid-nineteenth century was the accepted scientific theory."

"Is that what sparked Cayce's fascination with Atlantis?" Alyssa asked.

"The book touched on many controversies of that time." He held up a finger. "Darwin's theory of evolution, yes? Another is her description of mythical beings—*Masters*—who have undergone spiritual and physical transformations."

Alyssa tensed at the words: *Spiritual and physical transformations?*

"What kind of transformations?" she asked.

"Sadly, not much of it is known. Nevertheless, the book served as blueprint for Cayce's claims about advanced race that influenced development of mankind." He lowered his voice. "It was promise of channeling power of this advanced race that inspired likeminded individuals to gather together into group that became Society." He leaned forward. "Individuals who were wealthy enough to fund his research."

Alyssa processed his words. "Are there copies of this book?"

"That *was* my reason for asking you to come here. Fortunately, this library holds one of three last surviving examples of original manuscript," he said. "The document is in basement."

He pointed to a door at the far end of the hall. "We can take stairwell."

Alyssa didn't need the silent warning in his eyes. Her mind and body were on full alert.

She slid her chair back and stood when she spotted the man on the stairwell. His casual clothes belied the predatory gait and flinty eyes as he stalked toward them.

Konrad leaped up. "Run! There are more downstairs!" he cried out and charged the man on the stairs.

The man sidestepped Konrad's clumsy attempt to stall him and drove a fist into the small man's gut, dropping him like a stone.

Alyssa leaped across the table and dashed between the stacks, the flinty-eyed man at her heels. She heard a door open and the sound of footsteps rushing to the far end of the stacks. A moment later, another man appeared in the aisle, cutting off her escape. He was short and bald, with a neck like a bulldog.

She staved off panic, her mind racing faster than her legs. She looked desperately for a break in the bookshelves between her and the man before her, but she was trapped in a tunnel of books with flinty-eyes breathing down her neck.

She glanced up, inspiration striking.

Alyssa forced her legs to pump even faster. The man at the far end of the aisle braced himself, a cold smile on his face, as if welcoming the challenge.

In mid-stride, Alyssa launched to the bottom shelf with her left foot, then to the next higher shelf across the narrow aisle with her right. The man's smile wilted into an expression of bewilderment as she bounced between the shelves, climbing higher with every stride until she reached the top. The short man jumped after her, but his hand found only air.

Alyssa balanced on the top of the huge bookshelf. She spotted the tall doors to the outside.

The terrace!

She jumped to the neighboring bookshelf then the next, leaping across the aisles, chased by the curses of her pursuers as they doubled back in the aisle. She jumped from the last bookshelf onto a table and rolled to the floor. As she gained her feet, a hand clamped around her throat.

"That will be quite enough," the voice of a third man rasped into her ear, the Eastern European accent turning his *w* into a *v*.

The thud behind her came without warning. The man slumped to the floor. She spun.

"Knowledge is power, yes?" Konrad said, grinning, holding a massive book. "Now, go!"

Konrad's grin twisted. The flinty-eyed man appeared behind him, a bloody knife in his hand. Konrad sagged, his gaze locked on Alyssa.

The images popped into her head unbidden, flashing across her vision.

The attacker's blade sinks into my beloved's chest.

She slumps to her knees, the crimson stain growing larger.

Alyssa's senses sharpened. The breathing of the second man behind her gave him away. She dropped into a crouch and twisted, keeping one leg extended, sweeping his feet from under him. He yelped and tumbled to the ground, his head cracking into the slate floor.

Flinty-eyes charged her with the knife, his face warped in a snarl. She stepped aside and spun behind him. She drove the side of her foot behind his knee then grabbed his hair and yanked him to the ground, trapping his legs beneath him. She crushed his knife hand under her right foot. Her heart pounded in her ears as adrenaline surged through her body.

The sound of alarms fills my head.

Hathor.

Imset...

She dropped and drove her left shin into his throat. He wheezed, eyes bulging.

You took my son from me!

He flailed, trying to break her crushing hold, but Alyssa didn't relent her pressure. The man's movements turned more desperate then slowed.

A voice broke through her red haze. "Stop!" Alyssa faced the source, panting.

The security guard rushed up the wide stairs.

She bounced up.

The man on the ground gasped, sucking in great gulps of air, his face aghast with fear.

"Stop!" the guard yelled again.

She took off across the hall. The guard tried to block the stairs, but she leaped on a table and onto the stone balustrade between the mezzanine level and the lobby. She sped along the railing and through the tall door onto the terrace. She jumped over the railing and crashed onto the roof of her SUV, rolling down the windshield and the hood.

Alyssa dove inside and started the car. She threw it in gear and peeled out of the parking spot. Breathless, she slung the car onto the river walk and accelerated hard, swerving before the rear tires gained traction. She kept driving, her brain on autopilot, eyes darting to the rearview mirror, until she was sure nobody had followed her.

She pulled into a deserted parking lot and stopped.

Alyssa sat with her hands locked tight around the wheel, staring dead ahead, her breathing growing heavier. Her vision blurred. She didn't realize she'd been crying until she felt the sweatshirt pasted against her chest. The trembling came unsought, welling up from deep inside, as buried memories threatened to claw their way to the surface.

She covered her head with her hands, struggling to keep her composure. Slowly, the daze cleared, and the trembling stopped, allowing her to gather her thoughts. Alyssa inhaled deeply then pulled out of the parking lot and headed for the expressway.

———

Dr. Yuri Korzo pushed the thick glasses up the bridge of his nose and leaned closer to the display of the high-throughput DNA sequencer. A bead of sweat rolled down his right temple and clung to his jaw for a second before dropping to the workbench below.

He wiped it off, absentmindedly, his gloved finger leaving a wet trail on the black, smooth surface. He studied the output. For several seconds the synthesized sequence appeared stable, the nucleotides building on the molecular scaffolding he had designed from the original sample. He held his breath. Then the double helix collapsed on itself like a house of cards.

Damn it!

He bit back another curse and an even greater urge to put

his fist through the thin monitor. Four months of working on duplicating the genes he had found in the girl's blood, and he was not one step closer. The sequences were too long, too complex to synthesize. At this rate it would be years before he'd see any real progress.

Years I don't have.

He glanced at the time. Today could change everything, but they were late with the update. Late was never a good sign.

After Professor Geoffrey Baxter's death, the Society asked him to continue the American scientist's work, and Yuri jumped at the opportunity. Though well aware of the consequence of his failure, the temptation was too great. And it wasn't only the money that drove his decision. The image of the ancient bioweapon reacting to Alyssa Morgan's genes was etched into his mind as if he had just seen it yesterday and not four months ago. It was molecular poetry. Beauty and power. Rather than ravaging the girl's DNA, the lethal weapon displayed the most striking example of symbiosis he had ever seen. Since he first witnessed it, he knew he would not rest until he discovered everything about it.

The final motive for taking on this task was even more personal, and darker, one for which he needed to stay close to the Society, no matter the cost.

They will pay for what they took from me.

The grief threatened to surface when the phone rang. He forced the emotion down and answered the phone.

"The girl escaped," the voice on the other end said.

This time he didn't bite back a second curse.

"We had the exits blocked. She—"

He screamed and threw the phone across the laboratory. He sank onto the lab stool.

Not for the first time, he questioned the wisdom of his decision to accept the Society's offer. He forced himself to calm down. He'd known it was going to be difficult. They had been forced to abandon the research lab with minutes notice to escape the raid. He barely had time to copy the sequences onto a thumb drive before Interpol swarmed the place. Thanks to his quick thinking, he had the blueprint of what he was after, but reconstructing and synthesizing entire genes was another story all together.

He planted his elbows on the bench and pressed his face into his palms. He had to succeed. His thirst for revenge drove him, motivated him more than their threats, more than the thrill of discovery, even more than the money.

He lost track of time. The sound of the door closing behind him snapped him out of his thoughts. He turned and stared into the most striking pair of eyes he had ever seen. Deep, golden irises gazed back at him, appraising him with a sense of bemused curiosity, like a master appraising a new pet. He should have felt insulted, but instead, he found her gaze hypnotic, both irresistible and impossible to hold.

The woman entered the lab. She moved with a leonine grace, the long white chiffon dress fluttering as it traced the fluid movements of her lithe form.

"Dr. Yuri Korzo," she said. It was a statement, not a question.

He slowly found his voice. "How... how did you get in here?"

She approached and studied the display.

"This… this is confidential data," he stammered. "You cannot—"

"The HOXB allele is disrupting the beta exon, causing a loss of function. The genetic sequence also lacks the transcription factor binding sites you were expecting."

He stared at her slack-jawed. "How… how can you know?"

She lifted a vial filled with a red liquid.

When he didn't move, she said. "Run your analysis on this."

Yuri felt himself unable to move.

The woman's lips tensed for the briefest moment. "Do as I say."

Yuri flinched at the admonition. He grasped the vial and moved to the sequencer. He pipetted a small amount of the red fluid into the machine then keyed in the start cycle.

After several moments, the data flickered on the display. Yuri's brain took a moment to make sense of what his eyes saw. The genetic markers of this sequence matched the genetic markers of the girl almost perfectly.

"Where did you get this?" he breathed.

"I know the reward promised to you by the Society if you succeed in synthesizing the ancient genetic elements that you found in the girl's blood," the woman replied. "I also know the price of failure." She held out her hand for the vial.

Yuri gripped the vial tightly. "What do you want from me?"

"You want to make them pay for what they have done."

"What are you—?"

The woman pointed to the vial in his hand. "You will get as much of this as you need to complete your task—and to have your revenge."

Yuri's mind reeled. "The blood is only one part of the

process. To unlock it completely, we also require the ancient bioweapon."

"And you shall have it."

"How?"

The woman remained silent, regarding him with perfect posture.

Yuri contemplated. Finally, he asked, "And what do you want in return?"

The woman's lips curved into a thin smile.

ALYSSA PULLED her car into a parking spot at the MediaMarkt electronics store. She waited for several minutes, scanning the lot for anything unusual before hopping out. She had traded the SUV for another vehicle since the incident in Prague two weeks ago and continued to stay on the move and off the grid as much as possible. She had kept her phone turned off for fear of being tracked. Her only means of communication had been daily emails to her dad and Paul sent from electronics stores or Internet cafes.

A week ago she received the message she'd been desperately waiting and hoping for. It was from Konrad. He survived the stabbing and had been released from the hospital. Apparently, the three men had arrived just before she did and coerced him into collaborating with them. Despite what could have happened, Alyssa was too thankful and happy to hold a grudge against the old man—too many people had been hurt because of her.

Her dad and Paul wanted to know all about what happened, of course. And, of course, she didn't tell them the whole story. There was no reason to worry them more than they already were.

She stepped through the sliding glass doors of the store, and her senses were assailed by a torrent of humanity and electronic noise and images. Hundreds of TV screens crowded endless aisles edge-to-edge, playing the latest movies and live high-definition streams. A medley of a dozen songs blared concurrently from speakers that lined the entire back wall of the store. To her left, shoppers pried and prodded any type of electronic appliances, large and small. Alyssa resisted her urge to turn on her heel. Instead, she turned right and headed for the section with the laptops.

As she passed the row of the TVs, one of the images caught her attention. She did a double take.

Is that the museum?

She stopped and stared at the broadcast. It *was* her dad's museum! She stared at the video and tried reading the story captions, but it was like trying to make sense of a goulash of consonants and vowels, sprinkled with random dashes and dots.

"Excuse me." She tapped a middle-school-aged girl on her shoulder. The young girl glanced up from underneath the visor of a pink baseball cap and took out one of her earbuds. "Do you speak English?" Alyssa asked.

"Ya know it," the girl replied with a perfect California sitcom accent.

Alyssa pointed at the TV. "What are they saying?"

The girl took out the other earbud and listened for a few

moments. "Something about a break-in at a new museum in Cairo—I think."

Alyssa felt the blood drain from her face. Before the startled girl had a chance to react, Alyssa rushed to the nearest laptop and popped up a web browser. She clicked on the news link.

Her breath caught in her throat when she read the headline:

NEW CAIRO MUSEUM TARGETED IN ATTACK.

Her hand trembled as she scrolled through the story, scanning it.

"...Cairo's newest National Museum of Archaeology was targeted in an attack on Friday morning... The Egyptian military has secured the building and is preventing onlookers from loitering in its vicinity... Clues remain scarce, but social media has been quick to put forth a multitude of suspects... employees of the museum, foreign governments, and a 'psychotic billionaire cult' who may have played a role in the outbreak of the Horus virus several months ago... The minister of antiquities has issued a statement that the museum shall remain closed for the foreseeable future pending further investigation... This unusually coordinated and violent attack that left several individuals seriously injured..."

Alyssa whimpered. She raced out of the store and into the parking lot. Her hands trembled as she fumbled for the keys, and she unlocked the car. She snatched her phone from the glovebox and powered it on.

Come on, come on! Her palm tapped against the door as the phone booted up. After what seemed like an eternity, the home screen appeared. The instant the cellular connection established, a flurry of text message and voicemail notifications appeared. She hit the speed-dial for her dad's mobile.

He answered on the second ring.

"Dad!" she cried. "Are you okay?"

"I'm fine, Ally," he said. "I'm all good."

She exhaled a breath she didn't know she was holding, then she crumpled into the seat and began sobbing as everything that happened over the last few weeks caught up with her all at once. "I was so worried. When I read what happened…" Her voice choked with tears.

"I'm so sorry," he said. "I tried letting you know right away. I left you messages. They weren't going through."

"I know, I know… I'm so glad you're okay." She paused. "The crystal?"

"They got it," Kade replied. "I'm sorry."

Alyssa's chest tightened.

They got the crystal?

"Ally…" Kade wavered. "Something else happened. Something bad."

Like that's not bad enough?

"There was an attack at the genetics institute."

"What?" she gasped. "When? Is Kamal all right? Did anybody get hurt?"

"Kamal is fine. It happened a couple weeks ago. Some people got hurt, but they're fine now. The ministry has been trying to keep it quiet. They wanted to avoid a panic."

He hesitated then added, "Samples of the virus were stolen."

Alyssa's hand clamped around the phone.

"A couple weeks ago? The virus? But Kamal promised to destroy—"

"He kept samples. In case of an outbreak. The government wanted to be prepared."

"Did you know about it?" she asked, an edge to her voice, her concern temporarily forgotten.

"No, of course not," Kade replied. "I would not have allowed it. The ministries raised the alert. They are worried about a potential bio-attack."

Alyssa tried to make sense of the onslaught of information. "First the institute, now the museum. Is it the Society?"

"I don't know," Kade said.

"If there is another outbreak, they may need more of my blood."

"Coming to Cairo is the last thing I want you to do—for your safety. But I know I can't talk you out of it." He paused. "I will be glad to see you."

Alyssa's smile was distracted. "Me too."

"How are you holding up?"

"Just peachy," she replied, trying to keep the sarcasm out of her voice.

"Are you safe?"

Alyssa glanced out at the balding security guard lumbering along the parking lot. He gave her a friendly wave.

"I've got my own private security." Alyssa returned the wave.

"Are you eating enough?"

"Daaad…" She suddenly realized how hungry she was. She spotted a box of Pop Tarts in the back seat and reached for it. Her shoulders slumped when she found it empty. She tossed it aside, sighing.

"Ally," Kade said.

"What?"

"Be careful."

"I've been staying low—and on the move."

"Something is happening. I don't know what, but you have to stay sharp."

Alyssa exhaled. "I'll see you soon."

She ended the connection and put the phone in her pocket. She sat in the seat for a few minutes before she started the car and headed for the airport.

———

Dr. Yuri Korzo's palm was a white-knuckled vise around the handle of the metal briefcase on the passenger seat. He pulled up the armored Cadillac Escalade to the dimly lit portico of the Cairo estate and stepped out, lifting the lethal cargo with him. The cool desert air did little to stifle the panic churning inside his gut, threatening to spew out all over the rosebushes decorating the sandstone driveway.

It will be over soon.

He dabbed his forehead with a handkerchief and scurried to the ornate entrance, clutching the briefcase to his chest. Two men flanking the double doors stepped into his path, the contours of their muscles and the automatic weapons bulging beneath their tailored suits.

"You're late," one of them said.

Yuri bit back the response that lingered on the tip of his tongue. *Do not get distracted.* "Then get out of my way," he simply replied.

"Is this it?" The second man pointed at the briefcase.

Yuri stared at him silently.

The first man shrugged and lifted his wrist to his mouth. "He's here," he said into the concealed comm.

A moment later the tall door opened, revealing the inside of the mansion.

What if they change their minds?

He pushed the thought aside and entered. He paced through the lavishly decorated entrance hall and into a room with a dozen well-dressed people, all talking in excited tones. A hush fell when he appeared in the doorway. All eyes turned on him.

A dark-haired Asian woman in an elegant blue suede dress approached, a champagne flute resting lazily in her hand. Her almond-shaped eyes glinted like polished jade, and her face looked a decade younger than it did when he saw her only several days ago.

"Dr. Korzo," she said, smiling in a warm greeting, "we have been anticipating your arrival."

"Good afternoon, Madame Chen." He inclined his head. "You look well."

"A credit to your acumen." She absentmindedly caressed her arm where he injected her with the ancient genes retrieved from the golden-eyed woman's blood. "It is as if my body and mind have awakened from a lifelong slumber."

Yuri's lips turned into a smile at her words. It was genuine. They had no idea about the other woman. Two weeks ago, he reported to them that he had successfully synthesized the ancient genes from the saved data. Elated about his progress, they allowed him to inject them with the ancient genes. The results have been more than favorable, securing their trust and allowing him to keep up his deception—and keep them oblivious to the fate they would soon face.

Madame Chen misread his expression and placed a warm hand on his arm. "You have brought great success to us. If Professor Baxter were still with us, he would be proud of your accomplishment."

If that bastard was still alive, he'd take credit for every single thing I've done, Yuri thought, struggling to keep the disdain from his face.

The woman was oblivious to the change in his expression. She surveyed the faces gathered around her before continuing. "Tonight marks the end of a long journey, begun by Edgar Cayce and Francis Chaplain many decades ago. A journey continued by Walter Drake and his son William. Tonight, we honor their legacy—and sacrifice."

Yuri's chest throbbed at the pang of a memory as she raised the glass at him and they clapped and sipped on their thousand-dollar champagne. His jaw tightened. *You know nothing of sacrifice.*

The woman motioned him to the rosewood table in the center of the room. He rested the briefcase on it, surprised at his relief to be free of its burden, and flipped open the locks. The silence in the room was complete as he lifted the lid and the contents came into view. Two dozen auto-injectable syringes filled with a clear fluid were tucked snugly inside their foam cutouts.

"The Horus virus," Madame Chen whispered, unable to keep the awe from her voice.

Yuri lifted his hand to his mouth to hide his sneer. To call the ancient bioweapon a virus could not begin to do it justice.

There was so much more to this magnificently engineered, lethal marvel.

His thoughts were interrupted when a dark-skinned man took a step forward. He scrutinized the syringes, the eyebrows in his wide face drawn into a scowl. "You are certain this... ingredient... is essential to the process?" His deep voice rang with a rich African accent.

Yuri lifted one of the autoinjectors from the briefcase. He swept his gaze around the room. *Tread lightly*, the golden-eyed woman's words echoed in his head. *Don't push them.*

Still, he could not fail. Not now, when he was so close. He took a breath. "Four months ago, I exposed Alyssa Morgan's blood to a sample of this virus." He recalled the image of the virus repairing the DNA strand. "The results were... unexpected. I have never seen that type of reaction at a molecular level."

"We are well aware of your work—" the African man interjected.

Yuri lifted his palm to silence the interruption and continued. "The ancient genes, the same genes that have been causing the changes in your bodies, were synthesized from the genetic markers of the Morgan girl's blood. These are the same genes that will not only protect you from any harmful effects of the ancient weapon, but will also allow you to fully awaken your Hybrid consciousness—just like they did in Alyssa Morgan."

"We are putting a lot of faith into your words," the African man said.

A tall man wearing a traditional Middle Eastern *gabaya* stepped forward. "Have you looked at yourself in the mirror, Fuad?" he asked. "Do you not feel better than you have in decades? The ancient genes have already begun bonding with our bodies at the cellular level. Don't deny the changes."

"I also cannot deny that this is the same virus that four months ago brought us to the brink of a worldwide epidemic," Fuad countered. "I do not believe my apprehension is without merit."

Yuri swallowed around the lump in his throat before speaking. "You are correct, this is the same substance that caused the illness of Kaden Morgan. Released in battle, this… weapon was meant to destroy the enemies of the Hybrids and at the same time give strength to their kin and heal them." He paused. "Just like the Hybrid's own blood was meant to safeguard them, the ancient genes placed inside you have already bonded with your genome and will protect you—and complete the transition."

Silence filled the room. Madame Chen placed her champagne on the table. She approached Yuri and took the autoinjector from his hand. "We have been through this before," she said. "Dr. Korzo's reasoning is sound, and his science is beyond reproach." She examined the device with a faraway gaze. "William Drake risked, and sacrificed, everything so we could be here. I, for one, will not tarnish his legacy with doubt or fear." She took a deep breath and returned the syringe to Yuri then held out her arm to him.

Yuri struggled to control his breathing as he accepted the device and cradled her forearm with his other hand. It would take fifteen minutes for the virus to spread through her body and for her to become infectious. He needed to be out of this room in ten.

He placed the tip against her skin.

"Are you ready?" he asked.

She nodded.

He pressed the trigger, driving the tiny needle into her arm and emptying the contents of the vial into her body. He felt her body tense then relax.

"It is done," he said.

For several moments nobody spoke or moved, then the man in the *gabaya* plucked out a second device. He passed it to Yuri and rolled up his sleeve.

"For William Drake," he said. Yuri pressed it against him and squeezed the trigger as another man lifted a third syringe and approached him.

For William Drake.

For my son's murderer.

Soon he would have revenge on the other person responsible for robbing him of his only son.

Alyssa Morgan.

———

YURI HUNKERED behind the wheel of the SUV, his heart pounding even faster than the car speeding away from the mansion. The sense of accomplishment slowly gave way to the true notion of what he had done. He pushed that thought out of his mind and dialed her number.

"Yes?" Yuri tensed at the sound of her voice.

"It is done," he said.

"You did well," she replied. He exhaled, overcome with an unreasonable sense of pride—and relief. There was no going back. The woman was now his only means of staying alive. He was aware of what the Society would do to him if they learned what he had done. Still, it did not compare with his fear of disappointing the woman.

"You know what to do," she said. "One of them must survive long enough to be useful."

"I understand," Yuri replied. He disconnected the call and dialed the emergency number of the El Aini hospital.

ALYSSA'S HEART pounded against her chest. She glanced back, waving her arms. "Come on, Mom, Dad! Hurry up!"

She whirled and bolted for the entrance to the aviary.

"Slow down, Alyssa!"

She barely heard her dad's voice as she dashed through the door of the enclosure. Alyssa spun, breathless, taking in the sight of the birds all around her.

They're beautiful! So many colors!

"Look at the cockatoos!" Her friend's eyes twinkled, and she took off for the cage with the squawking animals. Alyssa turned to follow then froze. A majestic bird sat alone, perched on the highest branch. The creature seemed to catch her gaze. It cocked its head.

Alyssa's stomach fluttered. She moved slowly to the cage, stopping at the sign. She sounded out the letters.

L-a-n-n-e-r F-a-l-c-o-n.

She cranked her neck. Before she realized what had

happened, she stepped forward and squeezed her arm through the mesh wiring separating her from the falcon.

"Alyssa! Don't!" Her dad's alarmed cry scarcely registered.

Without warning, the falcon swooped down from the branch, landing on her arm. She felt its talons against her skin, pinching, but not breaking it. It cocked its head again as it locked its golden eyes on hers.

Alyssa held her breath. She was weightless, a soothing warmth radiating through her body, tingling her skin. She turned to her parents, beaming.

"He likes me!"

"Easy, Alyssa... don't make any sudden moves." Her dad closed in slowly. Her mom watched her, a calm, faraway expression on her face.

"Don't worry, Daddy. He won't hurt me." She turned back to the falcon, her heart humming with excitement. She felt her dad's hands on her shoulders, tugging her gently back toward him.

"No, Dad, wait!" she said, resisting. The falcon shifted uneasily.

"Alyssa, now," he said.

She turned to her dad in protest then looked up at her mom. She gave Alyssa a reassuring smile.

"Listen to Daddy, sweetheart," she said.

Alyssa's gave a dejected sigh but stopped resisting. Her dad pulled her back and into his arms.

The falcon's screech echoed in Alyssa's ears as the bird spread its powerful wings and took flight.

———

ALYSSA STIRRED awake at the squeal of the landing gear hitting the runway. The plane pitched gently forward until the front wheels touched the ground with another bump. She barely noticed the familiar sound of the thrust-reversers as the plane decelerated rapidly.

"Ladies and Gentlemen, Egypt Air is pleased to welcome you to Cairo. The local time is 10:24 a.m. We hope you had a pleasant trip with us and…"

Alyssa closed her eyes and leaned her head into the seat as the flight attendant continued her well-practiced announcement. For the hundredth time since the call with her dad, she racked her brain about the break-ins. Was the Society involved? Their quest for the ancient genes made them the obvious suspects. Or was it somebody else with other, even more nefarious reasons? She shuddered as she thought of the implications. And why would Kamal keep the virus in the first place? She stared out of the window, chewing her lip, as the plane approached the gate.

An hour later, she wasn't any closer to a solution as the automated sliding glass doors opened before her and she paced into the arrivals area. The crowd facing her was a sea of bobbing heads, anxious to get a first look at their visitors. No matter to which continent she traveled, the scene was always the same.

No welcomes without goodbyes, she thought wistfully, *and no goodbyes without welcomes*.

The rueful smile evaporated from her face when she spotted her dad. She threw her arms around him.

"Woah, kiddo!" Kade called out.

"I'm so glad you're okay," she said, holding him tight.

Dozens of feelings and thoughts coursed through her mind, but she pushed them aside. There would be time for them later.

They stood for several seconds in silence, neither willing to break the moment. Finally, Alyssa tightened her embrace one last time then stepped back reluctantly.

"What happened?" she asked.

"The people involved in both attacks knew what they were doing," Kade said.

"Was it the Society?"

"It's too early to be certain. Interpol is collaborating with Egyptian law enforcement to investigate all possibilities."

"Why was the break-in at the institute kept a secret?"

"The ministry feared a panic, with good reason. Now that the information is out, people are scurrying to shift the blame." He shook his head. "It's the biggest game of CYA I've ever seen."

"CYA?" Alyssa asked.

"Cover your a—"

Her dad's phone rang. He picked it up and listened for several seconds.

"Are you certain?" he asked, his face tightening.

"What?" Alyssa asked, but her dad waved her off.

"We will be there as soon as we can."

He disconnected and stared at Alyssa. "That was Kamal. We need to go to the hospital," he said, his voice tense. "Now."

———

THIRTY MINUTES LATER, Alyssa and her father stood next to

Kamal as he used his keycard to access the infectious diseases floor.

"The hospital is on level two alert," he said as the elevator ascended. "All critical floors are accessible by keycard access only, and all rooms are locked with a code."

They exited and paced along the corridor, stopping in front of a door. Alyssa stood back and watched Kamal's fingers as he entered a six-digit PIN into the keypad.

The door unlocked, and they entered the anteroom. Alyssa winced at the burn in the pit of her stomach as the image of her father lying in the same pressure-controlled suite surfaced in her mind.

She shook off the thought and focused on the woman in the bed. Despite the oxygen mask on her face, her Asian features were distinctly elegant and fine. Her age was impossible to guess.

Kamal studied the reports on the computer display, his face a glum mask.

"Who is she?" Kade asked.

"We don't know," he replied. "An anonymous call earlier today alerted us to a remote compound outside the city. When the medical crew arrived, they found over twenty deceased individuals. She was the only survivor."

Alyssa's hand flew to her mouth. "That's horrible."

Kamal took a deep breath. "The diagnostic tests revealed that her infection is consistent with the Horus virus."

"The stolen virus?" Kade asked.

Kamal nodded, his face turning even darker.

"Has anybody else been exposed?" Alyssa asked.

"We don't know. Mercifully, based on the tip, the medical

team followed infectious disease protocols when they arrived, and the compound has since been quarantined. We are keeping all of this information contained."

Alyssa gave a small sigh of relief. "You'll be able to cure her, right? And any others that may have been exposed?"

For a moment, Kamal's expression was completely unreadable. He opened up an image on the screen and motioned them closer.

"What I'm about to tell you hasn't gone beyond the attending physician in charge and the critical care team," he said. He inhaled deeply, as if steadying himself for what he was about to say. "The cure we devised from your blood several months ago doesn't seem to be effective against this strain. The virus appears to have... mutated."

"What?" Alyssa felt the dread rising inside her as the blood flowed from her face. "But how—?"

"It's too early to say. We are not certain if it was the result of a natural mechanism—or deliberate manipulation."

Alyssa stood transfixed, trying to process the information.

"There is more." Kamal flashed through several windows, stopping at two side-by-side images. "The team ran extensive tests on her blood." He faced Alyssa. "The patient's DNA fragments, they match up with the ancient fragments we found inside your DNA."

Alyssa stared from the computer to the woman in the hospital bed.

"She has Hybrid DNA?" she asked, blinking. "But that's impossible. If she did, she shouldn't be ill. She—"

"We repeated the tests several times," Kamal said. "There is no doubt. She shares those genetic markers with you."

Alyssa gaped at him. "What does that mean?"

"It's too early to say," Kamal replied.

"We have to try to find out where she came from!" Alyssa pleaded. "And what's happened to her!"

"We tried talking with her," Kamal said. "She is too weak. We may try again in several hours, while we monitor her condition."

"But it may be too late by then!" she pushed.

"We have to prioritize the patient's well-being above all else."

Alyssa glared at him, pressure rising. "How could you do this, Kamal? Violate our trust?" The words were out before she could do anything about it.

Kamal froze and held his breath, his lips stretched thin with tension. Kade jumped in, "Alyssa, I know you're upset—and tired—but Kamal had his reasons."

"Don't patronize me!" she spat, her frustration getting the better of her. "And don't you take his side in this. For all I know you knew what was happening all along."

"Your dad didn't know anything about the virus, Alyssa," Kamal said. "I know how upsetting this must be for you, but please understand we didn't have another option. We had to be prepared in case something similar happened. We couldn't take the risk of it catching us completely off guard like it did last time."

"You gave us your word that the virus and my blood would only be used to create a cure for the outbreak! And that the virus would be destroyed as soon as we knew we were safe."

"The directive to pursue the research came from the highest

level. We're a government-funded facility, and we have to abide by certain rules."

"I don't care about your rules!"

Kamal lifted his palm. "I'm afraid that's all we can do for now. I wanted to share with you all I had because you deserved to know. A team from Interpol is on their way to take over the investigation."

Alyssa threw up her hands in exasperation. "I can't believe…" She trailed off as she spotted a purse inside a plastic drawer in the corner of the room.

She put her head down and swallowed.

"I'm sorry. I was out of line." She looked from Kamal to her dad. "You're right, the jetlag and lack of sleep are getting the better of me. I know you're doing all you can."

Kamal gave her a small smile while Kade stared at her with raised eyebrows.

"I think I need to cool off, splash some water on my face." She moved to the door. "I'm going to find a restroom."

Kamal nodded. "We'll wait in the hallway."

Alyssa stepped out and paced along the corridor to the restroom, gears spinning, forming her plan. Her idea could get her in serious trouble, but she didn't have much choice. She needed to find out as much as she could while she was here, as long as she still had access to the evidence.

She found a restroom, splashed some water on her face, and hurried back to Kade and Kamal. The men stood in the hallway, waiting.

"I don't know about you, but I'm starving," she said, rubbing her stomach. "I think some food and a nap might be just what I need right now. Does the cafeteria still have my favorite meal?"

"The oatmeal with dates?" Kamal laughed. "Half the hospital staff would go on strike if they stopped serving it." He checked his watch. "I have a few more minutes and could go for a bowl myself. And it will give us a chance to catch up."

They walked back to the elevator. As they stepped through the doors, Alyssa fumbled through her pockets.

"Shoot!" She slipped her arm between the doors, barely stopping them from closing. "I must have left my phone in the restroom." She rubbed her head. "All this news on top of the jetlag. My mind is all over the place. I'm really sorry…"

Kamal gave her a reassuring smile. "No worries," he said. "We'll wait for you."

"No, no… please don't. I feel really silly and already made you wait. I know you don't have much time."

Alyssa hopped out of the elevator and rushed for the restroom. "I'll catch up with you in the cafeteria," she called out over her shoulder as the doors closed. "Get me a big bowl. Extra dates!"

Her heart raced as she waited for the doors to close, then pivoted and made for the room. She checked the hallway then entered Kamal's PIN into the pad. She had seen him enter the digits from across the hallway when they had first arrived.

These new optics are coming in handy…

The door unlocked with a click. She slipped through and closed it behind her. She donned the biosafety gear and opened the drawer. The purse was sealed inside a plastic bag. Despite the mask, Alyssa held her breath as she opened the bag and the purse. Her fingers tingled with anticipation when she spotted a mobile phone. She turned it on.

Locked. Of course.

Alyssa glanced through the window at the woman inside the sealed room then back to the phone.

For half a second, she tried to convince herself to put the phone back and go down to the cafeteria. Her good judgment left as quickly as it had arrived.

I won't get another shot at this.

She glanced over her shoulder into the corridor. It looked clear.

This may not be the brightest idea I've ever had.

Before she could change her mind, she crossed the room to the inner door.

Let's hope the same PIN works on the inside door.

She entered the number, and the door opened with a whispered whoosh. Her hair stirred with the familiar sensation of air flowing into the negatively-pressurized environment to ensure that no airborne particles escaped the inner room.

As the door automatically closed behind her, Alyssa approached the bed. It stood in the center of the room, surrounded by a clear plastic partition. Wires trailed from under the sheets to a bank of equipment, monitoring the woman's vital signs. An intravenous line dripped a slurry of saline and medicines into her. Close up, the woman looked older and even more frail. Her skin was stretched paper-thin across the bones of her face. Each halting breath left a trail of condensation on the inside of her oxygen mask.

Alyssa swallowed and brought the phone to the woman's

hand through the plastic. She guided the woman's thumb to the home button on the phone.

Alyssa cracked a smile when the phone unlocked.

A new text message icon bounced on the home screen. She pressed it.

"Valediction," she whispered, reading the one-word message. *What does that—?*

She yelped as the woman grasped her arm through the plastic. She tried to pull back, but the woman was much stronger than Alyssa had expected. She sat up in bed and locked her eyes on Alyssa's, looking straight through her.

Alyssa tugged again, finally yanking her arm free. The sudden movement unsettled her, and she toppled backward, flinging her arm over her head, losing grip on the phone. Wide-eyed, she followed the phone's trajectory as it flew across the room and crashed at the door.

Oh, f...

Alyssa raced across the room and retrieved it. The screen was completely busted.

This is bad...

She scampered into the anteroom and threw everything back in place. She ripped off the safety gear and stuffed it into the biohazard container then dashed out into the corridor, cold sweat running down her back. In her rush, she didn't see the elderly nurse watching her through narrowed eyes from the far end of the hallway before lifting a phone.

———

Alyssa rested across from her dad, her breathing finally

settling back to normal. She hoped she hadn't looked too guilty when she met up with him and Kamal in the cafeteria. Kamal was called away shortly after she arrived, leaving her and Kade by themselves. She replayed the word in her mind. *Valediction.* What did that mean?

Alyssa took a bite of the oatmeal, chewing the dates, the explosion of flavor temporarily derailing her contemplation. *How can they make oatmeal taste this good?*

She shook off the thought and turned to her father as he picked at his own bowl.

"Does the word *Valediction* mean anything to you?" she asked.

Her father glanced up. "Valediction?" He thought for a few moments. "No, should it?"

"I'm not sure," Alyssa said with a shrug.

"Why do you ask?"

Alyssa swallowed a spoonful of oatmeal. "Uh… just wondering." She quickly took another bite and chewed intently, suddenly discovering great interest in the exact number of dates in her bowl.

Her dad cleared his throat. "You may have been able to fool Kamal, but I know that face."

Alyssa counted six more dates then raised her head. "Promise you won't get upset?"

A ghost of a smile appeared at the edge of Kade's lips. "Asks the descendant of Ra?"

"I'm serious," she said. "I think I may have done something stupid."

Kade's face darkened. "What is it?"

Alyssa told him.

Kade stared at her in silence for several moments then said, "Well, I give you props for creativity."

"I know the Society is involved."

He was quiet for several moments more. "That may be true, but it's too dangerous for you to get involved... too." His voice faded out, the last word barely audible.

She placed her hand on top of his palm. "I understand how you feel, but after everything we've been through, you can't expect me to just sit back and twiddle my thumbs."

He shook his head slowly, a grim twist to his mouth. "No, Ally, you don't know how I feel," he whispered. He turned his palm and took her hand in his. "I will not lose you as well. I want you to stay out of it."

"You can't be serious!"

Instead of answering, Kade reached into the brown shoulder bag that doubled as his briefcase and pulled out a small box.

"I can't have you getting involved because I need you to keep this safe." He passed it to her.

Alyssa's fingers tingled as she opened the box and unwrapped an object from a soft cloth. She froze when she recognized the triangular shape.

"I thought it was stolen!"

"After what happened at the institute a couple weeks ago, I was worried they may strike the museum next, so I hid it."

Alyssa fixed Kade with a steady gaze, a new measure of respect in her eyes.

"You took good care of it last time," he said. He moved closer, lowering his voice. "Both break-ins had help from the inside. Nobody is above suspicion. It's only a question of time before they come knocking at my door. I have a feeling it will be safer with you than with me."

"Does anybody else know?"

"Just you and me." He motioned with his head over her shoulder, and his face tightened. "Better put it away."

Alyssa glanced back. A group of people entered the cafeteria and eyed their table. A woman in the group, a nurse, pointed to them and leaned to a man in a suit. The pair approached the table, trailed by two uniformed officers.

"Oh, no," Alyssa said, slipping the box into her backpack just before the group stopped at their table. The nurse addressed the man in the suit.

"That's her."

Kade sat up. "What is this about?"

The man glanced at Alyssa before turning to Kade.

"My name is Captain Ghassan. I'm in charge of security at this hospital. Is this your daughter?"

"Yes, it is," Kade said, his voice guarded. "What seems to be the problem, Captain Ghassan?"

"Nurse Fathi claims that she saw your daughter gain unauthorized entry into one of the restricted rooms," Ghassan said.

"There must be a mistake," Kade said.

"No, I'm certain," the nurse said. "It was her."

"She will come with us for questioning," Ghassan said. "Now."

Kade rose from the chair. "Like hell she will."

Ghassan tensed, and the guards tightened around them. The bustling cafeteria hushed as heads turned to their table. Ghassan held up his palm.

"Please, sir. Your daughter is accused of tampering with

evidence in an active investigation. It is regrettable, but due to the increased security precautions, we must detain her for questioning."

"I can explain," Alyssa started.

"Please come with us now," Ghassan said.

The two officers took Alyssa by her arms.

"Don't touch me!" she said, squirming.

"Get your hands off my daughter!" Kade yelled and shoved a guard off Alyssa.

Caught by surprise, the man stumbled backward, tripped over his feet, and fell.

A second of stunned silence was followed by an eruption of shouts and startled cries through the hall. The other guard released Alyssa's arm and rushed her father. Kade stepped aside and pushed the guard past him, using the other man's momentum to propel him into a food tray on the neighboring table.

"Go!" Kade yelled to Alyssa. Ghassan reached for her then grunted as Kade tackled him from behind.

"Daddy, no!" she yelled.

"Go, now!" Kade shouted as the scene disintegrated into chaos. Both guards gained their feet and rushed to help Ghassan. Alyssa clutched the backpack and leaped up, her heart in her throat.

"Stop!" Ghassan bellowed, struggling to work himself free of Kade, who used both arms and legs to keep all three men occupied.

Alyssa sprinted for the exit, weaving between tables. She threw a glance back. The guards pinned Kade down, twisting his arms behind his back. A metallic flash glinted. *Handcuffs.*

Alyssa stifled a sob as she flew into the lobby, drawing bewildered stares from physicians and patients alike. She barely avoided barreling into a young physician. He glared at her, baffled, as she sped past him and bolted through the tall revolving glass door into the street.

She ran for another half minute then slowed to a fast walk. Her heart worked to tear through her rib cage, and her entire body shook. The dull ache in her chest threatened to melt into sobbing tears. She held it back. She stepped into an alcove and took out her phone. She somehow managed to hit the speed-dial button.

"Alyssa?" a familiar voice answered.

"Paul!" she sobbed.

"What's wrong?" The concern in Paul's voice was immediate.

"They arrested my dad!" She couldn't hold back the tears any longer. "And it's all my fault."

"Alyssa, slow down. Where are you? What are you talking about?"

Alyssa took a deep breath. She told him what had happened.

Paul absorbed everything in silence. After she finished, he thought for several moments then said, "You need to get out of there, ASAP. Get a cab and head to the airport right away. Call me from the car."

"But my dad——" she started.

"Your dad can take care of himself. And he has Kamal."

"Okay," Alyssa said. "I'll call you back."

Two minutes later, Alyssa sank into the back seat of a cab. She dialed her dad. Voicemail. Sighing, she disconnected. She contemplated for a few moments, then dialed Kamal.

"Alyssa!" he called out as soon as he answered. "Where are you? I just heard what happened. What was all of that about?"

"I can't explain right now," she said. "How is my dad?"

"He was taken into custody for interfering with police officers."

"You have to help him. Please!"

"You have to come back now," he replied. "You're making things worse by running away, for both of you."

Alyssa looked at her backpack, the crystal inside it. "I can't do that," she said. "Promise me you'll take care of my dad."

"Alyssa—"

"You owe me. Promise me you'll take care of him!"

Kamal sighed. "I will contact the minister and call in a favor."

"Thank you," she said.

"One more thing," Kamal said.

"Yes?"

"The woman we saw earlier today. Her condition deteriorated." He swallowed. "We were unable to save her."

"She died?"

"Yes," he said glumly. "I'm afraid it's only a question of time before the news gets out about the virus—and the lack of a cure."

"I'm really sorry," she said. "I know you did your best."

"I know you will, as well," he replied.

Alyssa hung up. She took a deep breath and dialed Paul.

"Are you okay?" he asked.

"I think so," she replied.

"Where are you?"

"On my way to the airport."

"Good," he said. "You need to get out of the country."

"What if… Will they be looking for me at the airport?"

"I have an idea," Paul said, "but I don't think you're going to like it."

"I think my options are a bit limited at this point," she replied.

"George Renley," he said.

Alyssa's skin prickled. "Absolutely not. After what he did?"

"He has connections. If anybody can get you out, it's him."

"Paul, I swore to myself never to speak to him again."

"And that is completely understandable," he said. "I'm not asking you to trust him. And I know he will be eager to help you, to make up for what he did."

Alyssa was quiet for several long moments. She swallowed. "Okay, I'll call him."

———

LORD GEORGE RENLEY watched the distant rain clouds from the terrace outside his study. They churned across the sky, casting dark shadows over the woods on his three-hundred-acre estate. It would be pouring by mid-morning.

He leaned onto the marble railing, his body giving a small shiver at the chill of the stone against his skin. He frowned, lifted his hands and then balled them into fists. He brought them up. *Still strong.* Yet he could no longer deny the passage of time. It seemed only yesterday that he would charge to the docks at the first sign of a storm, casting off in his thirty-foot cutter to single-hand it through the white caps and measure his prowess and skills against the elements. Now—

His phone rang, snapping him back into the present.

"Yes," he answered. He waited several seconds for an answer. "Hello?" he said again, sharper.

"Lord Renley?"

He tensed at the sound of the voice. "Miss Morgan?"

"Yes," Alyssa said, her voice cold and measured.

"What can I do for you?"

"I need your help."

"I assumed as much. I imagine calling me must not have been an easy decision."

"I'm in Cairo. I need a way out."

Renley considered. "Could you elaborate?"

"My father has been arrested," Alyssa said. "And the police may be looking for me."

"I see," Renley said. "Is there anything else I should know?"

"People are getting sick," she continued. "The virus, it's been released again."

"What? Are they able to administer the cure?"

"It doesn't work."

"What do you mean?"

"I mean it doesn't work! And the woman, the last one who died, she had traces of Hybrid DNA," Alyssa continued, now seemingly unable to stop. "She shouldn't even have been sick in the first place, but—"

"Miss Morgan," Renley interrupted, trying to stay calm and ignore the heavy feeling settling in the pit of his stomach, "please slow down."

Alyssa continued as if she hadn't heard him. "She... she

just died. We think the Society was involved. Her phone, it said something about 'Valediction'—?"

Renley froze. "Miss Morgan," he cut in.

Alyssa kept going.

"Miss Morgan," he said, louder.

Alyssa stopped.

"Have you shared this with anybody else?"

Alyssa took a deep breath. "No. Wait. Yes. My father. And Paul. But that's it."

"Good." Renley exhaled. "I will make arrangements for your travel out of the country. Go to the private terminal at the airport. Somebody will meet you and escort you from there. And, Miss Morgan?"

"Yes?"

"It is of utmost importance that you do not share this information with anybody until you get here. I shall make arrangements for you once you arrive in England."

"Thank you," she said.

"I will see you when you get here." He disconnected the call.

George Renley stood for several moments, replaying the conversation in his head, then he picked up the phone again and dialed a number.

ALYSSA PERKED up in the plush leather seat as the silver Bentley approached the estate. The rolling English countryside with its treeless hilltops and old limestone farmhouses gave way to an ivy-covered stone wall and a winding path leading to the iron gates. The car pulled into the long driveway, flanked by rows of oaks crowned in rust and gold, swaying gently to the chilly autumn wind.

Alyssa chewed her bottom lip as she reflected on the past several hours. *So far, Renley has delivered on his promise.*

After the taxi dropped her off at the private terminal of the Cairo Airport, she was met and whisked away by a woman who had been waiting for her.

I suppose I was easy to pick out, rolling up in a cab among the Rolls-Royces and Bugattis.

Within an hour she was up in the air on a small private jet that Renley had chartered. She used the plane's satellite phone to try to call her dad, but hadn't been able to reach him. No better luck getting through to Kamal, either. She did reach

Renley, but he told her only that his driver would meet her at the plane and bring her to his home.

The limousine rolled to a smooth stop at the top of the circular driveway. A thin, distinguished looking man stepped out from beneath a covered alcove. Though he looked to be in his early seventies, he strode briskly to the car. The chauffeur opened her door as the man reached the Bentley. He wore a starched Windsor-style shirt, a black suit, and a silk tie.

"Good afternoon, Miss Morgan," the man said, offering a bow and white-gloved hand to help her out of her seat. He gazed kindly at Alyssa through a pair of round silver rimmed glasses that matched the gray in his hair. "My name is Jacques. I am Lord Renley's majordomo. I trust you had a pleasant trip from Cairo?"

What's a majordomo? she thought. "Uh, yes, thank you, Jacques," she managed to reply as she took his hand and stepped out. Jacques reached for her backpack.

"I got it, thank you," Alyssa said.

Jacques pulled back, the slightest look of surprise crossing his face before he nodded. "Of course, as you wish."

Alyssa tried not to stare at the structure looming proudly before her. The mansion grew out of the manicured lawn like an infant castle. Moss and ivy clung to its pale gray walls. At its threshold stood an ornate marble fountain, the soft gurgling of the water resonating in the surrounding silence. They approached an entryway that was sheltered under a wide archway supported by stone pillars.

Jacques opened the tall oak door, decorated in thick brass, and Alyssa passed into an imposing entrance hall floored in polished marble. The twenty-foot ceiling was arched high, and the walls were decorated in French tapestries and large paintings. A wide, curving staircase wound to the second floor.

So this is how the top one percent of the one percent live.

"May I get you anything at all?" Jacques asked, closing the door behind them. "Would you care to freshen up?"

"No, thank you," Alyssa replied. "I would like to see Lord Renley as soon as possible."

"In that case, please follow me. Lord Renley is expecting you in the library."

Alyssa followed Jacques through the marble-lined corridor, eyeing a painting.

Is that a Rembrandt?

Before she had any more time to ponder, they arrived at a wood-paneled door. Jacques slid it open and moved aside, bending slightly at the waist. Alyssa stepped through, and Jacques closed the door behind her.

The room was large and perfectly proportioned, with grand latticed windows overlooking the courtyard. Bookshelves lined the walls, floor to ceiling, interspersed with strips of dark oak paneling. A grandfather clock ticked on the right. Renley luxuriated in one of the two leather armchairs that were drawn up to the carved stone fireplace dominating the left wall.

He rose, putting aside the tablet he was holding. His salt-and-pepper hair was combed neatly back. He took off his reading glasses and slipped them inside his bespoke suit.

Of course he wears suits at home.

"Miss Morgan," he said.

With no small pain, Alyssa screwed a hint of a smile onto her face. "Lord Renley," she replied coolly.

Renley approached her. "I can only imagine the depth of

your resentment for me and my despicable actions several months ago. I have no excuses for my conduct during our last encounter. I only hope that you will consider forgiving me and that, with time, we may be able to re-establish a relationship of trust between us." He held out his hand.

Alyssa was taken aback. *I guess that's Renley-speak for "I'm sorry I was a bastard." Well, it's a start.*

"Thank you," she replied, a bit less cool, and accepted his hand. "But you know I have not come here to hear your apology."

"Indeed. And I promise that I shall share with you everything I know. Perhaps you would care to discuss it over dinner?" he asked.

Alyssa felt her stomach growling. She shed her coat and draped it over the chair. "I would like that."

"I understand the past several weeks have been... challenging," Renley said. "I took the liberty of inviting a familiar face in hopes of lifting your spirits." He pointed behind her as the door opened. She turned—and stared into Paul's grinning face.

Alyssa let the surprise freeze her for only an instant. She dashed up to him and threw her arms around his neck.

"What are you doing here?" she said, stepping back, staring at him. "What about Oxford?"

"I was granted a leave of absence to participate in field research." He glanced at Renley. "It seems a well-regarded alumnus donor placed a call to the administration."

She hugged him again, holding him tight. "I've missed you," she said. She broke the embrace after some time.

Alyssa faced Renley. "Thank you," she said.

"It is gratifying to see a smile on your face," Renley replied.

He cleared his throat. "Well, I shall leave you two to get reacquainted. Jacques will call on you to show you to your room shortly and summon you when dinner is served." He gave the slightest of nods before leaving the room.

Alyssa turned to Paul and caught him stealing a glance.

"You look..." he struggled for the word, "older." The pained expression on his face after the word came out of his mouth made her burst out laughing.

"I don't see you for four months, and this is the best you can come up with? Where did you spend your time? Nerd charm school?"

"Something like that," he said, his cheeks flushing with embarrassment.

Has it only been four months?

Alyssa eyed him up and down. His chestnut hair was longer, lankier across his forehead, and his face had grown leaner, making his cheekbones stand out and emphasizing his dark eyes even more. His shoulders were wider than she remembered, and his muscles rippled beneath his T-shirt as he slipped off his backpack and set it on a chair. He seemed more mature, harder.

She grinned and punched him playfully in the arm. "Geez, Paul. What have you been doing? Hitting the gym much between classes?"

He laughed self-consciously. "Well, after six weeks of physical therapy rehab, I got kind of used to the daily routine. I kept it up." He reached out to her, touching her cheek gently. "How about you?" he asked. "How are you holding up?"

She shrugged, her somber mood threatening to break through the surface again.

"Hanging on," she whispered, the expression on her face matching her thoughts.

He took her hand and led her to the plush leather sofa at the fireplace. He sank into it and pulled her beside him. They cozied up, facing the fire for several minutes, soaking in the heat and each other's presence. The dance of the flames and warmth of Paul's body next to hers went a long way to beat back the hopelessness that had begun to set over Alyssa during the last couple of days.

"Talk to me, Ally," Paul said.

Alyssa took a deep breath, searching for a place to start. "I've been having these dreams." She shook her head. "I don't even know if they are dreams. They seem so real. Just like... his memories. A couple of weeks ago I saw the night when his wife died and his son was taken." Alyssa shivered, not at the cold, but at the feelings that stirred up inside her. "It felt so real. When I wake up from them, I don't know what's real anymore." She felt burning behind her eyelids.

"You've been through so much. I'm not surprised—"

"That's not all," she continued. "I feel... like something is trying to break out. Like I'm losing control." She swallowed, looking down, unable to hold his gaze. "After that dream, I... I almost killed somebody."

"What?" Paul pulled back slightly, blinking.

She told him everything that had happened in the library in Prague. "All I could think of was Horus's loss. I felt this... *rage*..." She trailed off, her stomach clenching at the memory.

Paul reached for her hand again and cradled it, his touch and the silence helping to ease her tension.

After several moments, he asked, "Have you been able to find out anything else about the Hybrids?"

Alyssa pressed her lips into a tight line, thinking about the months of dead-end leads.

"No," she said, "but I haven't given up. Much to my dad's consternation."

Paul cocked an eyebrow.

"If it were up to him, I'd be hiding under a rock," she sighed.

"You can't fault him for that," Paul said. "Especially after what happened to your mom."

"How about what's happening to me now?" She pulled her hand back. "I'm not doing this because I'm bored, Paul. This isn't some wild goose chase!" she said, a measure sharper than she had intended.

Paul drew back, startled. The look in his eyes deflated her instantly. Her shoulders sagged.

"I'm sorry," she said. "It's just I'm really confused and scared... for my father, for me." She dropped her head, lips trembling.

Paul reached out and lifted her chin. She saw the play of mixed emotions in the soft concern of his eyes and worried lines of his lips. He knew how important this was to her, but the fear for her was plain to read. He put his arms around her and tugged her close. A long stretch of silence followed, with each lost in their own thoughts.

A soft knock at the door drew them back.

Paul gently pushed her back and stood. He extended his hand and bowed. "Would the lady care to join me for dinner?"

"I would be delighted," Alyssa said in her best impression

of the Queen's English and accepted his hand. "As long as the esteemed sir does not mind my bringing along a snooty chaperone."

———

TWO HOURS LATER, Alyssa watched Paul scoop off his last bite of the mouthwatering baklava while Renley sipped on his cognac. The pre-dinner catnap and hot shower went a long way to make her feel more like herself again. The scrumptious dinner didn't hurt, either. She leaned back in her chair and tugged back the sleeves of the blue sweater dress that Jacques had delivered to her room, courtesy of her host. It seemed like Renley was going all out to make up for what had happened in Cairo last summer. Still, Alyssa couldn't shake the feeling that he was keeping something from her. She took a sip of her water and eyed him, trying to read any hidden motives that might be hiding behind that stony façade.

It'll take more than an apology and a cashmere dress to make me trust you again, old man. Still, it was a damn good apology—and the dress was the softest thing she'd ever owned. *But still...* She wiped her mouth with the cloth napkin.

"The dinner was marvelous," she said. "Thank you again for your hospitality, Lord Renley."

"It is my pleasure," he smiled. "However, I am quite aware that you did not come here to sample the Renley estate cuisine, fine as it may be."

Alyssa nodded, grateful for the opening. "Do you have any information about the break-in at the institute?"

"After receiving your call, I made some inquiries. It appears that your initial suspicion was correct. The Society may have had a role in the events."

"I knew it!" Alyssa sat up in her chair.

"However," Renley continued, "there is more. Apparently, the Society received information—and resources—from a third party that enabled them to carry out the attack."

"A third party?" Paul asked.

"This is where the issue becomes somewhat abstruse," Renley continued. "The individuals who may have been linked to this third party are unable to disclose any additional information."

"Unable or unwilling?" Alyssa asked.

"They are dead," Renley replied. "The woman you saw in the hospital was the last survivor of that group."

"Do you know who she was?"

"Madame June Chen," Renley said. "She was one of Hong Kong's wealthiest individuals, with ties to most of the organized syndicates in that city. She was also rumored to be one of the largest antiquities collectors in that region, known to bend rules to obtain the objects of her desire."

"A woman after your own heart," Alyssa said, and regretted it almost instantly.

Renley's only outward expression of disdain consisted of the slightest downturn of his mouth.

Sensing the tension, Paul jumped in. "So, what happened? Did their deal go bad?"

"Or were they double crossed?" Alyssa added, happy to move past her cheap shot.

"Either one of those two scenarios appear to be plausible, based on the limited information we have," Renley replied.

"And no leads about this third party?" Paul asked.

"As of now, we seem to have exhausted our leads on this front."

"What about the message on her phone? Valediction?" Alyssa asked. "It seemed to mean something to you."

"Ah, yes," Renley said. "The heart of the matter."

"So, you know what it means?"

Renley took a sip of his cognac before answering. "Valediction," he said, "or, more precisely, *the Valediction* is the name of a sea vessel. A large yacht, custom built for the use of the Society. It has served as their mobile headquarters for over a decade."

"A Society yacht?" Paul asked.

"More a ship than a yacht, actually. It has been kept in international waters and is almost self-sufficient, with a large enough crew to cater to the needs of the members on board. It is being periodically refurnished with necessary supplies and crew rotations."

Paul whistled. "Those smug bastards. What better place for the members to get together, away from prying eyes and the reach of law enforcement agencies. Just please don't tell me it turns into a gigantic sub, like some Bond villain's toy," Paul said.

"No, nothing that exciting," Renley replied. "Though it is rumored to have state-of-the-art defenses and surveillance measures."

"Why *Valediction*?" Alyssa asked.

"In many ancient cultures, a rite of valediction, or parting, occurred when a young child left the comfort and safety of their home to venture on a journey of self-discovery. The child was only permitted to return after fulfilling a specific rite of passage, to be celebrated and accepted as a full-fledged member of their society. Those who dared to return prematurely or unsuccessfully were deemed unfit and were banished, or even killed."

"That sounds barbaric," Alyssa said.

"Survival of the fittest," Paul mused. Alyssa shot him a sidelong glance. Paul raised his palms. "Hey, I'm not saying I agree with it, but seems a fitting motto for the Society."

"Okay, so what does the message mean?" Alyssa asked.

"I cannot be certain," Renley replied, "but it could be a call for the members to gather on the ship. A type of beacon call."

"How can you know?"

"I cannot. However, the ship was designed to provide a safe haven for its members, especially in times of crisis. Furthermore, it also serves as a secure offline repository for the Society's documents and data. If there is any information about the third party, it would seem a logical starting point for their own investigation."

Paul slapped his hand on the table. "Brilliant. That settles it then. We just have to infiltrate a ship that belongs to a powerful, dangerous, and, not to mention, looney group of people, steal information from a completely offline and totally secure data repositorium, oh, not be seen by the ultra-sophisticated surveillance and highly trained guards, and *if* we manage that, escape all the aforementioned minor inconveniences on the way out, and be home before supper. Good thing I brought my spandex tights and cape. When are we leaving?"

Alyssa looked at him intently. She chewed her lip, pondering his words.

Paul stared back at her. "I was kidding..." He shook his head, exasperated. "And I don't really own spandex tights," he added.

"Do you have any other suggestions?" she asked.

"No, I don't, but I'm also not in a hurry to be caught by the Society—again. I don't have very fond memories of my last time as their guest." He rubbed his left arm for emphasis. "There's no way we can sneak aboard that ship."

Alyssa's shoulders slumped, knowing he was right.

"There may be another option," Renley said. "Pardon me." He motioned Jacques over and whispered in his ear.

Jacques nodded.

"Ah, splendid. Please show him in," Renley said.

Alyssa looked up at him expectantly as Jacques left the room.

"The *Valediction* is catered by an extensive crew," Renley continued, unperturbed. "In the past, I have provided references to several of my staff to serve aboard. Since I believe my word still carries a certain weight, I may be able to create an opportunity for you to get aboard under the disguise of two new crew members."

From his expression, Paul took little consolation from Renley's words. "Go on the Society's ship, pretending to be part of their crew?" He lifted his arms in exasperation. "Are you out of your bloomin' mind?" He blushed at his words. "With all due respect," he added.

Alyssa put a hand on Paul's arm. "Do you think this could really work?" she asked Renley.

"Well, there is the matter of training you two to be stewards," he replied. "And of altering your appearances sufficiently to not be recognized. The latter being the smaller of the two matters, I should wager."

Paul laughed out loud.

"What's so funny?" Alyssa snapped.

"Nothing," he had a hard time keeping a straight face, "it's just that picturing you as a chamber maid…"

Alyssa punched him in the arm. "Watch it!"

"Ouch!" Paul said, rubbing it. "Easy there, divine one. No smiting the mortals."

"Even if we somehow managed to get on board as part of the crew, how would we access the information?" Alyssa asked.

Renley's eyes crinkled with a hint of smugness. "I took the liberty to solicit an outside expert opinion. I was advised that if you were able to obtain physical access to the hardware, a remote connection could be established that would allow a third party to successfully hack into the data server."

"Did somebody mention 'hack' and 'data server' in the same sentence?"

Alyssa whirled at the voice ringing from the doorway. Her lips stretched into an ear-splitting grin. "Clay!" she yelled. She jumped up and rushed to him, wrapping him in a tight hug and planting a big kiss on his cheek.

"Now that's a welcome that's worth leaving my desk at the WHO at a moment's notice," Clay said, flashing a wide, toothy grin and returning the warm embrace. "Well, that and the daily 'stipend' from Lord Renley that's worth more than my monthly fellowship."

Paul came up and shook his hand then pulled him into a bearhug. "It's good to see you, mate," he said.

Clay patted Paul on the back affectionately then strolled up to Renley and shook his hand.

"Thank you again for the offer, Lord Renley," he said. "It looks like I was interrupting something important."

"On the contrary, Mr. Obono, your timing was impeccable, just as I had hoped it would be," Renley said. "We were discussing the electronic security challenge I had outlined to you. Were you able to review the specifications on your way?"

"Ah, yes," Clay said. "Well, sounds like it'll be a doddle, if somebody can get their hands on the network port of that server. We hook up a remote gateway, sprinkle on some home-grown technomancy and Bob's your uncle—we're in." He ruffled his thick curls. "So, what server are we going after and how do we get to it?"

Alyssa filled him in on the plan. After she finished, he stared at her, unblinking, his mouth slack. After several seconds he shook his head in dismay.

"You are still just as nut-cracking bonkers as you were when I last saw you. That ten-thousand-year old Ra juice apparently doesn't add any bonus points to your wisdom." His eyes darted to Paul. "And you're going along with this?"

"Clay, something is happening," Alyssa jumped in before Paul had a chance to reply. "There was a break-in at the genetics institute. The Society stole the virus. Two weeks later twenty of them turn up dead, infected by the virus, like they were part of some weird ritual." Alyssa swallowed. "And that's not all. Their genes contained Hybrid markers."

Clay stared at her. "What? How?" he asked.

She shrugged. "That's what we're trying to find out."

Clay shook his head, trying to make sense of what he heard.

"Still, we have stocks of the cure at multiple WHO sites throughout the world. Even if another outbreak were to occur, it would only be a question of time before the cure would be administered to all infected individuals. It's not going to catch us with our breeches around our ankles again."

"There is no cure," Alyssa said.

Clay's face dropped. "Come again?"

"The cure that was developed for the Horus epidemic isn't effective against this strain," Alyssa replied, her face glum. "There is no way to stop the virus."

Clay stared at her wordlessly. He sank into a chair. "We're royally bollocked."

———

YURI KORZO WAITED as he was instructed. The shirt was pasted to his back, the humidity mixing with his own perspiration.

His heart sped up when he saw a car approach in the distance. The white Mercedes Maybach rolled to a smooth stop alongside Yuri's SUV, and a tall man wearing a black suit and sunglasses exited from the passenger seat. He opened the rear door and beckoned Yuri inside.

Yuri swallowed around the lump in his throat and approached the car. The golden-eyed woman glanced at him from the rear seat. Yuri slipped into the opulent leather next to her, and the man closed the door.

The woman studied him in silence for several moments before speaking. "You did well in Cairo," she said. "You have dealt the Society a significant blow."

No less than they deserved after taking my son from me. He simply nodded.

"I am aware that altering the virus in such a short time frame was not an easy task," she continued.

"It could not have been done without your guidance," Yuri replied, truthfully. The technical knowledge the woman had shared with him went beyond anything he had ever seen.

"I require another modification," she said, handing him a tablet.

Yuri scrolled through the document. He stared at the specifications for several moments before grasping the potential implications. He gaped at the woman.

"The applications of this would be—"

"Limitless," she completed.

He did not deem her words an exaggeration. *Still...* "The technical challenges are… significant," he said.

"I am not interested in excuses," the woman responded. "The information I shared with you until now is trivial compared to the knowledge I hold."

"I will do my best," he said. "If it can be accomplished, it will be done."

"Of that I am certain," she said. "Grief and revenge are powerful motivators."

And common enemies make unlikely allies, he thought wryly.

"If you are successful, this will help us wipe out the Society," she said, dismissing him.

Or anything you choose to… he thought as the door opened and he stepped out.

———

ALYSSA TRUDGED UP THE STAIRS, barely able to keep her eyes open. Paul and Clay walked on either side of her, not looking any better than she felt. Her head buzzed with the new information and the presence of her trusted friends. They had discussed several options deep into the evening but decided to postpone any decision until tomorrow morning when they could think about it with clear minds. Right now, all she could think about was the plushy bed in her room.

They crossed the long corridor and stopped at her bedroom door. She faced Paul.

"I'm glad you're here," she said, wrapping her arms around him. She turned to Clay. "And you." She gave him a long hug. "I don't know what I would do without you two."

Clay gave her a tired smile.

"Get some sleep," Paul said. "We have some decisions to make in the morning."

She nodded and stepped into her room. She fell into the oversized mattress, yawning deeply and stretching out her arms and legs as far as they could go, relishing in the softness and fresh smell of the linens.

Ahh… a little slice of—

The soft knock on the door interrupted her brief respite.

"Whatever it is, it can wait until tomorrow," she mumbled, half asleep.

The knocking repeated, louder.

She groaned. "*Leammelone…*"

The knocking turned into banging.

"It is time—*Horus.*"

MY EYES SNAP open at the words, the voice harsh and guttural.

So'bek lifts his ceremonial *was* staff as the last echoes of its rhythm against the marble floor fade into the recesses of the great hall. More beast than man, his towering figure dwarfs my small body, looming above me from behind the sacred shrine. His reptilian eyes stare down from beneath his hood as I kneel in the center of a triangle facing the altar.

Three individuals hold stations at the three vertices of the triangle. Even though my blood is too young to have been blessed with an animal sentinel, I can sense their presence, soothing me and giving me strength for the trials I am about to face.

A ring of Hybrids surrounds the four of us, dressed in white robes, their faces solemn, but their eyes warm and reassuring. I take comfort in remembering my mother's words that no Hybrid has been rejected by a sentinel since before I was born six years ago. Still, the thought that I may be the one makes my stomach heavy with fear and nausea.

So'bek nods. I rise and turn right until I face the first member of the triad that surrounds me. It is my mother, the queen of our people.

"Isis, Daughter of Ra," So'bek's voice rings through the chamber, "what parting gift will you bestow upon this child as he embarks to face the Trials?"

She steps forward and peers down at me, her feline eyes calm and full of confidence. Her hands hold a golden amulet. I bow my head, ready to accept her gift and blessing as she hangs the talisman around my neck.

"Your animal sentinel will find you," she says, the warmth of her voice matching the love in her eyes, "and you will return home safely." She places her hands on my forehead in the traditional blessing of our people, her forefingers and thumb forming the sacred triangle that represents the rays of the sun.

I wait until she lifts her palms then turn to my right again and face my father, our king and sovereign ruler of the Hybrids.

"Osiris, Son of Ra," So'bek's voice rings out again. "What shall be your parting gift to this child?"

My father regards me for several heartbeats, the fierceness in his golden eyes giving me strength. I lift my head and hold his gaze, unblinking. An acolyte approaches him with a tablet of black ink and a golden reed. He dips the reed into the ink and traces a cartouche on my forehead. I feel its power and warmth spreading through my body, melding with the amulet around my neck.

When he speaks, his voice is deep and full of pride. "You are Horus. Son of Isis and Osiris. You shall know no fear."

I bow my head, and he repeats the blessing of our people.

I turn to the right a third time and face the front of the triangle once again, gazing at the child who completes the triad. He is my companion, my most trusted friend. I look into his blue eyes.

"Set, Prince of the Pure Ones," So'bek calls to him. "What shall be your parting gift to Horus?"

Set approaches me and holds an onyx dagger before me. I grasp it with my right hand. It is heavy and cumbersome in my young grip, but I know it is perfectly balanced and shall fit my hand flawlessly as I mature. Forged by the Pure Ones' royal master smiths out of ore that fell to our island from the sky, its edge is sharper than any hardened steel and more durable than gold.

"May this dagger drink of the blood of those who shall attempt to harm you or your kin," Set says, the solemn words at odds with his young voice.

Our gazes catch and one corner of his mouth tugs into a sheepish smile.

"Brothers forever," he says, and he repeats the triangle blessing of my people.

"Brothers forever," I reply.

So'bek lifts the *was*. "The parting gifts of protection, courage, and strength have been bestowed upon you by those you love," he calls out. "May they guide your journey as you enter the Trials of Valediction. May they help you and your sentinel find each other and bring you safely back home."

So'bek lifts the *was* and strikes the marble three times, and the circle around me parts as the sound rings out.

———

THE KNOCKING GREW LOUDER.

"Miss Morgan," Jacques's voice rang through the door.

Alyssa's brain took a moment to make sense of the words.

"Miss Morgan," Jacques repeated. "Lord Renley kindly requests your presence at the breakfast table."

What? I just…

Any lingering haze of sleep vanished from Alyssa's mind. She opened her eyes—and blinked at the bands of bright sunshine flooding in through the wooden shutters.

"Miss Morgan? Is everything in order?"

"Yes… yes, thank you, Jacques," Alyssa managed to mutter. "I will be down as soon as I can."

"Very well, Miss," he replied.

Alyssa sat up. She still wore last night's clothes, and the bed covers were tucked in. She checked her phone. Seven forty-five in the morning.

A cold wash swept through her, raising goose bumps on her arms.

What is happening to me?

She sat up and hugged her knees tightly, tears threatening. A pressure built inside her chest. She fought back the tears and sat perfectly still, too afraid to move, waiting for the pressure to pass. When it did, she took a trembling breath, trying to clear her mind, then slid her feet to the floor and lumbered to the bathroom.

PAUL AND CLAY hunkered down at the table, engrossed in their Eggs Benedict. They glanced up and mumbled a quick greeting when Alyssa entered the room before turning back to their plates.

Boys... Alyssa thought.

Renley stood. "Good morning, Miss Morgan. I trust you had a restful night."

"I need coffee," she said and plopped into a chair.

Paul looked up. "You okay?"

She shook her head. "I don't know."

"What is it?"

She held up her hand and waited for Jacques to pour a steaming cup of coffee from a silver pot and set it in front of her.

"I am more of a tea drinker, but Jacques assures me it is quite palatable," Renley said. "I hope he brewed it to your satisfaction."

She took a sip and let the richness of the taste spread through her mouth.

"It's delicious, thank you," she managed to reply.

"Another dream?" Paul asked.

She nodded then took another couple of sips.

"Want to talk about it?"

Alyssa shook her head.

Renley cleared his throat. "Have you considered our next course of action?" he asked.

"Please tell me that sleeping on it put some sense into you," Clay added, pleading.

"Do we have any other options?" Alyssa asked.

Silence filled the room.

"Very well," Renley said. He gave a brief nod to Jacques who stepped out and returned a few moments later. A tall, middle-aged woman wearing a black floral dress accompanied him.

"This is Mrs. Brandenthorpe," Renley said. "If you and Mr. Matthews are to have any chance of succeeding aboard the *Valediction*, you must have at least a working knowledge of the etiquette and manners becoming of a steward."

He nodded at Clay. "Mr. Obono, here, will assume the role of your principal during your education."

Clay chuckled and reclined in his chair. "Brilliant! I always wanted to have minions!"

Alyssa grumbled. "Call me minion one more time, and you'll be wearing this coffee in your lap."

"Miss Morgan!" Mrs. Brandenthorpe gasped. "First rule: we never, ever talk back to our principals."

"But he started it!" Alyssa said, exasperated. She looked to Renley for support.

Renley turned and headed for the door. "I shall leave you to it, then. I have some phone calls to make."

"But…" Alyssa trailed off.

Clay grinned at her shamelessly.

"He's so going to enjoy this," Paul moaned.

Mrs. Brandenthorpe moved into the middle of the room. She possessed a long face with a deeply etched forehead, a road map to decades of furrowed brow. Her pointed nose held a pair of floral-print glasses, from which she seemed to look down at them, sized them up with poise that conveyed class, intelligence, and motherly concern all in one.

"If I may have your attention, then," she began. "I shall attempt to convey to you an abridged account of stewardship, including international protocol, proper salutations, clothing and valet care, and culinary expectations. We shall start with instructions on the silver service."

"Silver service?" Alyssa asked.

Mrs. Brandenthorpe gave a heavy sigh, the look of disappointment making Alyssa feel like she just spilled tea on the woman's favorite table cloth. "Silver service, my dear Miss Morgan, is the highest form of stewardship. It is the cornerstone of…"

Alyssa clenched her jaw as Mrs. Brandenthorpe continued her lecture.

Perhaps being captured by the Society isn't the worst that can happen to me.

THREE HOURS LATER, Alyssa struggled to ignore her grumbling stomach—and the random impulse to stick a fork in her own eye as Mrs. Brandenthorpe reviewed the key facets of the bishop's hat napkin fold. *If I have to fold that napkin one more time—*

"Miss Morgan?" Mrs. Brandenthorpe looked at her expectantly. "Shall we run through the serving order while practicing our folds?"

"Of course," Alyssa said, contorting her face into a smile. "We start with the principal, who will be seated at the head of the table," she recited. "Serve from the left, clear from the right. Use the right hand to clear a used plate and left hand to slide in a fresh plate."

Mrs. Brandenthorpe nodded. "Very good, Miss Morgan. Except when...?"

Alyssa stared at her. "Except when... uh..."

The woman waited a moment before turning to Paul. "Mr. Matthews?"

"Except when the patron is obstructing," he replied. "We never lean across the patron. To avoid it, we remove plates from the left."

"Outstanding, Mr. Matthews," she replied, giving Paul a satisfied smile and simultaneously raising an eyebrow at Alyssa. *How did she do that?*

The woman moved to the table. "Now, shall we put your freshly acquired knowledge into practice?" She faced Clay. "Mr. Obono?"

Clay looked up from the laptop and sat up straighter in the chair at the head of the table.

"Would you care for lunch now, sir?" she asked him.

"Would I ever!" Clay exclaimed. "I'm starved like a —"

Ms. Brandenthorpe raised another eyebrow, and Clay cleared his throat. "I mean… Yes, ma'am. Indeed, I would."

"Miss Morgan, Mr. Matthews, if you would be so kind." She pointed to the table.

If there was a Hell, Alyssa spent the next hour in it, having Mrs. Brandenthorpe draw attention to every single misstep while she and Paul served lunch for Clay and his six imaginary VIP friends.

Alyssa shot an envious glance at Paul, who seemed to move around with ease and grace.

How is he so good at it?

By the time it came to clear the plates, her brain felt like it was going to explode, and she was slowly losing the struggle with the pounding inside her temples.

"Miss Morgan!" Mrs. Brandenthorpe exclaimed.

Alyssa jolted, almost dropping the stack of plates.

"We do not stack the tableware! That may cause undesired clinking. Please watch Mr. Matthews."

Alyssa's nostrils flared. *I'll clink—* She bit her lip and kept her mouth shut.

"And what is the final step before dessert is served?" the woman asked.

Alyssa stared at her cluelessly. Paul shrugged.

"Crumbling the table, of course," Mrs. Brandenthorpe exclaimed, her voice ringing out enthusiastically. "It is the key to freshening up before serving pudding." She handed Alyssa a thin brush and put her hand on Alyssa's wrist. "We use small movements of the wrist to remove the crumbs, like so, while—"

Alyssa snatched her wrist away from the woman's hand.

"Enough!" she threw her hands up in exasperation. "I can't take this anymore!" She flung the brush across the room.

Mrs. Brandenthorpe recoiled, gasping. "Miss Morgan!" she said, her face a mirror of indignation. "Such an outburst is not becoming of a silver service stewardess."

"The Society may be planning an epidemic, and I'm learning about crumbling the table!" Alyssa shrieked. "We don't even know if Lord Renley will be able to get us on board that friggin' boat!"

The woman stared at her as if Alyssa had just stepped on the Queen's corgi.

"It's more of a ship," Renley's voice rang from the door, "and the answer to that particular question appears to be yes."

Alyssa whirled. "I'm sorry…" she started, heat flushing her cheeks.

"Fortunately, as I had hoped, my word still appears to carry some influence within certain circles of the Society," Renley continued, seemingly unperturbed. "I was able to recommend you both for positions as junior stewards. You will start tomorrow."

Paul's plate hit the table with a loud clang. "Wha-what?" he stammered. "Tomorrow?"

"There is a helicopter in Tenerife that is scheduled to leave for the *Valediction* in eight hours," Renley said. "I suggest we do our best to ensure you are both aboard that flight."

Paul stared at him, swallowing hard. "But we don't have a plan yet. And there's so much more to learn!"

"The jet will take you to Tenerife. We can discuss the plan en route," Renley replied.

Alyssa's eyes lit up. "Then we'd better start getting ready!"

She ripped off her serving apron with a flare and handed it to Mrs. Brandenthorpe with her best imitation of a deep curtsy then spun and raced out of the room.

Paul's eyes ping-ponged between Mrs. Brandenthorpe and Alyssa's back. "But we haven't even finished our crumbling lesson!" he called after her, his voice cracking.

THE ATLANTIC OCEAN stretched in all directions beneath her, the fading sunlight scattering diamonds across its surface. Despite the heavy sound-dampening headset that covered Alyssa's ears, the hour-long pounding of the propeller blades had begun to rattle her brain as the helicopter swept through the air, a thousand feet above the whitecaps.

She turned from the window and glanced across the cramped, four-passenger cabin at Paul—

James. Not Paul, she reminded herself. *James Truman. From Chester.*

He rested in the tight seat across from her, eyes closed, his head drooping onto his chest.

How can he sleep through all this noise and shaking?

She studied his face, still trying to get used to his freshly cropped short hair and cleanly shaved chin. Renley said that, as junior stewards, they would be unlikely to run into any Society members during their short stay, much less any who might actually recognize them. Still, they weren't taking any chances. Her own transformation had been no less dramatic than Paul's. She scrutinized the reflection of her made-up face and blonde curls twisted into a French braid. She pushed the red-rimmed glasses over the bridge of her nose. In addition to aiding in her disguise, the glasses contained a miniature camera in the left temple. Their only links to the outside were two sets of military-spec communication units disguised as Bluetooth earbuds. Once they hooked their phones into the ship's Wi-Fi, the earbuds should allow them to piggyback an encrypted signal over the yacht's satellite uplink and communicate with Clay. *At least, that's the plan.* Alyssa hoped he was right, or they'd be completely on their own.

Her throat tightened at the thought of falling into the Society's hands. It was that possibility that convinced her to leave the crystal behind with Clay. She was reluctant to part with it, but knew it was the safest thing to do. She hadn't even told Paul about the crystal. The fewer people knew about it, the better.

"There she is, boys and girls," the pilot's voice rang in her headset, interrupting her thoughts. "Starboard side, two o'clock."

Paul jerked awake and glanced out the window. Alyssa twisted in her seat and followed his eyes. She gasped. Despite Renley's description, seeing the ship in real life was every bit as striking as he had predicted it would be.

The *Valediction* was the largest superyacht in the world. Even though it was privately owned, the details of its design and functions were as tightly guarded as the specifications of a top secret military vessel. At over six hundred feet long it was almost twice the length of a football field, with a complement of over a hundred crew, all highly screened and sworn to secrecy. The hull was painted a deep metallic silver that shimmered in the fading sunlight. The superstructure above the hull was completely enclosed by a sleek arrow-shaped glass dome that hid the deck and made the yacht appear more like a spaceship than a boat. Rising from the top of the glass, four Doppler radar domes and an array of antennas completed the unearthly look.

The young man sitting next to Paul craned his neck across the narrow isle to steal a glance out of Paul's window.

"Crickey, that's one mother of a ship," he blurted out, his thick accent ringing through her headset. Dan Malone, the lanky Aussie with a craggy nose and eyebrows that could have passed for a pair of bushy caterpillars, gave Alyssa a boyish grin and a shameless wink when he spotted her glance. He was as talkative as he seemed eager to start his twelve-week rotation as the kitchen porter and only stopped running his mouth after the pilot told him to cut the chatter.

"It is impressive," the fourth and final occupant of their cabin said. Lisa's pinched-lipped expression and tight ponytail matched the rigid posture she'd held throughout the entire flight. A twenty-year-old from Switzerland, she spent the last two years serving as a *hofdame*, or court lady, for a Danish noblewoman.

Alyssa turned her attention back to the ship, its structure rising out of the water, reflecting the fading sunlight like an island.

Without warning, a cascade of images blinded her, frozen snapshots of another life, popping like camera flashes in her head.

A tall spire rising high above the water... The wind whips into me as I plunge to it, the tower growing larger and larger in my vision—

Alyssa gasped.

"Jane!" Paul's voice snapped her back. "Are you okay?"

Alyssa's breath caught in her chest. She swallowed to gain her voice. "I... I'm fine," she said. Dan and Lisa eyed her with concern.

"Everything okay back there?" the pilot asked.

"I'm good," she mumbled. "Just... feeling a bit motion sick, that's all."

"Hold it together," the pilot said. "We'll be wheels down in two minutes."

Paul frowned, looking entirely unconvinced, as Lisa slipped her hand into the side pocket of the seat. She fished out a paper bag.

"Here," she said, giving Alyssa a small smile. "Just in case."

"Thank you," Alyssa glanced down, avoiding Paul's gaze, but could feel his eyes on her. She curled her fingers into tight fists to keep her hands from trembling.

The helicopter circled the ship once and swung around for a landing. A section of the glass canopy slid open, and a circular platform rose up. The canopy appeared to grow larger beneath them as the pilot lowered the chopper onto the ten-foot H stamped on the white helipad.

Only now did she get a true sense of the vessel, a glass island in the middle of the ocean. They set down with the slightest of bumps, then the engine noise cut out, and the rotors began spinning down. Alyssa let out a breath she didn't realize she was holding.

She flinched as the platform shuddered and descended into the ship, the glass hatch slowly closing above them. As it sealed, her eyes met Paul's. The expression in his face mirrored her own thoughts.

We're in the lion's den.

———

ALYSSA GLANCED into the eyes of the most physically intimidating man she had ever seen. He was tall, fair-haired, big as a bear and twice as mean looking. His gaze rested calmly on her from beneath the visor of his military style patrol cap that matched the fatigues straining to contain his bulk. The smell of burned aircraft fuel stung her eyes, but she kept his gaze unblinking as he sized her up. Several long seconds later he moved past her to Paul, who stood on her right.

Five minutes ago, the four of them had exited the helicopter and were ordered to line up, keep silent, and await further instructions. A short while later, this mountain of a man entered the small hangar, accompanied by a diminutive woman dressed in a white coat, carrying what looked like a small cooler. Her short auburn hair was combed neatly into a boyish cut.

The man pointed at the woman. "This is Ms. Agnews, our chief nurse. My name is Sergeant Maxwell Torin. I am head of security on the *Valediction*." His voice was measured, his speech surprisingly eloquent. "The safety and well-being of the members and the crew have been placed in my hands. I will protect both from any external—" he swept his gaze over them —"or internal threats." He clasped his hands behind his back. "Any questions?" His eyes rested on Alyssa.

"No, sir," she said.

He moved closer to her until her view was fully obstructed by his chest. She craned her head.

"You may address me as Sergeant, Sergeant Torin, or even Mr. Torin," he said, "but please do not call me 'sir.' I work for a living."

She swallowed hard. "Yes, Sergeant," she said.

He let his gaze linger on Alyssa for another heartbeat before nodding to the woman behind him.

"Ms. Agnews," he said.

The woman pointed to the metal bins before them. "Please empty your pockets and place all items into the tray directly in front of you," she said.

Alyssa deposited her purse and phone into the tray and glanced to Paul. He pulled out his headset and placed it into his tray along with his phone and wallet. The case of Paul's phone looked like a standard battery case, but it contained a highly sophisticated digital lockpick. The slim electronic skeleton key was controlled by a decryption software app on the phone that was disguised as a word puzzle game. Fortunately, Renley was able to warn them about the tight security protocols, and Clay assured them that the devices would stand up to even the most rigorous inspection.

Sergeant Torin waited for them to finish, then reached to his belt and pulled out a metal detector wand. He motioned Lisa to him. She stepped forward and spread out her arms. He tracked the wand across her body while the woman carefully inspected the contents of Lisa's tray. A few moments later he motioned her back. He waved to Alyssa.

She approached him and copied Lisa's posture. She held her

breath instinctively as he inspected her. When he finished, he pointed to Paul and then Dan. Ms. Agnews gave a slight nod.

"You may retrieve your items," he said.

Well, that wasn't so bad, Alyssa thought, reaching for her purse and phone.

"The final security measure ensures that you stay within the authorized boundaries of the vessel," Torin said. "Due to some unfortunate events that occurred in the last several days, we have increased our security protocols."

Ms. Agnews opened the cooler and lifted a device that looked like a cross between a hypodermic needle and a pistol.

"This is a hypodermic injector," she said. "It deposits a micro-tracker under your skin that will allow us to monitor your whereabouts while you're on board. This measure has been put in place for the safety of the ship and for your own protection."

Alyssa froze. Her mind raced as their plan threatened to derail in front of their eyes. Renley had told them about electronically locked tracking bracelets, and Clay had already instructed them on how to crack the locking mechanism. They were not prepared for this.

How am I supposed to get into the server room with a tracking device inside me?

Paul placed a calming hand on her arm, as if sensing her thoughts.

Ms. Agnews caught the exchange.

"I know it sounds scary," she said, misinterpreting Alyssa's alarmed face. "But please rest assured that this device is completely harmless. It's only the size of a grain of rice, and the injection isn't any more painful than getting a flu shot." She gave a reassuring smile. "Now, who wants to go first?"

For several seconds nobody moved. Finally, Dan stepped forward. "Ah, hell, let's just get this over with."

An acid churning had begun in Alyssa's gut. This could not be happening. All of their planning and hard work was going down the drain. The hangar appeared to close in around her. They were trapped, and now the Society was going to be able to track her every move. Their plan—

"Ow! Fu—" Dan cried out before catching himself. He glared at Ms. Agnews and rubbed his forearm. "Flu shot, my arse!"

"You big baby," Ms. Agnews teased. "It'll stop stinging in a couple of minutes. If it doesn't, come by the med bay. I'll get you a Spidey Band-Aid to make it feel better."

Dan fell back in line, his face glowing red.

Paul moved up and rolled up his sleeve. Alyssa tensed, but she knew they didn't have a choice. Any objections would only cause suspicion.

Ms. Agnews sterilized Paul's forearm then reloaded the injector with another cartridge from the cooler and pressed it against his skin. He grimaced when she squeezed the trigger.

He stepped back. "See, nothing to worry about," he said to Alyssa, tugging the corners of his mouth into a smile, but she didn't fail to notice the concern in his eyes.

Alyssa took a deep breath and approached the woman. The alcohol tingled her skin as Ms. Agnews swiped the antiseptic pad across her forearm. Alyssa read the name on the side of the device. *Biojector.*

"Take a deep breath and let it out," Ms. Agnews said. "It'll be over before you know it."

It took all of Alyssa's willpower not to tear her hand from

the woman's grasp. The swish of the autoinjector merged with the sensation of a hot needle piercing her flesh. She opened her mouth to scream, but before she could make a sound it was all over. A dull pain remained that slowly transformed to an ache.

"All done." The woman placed an adhesive bandage over the injection site and patted her on her back. She waved over to Lisa. "Last but not least."

"I... I do not think I can do it," Lisa said, her Swiss accent exaggerated by her anxiety.

Alyssa realized that she had been so worried about them noticing her own apprehension that she didn't even notice Lisa's.

"I am very afraid of this," Lisa said, her face pale. "I... I wish to reconsider this assignment... please."

"Are you certain?" Ms. Agnews asked, eyes narrowing for an instant.

Lisa nodded.

"Very well," Ms. Agnews said. She glanced at Sergeant Torin.

"You will be placed on the next flight out to the mainland," he added. "However, since you refused the bio-tracker, you will be guarded at all times while on board."

Lisa nodded silently, stifling a sob.

Torin lifted his hand to his earpiece. "The other transmitters are functioning properly," he said, facing the other three. "You are now free to move about the sanctioned areas of the *Valediction*. Ms. Agnews will show you to your quarters."

He motioned to Lisa and said, "Please come with me."

Lisa followed him. Before she disappeared through the door, she turned, catching Alyssa's eye.

Ms. Agnews picked up the cooler. "Ready to see your cabins?"

"What about our bags?" Dan asked.

"Your bags will be delivered to you shortly," she replied.

Alyssa glanced at Paul. No doubt the delivery service was another opportunity to search through their belongings.

They moved to the far corner of the hangar, stopping in front an elevator. Ms. Agnews pressed a button to summon it.

Dan pointed to a glass elevator across the hangar. "Can we take that sweet glass one, instead?"

"That particular elevator is for the exclusive use of our guests," Ms. Agnews said, "and is off-limits to you. This is the crew elevator."

Dan's face sagged, but he nodded. The doors slid open, and they stepped inside. Alyssa marveled at the polished wood and matte bronze accents inside. *If this is the crew elevator, what does the other one look like?*

"We'll go directly to the crew deck," Ms. Agnews pressed the button for deck four. "You will receive a tour of the appropriate sections and an orientation briefing at 19:00 hours today."

Paul glanced at the number of the buttons and whistled. "Twelve floors? That's more than the apartment building I live in!"

Ms. Agnews smiled at him. "They're called decks. It's James, isn't it?"

"Yes, ma'am." He cringed. "It's safe to call *you* 'ma'am,' right?"

Ms. Agnews laughed. "Yes, James, you may call me ma'am."

"Whew," Paul said, mock-wiping his brow.

How does he do that? Alyssa stared at him, both envious and vexed at Paul's innocent charisma. Her mind wandered to their first meeting.

"Whatcha grinning at?"

She started at Dan's voice. "Just some memories," she replied.

"Cool. I have those, too, sometimes. Uh, I mean..." He grimaced at his own words and tugged at his collar, his face turning crimson.

Alyssa stared at him, trying not to laugh. "That's... great."

Mercifully, the elevator came to a stop. The trio followed Ms. Agnews into the hallway.

"Deck four, crew living quarters. They're aft—" she glanced to Paul—"that's the rear of the ship, James. Your mess hall, workout area, and the commons, which is our gathering area, are here as well." She motioned them to keep up, and they arrived at an intersection. "There is a small movie theater and lounge for your use." She pointed to the left. "The female sleeping quarters are on the port side—left as the ship is moving forward—and the male sleeping quarters are on the starboard side." She looked sternly from Alyssa to the two young men. "We have a strict policy against fraternization among our crew members." She gave a small smile. "But we also understand that we have a hundred young men and women aboard, so whatever you do, keep it to yourselves." Her face grew stern once again. "However, if it even appears to affect your work performance or cause any distress to your fellow crew, there will be consequences."

She pointed starboard. "Gentlemen, you're assigned cabin forty-eight. Just follow the numbers down the passageway."

Dan punched Paul playfully in the shoulder. "Awesome, roomy!"

"Oh, yay." Paul stifled a grimace as Dan took off for the cabin.

"Dibs on top bunk!" the Aussie yelled.

Paul shook his head and trotted after him.

"Don't forget, 19:00 hours, commons!" Ms. Agnews called after them. She turned to Alyssa. "Nice young men," she said. "I think they'll get along just fine."

They moved portside and arrived at cabin twenty-one.

"You were assigned to share your cabin with Lisa, but since she won't be staying, enjoy your temporary upgrade to a solo suite. You will find your crew manual on your desk and uniforms in the closet. Do you have any questions?"

"No, ma'am," Alyssa replied.

"Very well. In that case, I shall see you at 19:00 in the commons."

Alyssa entered the cabin and locked the door behind her. She leaned against it and exhaled deeply, studying the small compartment. A bunkbed occupied the wall on her left, and a narrow desk butted against the opposite wall, a chair shoved tightly underneath. Facing her was a door to the bathroom —*head*—she reminded herself.

At least I'll have it to myself. They needed all the breaks they could get. *I do hope Lisa is all right,* she thought with a twinge of guilt.

She peeled off the adhesive bandage from her forearm and gently rubbed her finger over the skin, pressing on the tiny bump. She needed to check in with Clay and Renley as soon as possible, so they could start devising an alternate plan.

She entered the bathroom and turned on the shower. She wouldn't put it past the Society to bug the crew cabins. The splatter from the water should drown out any words whispered into the headset.

Alyssa reached into her purse and pulled out the comm unit. Her fingers brushed a small plastic pill bottle. She lifted it out. Mixed among the anti-inflammatories and motion sickness meds hid their ticket off this ship. One of the capsules contained a partially inactivated strain of Norovirus, a nasty and highly contagious GI bug, and scourge of cruise ships. Ingesting this strain would give her symptoms that are manageable, but that mimic the full-fledged disease sufficiently to get them rushed off the ship. The plan was for Alyssa and Paul to take these as soon as they established the remote connection to the server, ensuring that they both were on the first available helicopter flight off the boat.

She put the pill bottle back into her purse and slipped in the earpieces. She waited for the Bluetooth connection to pair up, then tapped a game icon on the phone and typed in the password to start the scrambling software.

I sure hope Clay is as smart as we all think he is...

She chewed her bottom lip as she waited for the software to find the ship's Wi-Fi signal. She exhaled deeply when the icon turned into a smiley face—Clay's personal touch. She was online, piggybacking on the carrier signal to the satellite uplink.

"Clay? Clay, come in." She waited for several long seconds. Nothing. Her chest tightened. "Clay are you—?"

"Alyssa!"

She exhaled with relief.

"Are you and Paul okay?"

"Yes," she answered, "But we've got a problem."

Clay hesitated. "Uh-oh… What do you mean?"

"Those tracking bracelets Renley told us about… They replaced them with an implant."

"They what?"

"They tagged us with some tracker. I've got a friggin' chip stuck in my arm. And so does Paul!"

"Oh, not good… not good at all…" Clay muttered.

"You're not exactly inspiring confidence."

"Sorry… sorry… it's just… damn. Okay, okay. We can do this." She heard him take a deep breath. "Tell me all you can about this doofer."

"It was deposited with a… hypodermic injector, the woman called it. It looked like a cross between an old-style *Star Trek* phaser and a needle syringe." She tried to recall the name printed on the side of the device. "I think it said 'Biojector' on it."

"That's my girl!" She couldn't tell whether he was more excited at her recalling the name of the device or her making a *Star Trek* reference. "Tell me all you can about where they injected it and how big it is. Did they say anything?"

"Not much, only that it was harmless. It's about the size of a grain of rice. It's right in the middle of my forearm about a quarter inch deep. And itchy as hell."

"I'll see what I can find out about it, put some of Lord Renley's resources to good use."

"Thank you, Clay." She took a deep breath. "I gotta go. I'll call in as soon as I can."

"Sounds good. Do be careful."

"I'll try," she answered and removed her earbuds.

———

DAN WAS WHISTLING CONTENTLY, browsing through the kitchen uniforms hanging in his closet.

"Check it out, mate!" he said, turning to Paul with a grin. "How sick are these?" He lifted one up for Paul.

"Fully." Paul nodded approvingly. "I'm going to jump in the shower." He wanted to check in with Clay and report on the damn tracker.

"Right on," Dan replied and turned to the hats.

Paul knelt at his dresser and pulled a towel from a drawer.

"Hey, mate, you think I can go to the meeting in thongs?" Dan asked.

"What?" Paul whirled, mortified.

Dan lifted up a pair of flip-flops. "My feet are killing me."

Paul exhaled. "Ms. Agnews probably wouldn't approve," he said.

Dan's face sagged. "Yeah, you're probably right."

Paul shook his head and stepped into the bathroom and closed the door behind him, locking it. He started the shower and slipped in the earbuds then tapped on the icon on his phone.

The knock on the door interrupted him. "Hey, James, sorry to bug ya."

Paul took out one of his earbuds. "What is it?"

"Sporting one of those uniforms to the meeting should be cool, right?"

I wish I had his problems. "Better than thongs," Paul replied.

"Sweet!" Dan whooped.

Paul turned to the phone and lifted the earbud to his ear.

"Or you think it'll look like I'm trying too hard?"

Paul's hand froze. He shook his head. "I don't know, Dan. Why?"

"Well, girls like guys in uniform, right?"

I don't think that started with kitchen uniforms, but... "They sure do," he said.

"Cool—thanks, mate! You're a real pal."

Paul put the earbud in and turned to the phone.

"So—you and Jane," Dan's voice started from the other side of the door.

Oh, for goodness sake... "What?" Paul took out the earbud again.

"You're not, like, going steady, are you?"

Going steady? Where are we? Middle school? You want me to pass a note to her? "It's... a bit complicated," Paul replied.

"What do you mean?"

"I mean, we don't get to see each other that much, so... it's just complicated."

"Gotcha. Okay."

Paul turned back to the phone and put his earbud in. He started typing the password.

"So, like, would you say you're more together than you're not together?"

What does that even mean? "I don't know, Dan. You realize that's an odd question, don't you?"

"Yeah, yeah... I reckon so," Dan said. "Sorry... it's just... she's a fox, you know."

More like a tiger...

"Sooo, which one is it?"

"I don't know," Paul said, exasperated. "I suppose we're more together than we're not. Listen, I really have to get in the shower. I don't want us to be late."

"Right, right," Dan said, sounding dejected. "Cheers, mate... good talk."

Paul shook his head and put in the earbud. He typed in the password and waited for the connection to establish.

"Clay, are you there?"

"Paul!" Clay's voice rang in the headset. "Alyssa just checked in. She told me about the tracker." He relayed what Alyssa had told him. "How are you holding up?"

"Let's just say I didn't hit the jackpot in the roommate lottery," he said.

"What?"

"Never mind," Paul said. "The tracker?"

"I started digging into it. It's electronic. It'll have a weak link. We'll just have to identify it."

Paul nodded. "Good—"

The knock at the door made him jump.

"What now?" he said.

"Oy, sorry to bug ya, but I really have to take a leak. You gonna be much longer?"

Is this guy for real?

"What's going on?" Clay asked.

"All good," Paul whispered. "I gotta go. I'll check in again as soon as I can." He disconnected the call and slipped out the earbuds. He stripped off his clothes and jumped into the shower.

"Almost done!" he yelled.

"Much appreciate the swiftness. My eyeballs are floating, mate."

Paul cut off the water and stepped out. He quickly toweled off and wrapped the towel around his waist. He opened the door and barely made it aside as Dan stormed in and headed for the commode. He lifted the seat and started peeing.

"Crickey, that was a close one…"

Paul closed the door behind him. *It's going to be a long three days…*

ALYSSA PERCHED on the edge of the hard bench, sandwiched between Paul and Dan in the spacious crew community quarters, surrounded by idle chatter from the fifty or so other young men and women. Like Paul and Alyssa, most wore white pants and matching polo shirts as they crowded around five large tables that filled the sparsely decorated room.

The chatter dissolved into a faint murmur when Ms. Agnews paced in, appearing slightly more agitated than when Alyssa last saw her.

"We'll have to keep the meeting short today," she began without further ado. "Only senior crew will be required on the main deck this evening. Junior crew are dismissed until tomorrow. The ship's tour for new arrivals will take place tomorrow morning. You may take time to familiarize yourself with the ship at your leisure tonight. Remember, you are consummate professionals and expected to project it in deed and spirit. Dismissed."

She exited the room.

"What's going on?" Alyssa whispered to Paul as surprised mumbles and hushed conversations percolated through the room.

Paul shrugged.

Dan trotted up to them, his face glum.

"You okay?" Alyssa asked.

"I gotta report to the galley, stat." He sighed. "There goes my evening off."

"Any clue what this is about?"

Dan moved closer. "They've got me on duty in the ship's pantry. Apparently, some important blokes came in for a meeting on short notice, so everybody's scrambling."

Alyssa looked at Paul. Dan caught the exchange. He cast a knowing glance at Alyssa.

"Betcha you'll be glad to spend some time with your boyfriend."

Alyssa looked at Dan, surprised.

Dan's eyes darted to Paul. "I thought you said that you two were going steady."

"You said what?" Alyssa asked, cocking an eyebrow.

"No, I just meant that we've known each other—" Paul started.

"James," Alyssa interrupted, giving Paul a stern look. "I don't think Ms. Agnews would condone that kind of talk. We are expected to be consummate professionals and project it in deed and spirit."

"Oh, mate, I'm sorry…" Dan lifted his hands, slowly backing away. "I didn't mean to get you in hot water with your, uh… I'll catch ya later in the room." He spun and skirted away. "Cheers," he called back over his shoulder.

Alyssa smothered a laugh as she turned to the hallway. Paul dashed after her to her cabin. She closed the door behind them.

"Oh, man, you should have seen your face." She grinned widely, making her look like a little girl.

"You enjoyed that, didn't you?"

"Immensely," she answered, laughing, spurred by the challenge in his voice. "I'm sorry," she said, coming in for a hug.

He pushed her away playfully. "Get away from me," he teased. "Why would you want a hug? It's not like we're going steady."

"But we have been through a lot together," she said, her lighthearted mood darkening. She stepped closer, lowering her voice. "This meeting seems important. We may be able to learn something valuable."

"I had a feeling you'd say that," Paul whispered back. "I'm not even going to start telling you how crazy that idea is. Besides, we don't even know how to deal with these buggers," he pointed to his arm.

Alyssa moved back and asked, "How about a shower?"

"Wha-what?" Paul drew back before realizing what she meant. "Very funny," he mouthed.

They moved into the bathroom and locked the door behind them. Paul started the shower while Alyssa connected her headset to the phone and handed one of the earbuds to Paul. A few seconds later the click in her headset confirmed the secure connection to Clay.

"Clay, can you hear me?" Paul asked.

"Loud and clear," Clay responded. "How are you? How's Alyssa?"

"I'm fine," Alyssa said. "We're in my cabin. Did you get anywhere on the trackers?"

"I got a start. Looks like they're short-range radio frequency trackers that are activated by body heat."

"That's why they kept the cartridges in the cooler!" Alyssa said. "So, can we take them out?"

"It's not that easy. There's a failsafe. Once they're removed, they stop functioning."

"They stop working right away?" Paul asked.

"Uh… that's the part I'm still trying to figure out. It probably uses the same temperature sensor as the one activating it. Based on what I've read, my best guess is that if its internal temperature falls below thirty-five degrees Celsius, it goes offline."

"Best guess?" Alyssa said.

"I know, I know," Clay said. "I'll keep looking into it. For now, don't diddle with them."

"Thank you," Alyssa said. "We'll check in when we can." She ended the connection.

"We need to be at that meeting," she said.

"And I suppose you already have a plan."

"Well, not exactly a plan," she replied. "More of an idea that's cooking."

———

TWENTY MINUTES LATER, Alyssa peeked through the round window in the stainless steel door of the ship's pantry. She spotted Dan in the far corner, shoulders slumped, staring at a tablet in his hand and muttering to himself. She knocked on the window.

Dan looked up. His face went through a confused expression, then it brightened. He rushed to the door and unlatched it.

"Jane!" he said, busting out a grin. "Whatcha doing here? Got in a fight with your not-boyfriend?"

She returned the smile. "No, we're good. Just wanted to drop by and say hi, see what you're up to." She glanced past him. The room was the size of a small apartment. What seemed like thousands of boxes of food and drinks filled row after row of shelves. Straight ahead, a pair of thick metal doors led into what she presumed was the refrigerated section.

Looks like there are enough provisions here for a year.

"Wow, this place is massive," she said.

"Ain't that the truth." Dan sighed. "And not a soul to show me around. Everybody and their uncle are chasing their tails about those bigwigs that just arrived."

"Sounds important."

"Ya think?" He threw up his hands. "And I'm running late!" He pointed at a cart filled with bottles of alcohol and jugs of juices. "I gotta bring these up so they can stock the bar in the VIP lounge."

"I could help." Alyssa offered, trying to sound casual. "I could cart some things up while you finish here."

"I don't know…" Dan scratched his chin. "Probably should be doing it myself."

"It'll be our little secret." She gave him a coy smile. "Besides, what harm can there be in recruiting some help to get things done on time? It shows initiative."

He eyed the tablet and the items on the shelves. He rubbed

the back of his neck, his face betraying an epic internal battle. Finally, he nodded. "I suppose you're right."

Alyssa's stomach fluttered. She gave him a thumbs up.

She waited while he double checked his tablet and added a couple more bottles to the cart.

"All right, I think this is it," he said, "just bring it to the door and give it to the wait staff. We're not supposed to go inside."

"You got it." Alyssa saluted. "To the door."

"You sure you'll be all right?" Dan asked.

"I'm pushing a cart into the elevator and down the hall. I think I can handle it."

"Okay, okay. Just making sure. Cheers," he said, looking almost happy.

"Don't mention it!" Alyssa waved and pushed the cart out of the pantry and into the elevator. Her fingers trembled as she pressed the button for the VIP floor. The moment the elevator door closed, she unscrewed the lid of the jug with the tomato juice, popped the plastic foil, and set the lid back on top without screwing it on. She exited the elevator onto a plush rug that ran the length of the corridor to the wide, frosted glass double doors.

A young woman wearing formal waiter's attire eyed her as she approached.

Alyssa put on her most disarming smile. "Hi."

"Who are you?" the woman asked.

"I'm Jane," Alyssa replied. "I'm helping Dan with the delivery for the bar."

"Okay, I'll take it from here."

Alyssa picked up the tray with the bottles and jugs from the cart.

"Here they are," she said. "Club soda, pineapple juice, orange—"

"It's okay, just leave it," the woman reached for the tray.

"I'm glad to help," Alyssa moved the tray awkwardly to the other woman.

"Really, I'd rather you—" Her next words turned into a screech as the tray tilted and the bottles tumbled. The tomato juice squirted out of the open container, drenching her crisp white server uniform in bright red splotches.

"Oh, God! I'm so sorry!" Alyssa cried out.

The woman stared at the red mess on her uniform. "Look what you did!" she shrieked. "I can't go in there like this!"

Alyssa set the tray on the cart and grabbed the handle. "Run and get changed," she said before the other woman had a chance to fully recover. "I'll take this in."

"Junior staff are not permitted in the Cayce Lounge."

"We're already late!"

The woman pondered for a moment, a pained expression passing through her face. Finally, she nodded and rushed away.

Alyssa breathed in and out, trying to tame her heartbeat, which rattled in her rib cage as if trying to escape. Slowly, the panicky daze cleared. She took a deep breath and approached the door.

The frosted panels slid open, and she entered the room. Or, more appropriately, the great hall. The entire circular space was open, panoramic floor-to-ceiling glass walls surrounded most of its perimeter. On the left, a vacant, concert-size grand piano idled on black polished marble near the intricately carved mahogany bar. Facing it, a myriad of colorful, exotic fish darted in a massive, curving glass tank. A dazzling, multi-tiered crystal chandelier hung in the center of the huge space. Beneath it, eight people lounged on an ensemble of minimalist, black leather furniture, oblivious to her presence.

Just keep your head down. Stay invisible.

Alyssa pushed the cart along the spotless floor to the bar. The bartender, a tall man with almond eyes and wide cheek-bones, gave her a curious look, but kept silent as she stopped at the bar and began passing him the contents from the cart. She kept her head low, eyeing the group.

"The event in Cairo was a declaration of war!" An olive-skinned man wearing gold rimmed eyeglasses leaned forward in his armchair, the sleeves of his yellow Indian *kurta* tunic flapping as he waved his arms, agitated.

"We must not rush to judgment," a woman lounging across from him interjected. "We are still unsure of what exactly occurred." She was Asian with a faint, long scar that traced the left side of her cheek from her temple to her jaw.

"We know that two dozen of our own perished needlessly!" the Indian man countered.

They're talking about the woman I saw in the hospital!

A Middle Eastern man stood from the leather sofa. "As regrettable as the incident may have been, they knew the risk," he said. His face was all angles and hard corners; a trimmed beard defined a strong chin. He wore a slate blue suit with a maroon tie, tailored handsomely to his physique. His tone and body language implied that he led the meeting. "Harnessing the ancient power continues to be our greatest pursuit. But we must learn from our past. Madame Chen and her followers prioritized swiftness over prudence." His face darkened. "And once again that course led to peril—just as it did for William Drake."

He lifted a finger to the bartender who nodded and handed Alyssa a bottle of red wine and a corkscrew, pointing at the man.

Alyssa stared at the bartender, a shiver running down her spine.

"Go," he whispered and mimicked a pouring motion.

Alyssa stood, frozen.

"Now!" he mouthed, snapping her out of it.

She crossed the room to the sitting area, her trembling legs making it hard to keep a straight line. She showed the bottle to the Middle Eastern man who gave the slightest nod without glancing up. She stepped back to work on the bottle.

"We must not disregard the possibility that what occurred may have been an accident," the Asian woman said while Alyssa fumbled with the bottle. She finally managed to peel back the foil and twist in the corkscrew.

"That may be wishful thinking in the face of the facts," the Middle Eastern man said as the cork came out with a quiet pop. Alyssa placed it on the table, and he picked it up and played with it absentmindedly while Alyssa poured a taste. "I'm afraid the situation may be more complicated and grave than we recognize," he said.

He picked up the glass and swirled the wine around then took a sip and set it back down. "What reports have we from the site?" he asked, facing a slight, bespectacled man.

Alyssa held her breath, struggling to keep her hand steady as she filled the glass.

"The team dispatched to Cairo is still piecing the events

together," the man answered. "Preliminary reports indicate that the meeting took place as scheduled. It is less clear what occurred afterward."

The Indian man stood up. "What of the reports that rather than synthesizing the genes himself as he claimed, Dr. Korzo obtained the genes from a Hybrid female who—"

Hybrid female?

The bottle almost slipped from Alyssa's hand and clinked against the wine glass as the Middle Eastern man lifted his hand to silence the Indian man. Alyssa cringed at the discontented look he gave her before he turned to the other man.

"We can discuss this matter further at an appropriate time," he said. "In private." He gave Alyssa a dismissive wave.

She nodded shyly and set the bottle of wine on the table.

The Indian man continued, "Be that as it may, this pursuit—"

"Enough," the Middle Eastern man silenced him. He shifted his gaze across the room. "Do we have access to Yuri Korzo's research files, Dr. Tibaldi?"

Alyssa followed his eyes. An Italian-looking woman with long dark hair glanced up at him, and her eyes met Alyssa's for an instant. Alyssa cursed herself and looked down quickly, but not before she noted the strange flicker crossing the other woman's eyes. Alyssa turned and paced to the door.

"Dr. Tibaldi?" the man repeated.

"Yes, right," the woman responded, sounding distracted. "Unfortunately, it appears that much of the research has been lost and—" The rest of the sentence was cut off as Alyssa exited the room and the sliding glass doors slid shut behind her.

Alyssa's heart hammered in her chest as she paced down the

hall to the elevator. That Italian-looking woman, Dr. Tibaldi, she was there in Cairo four months ago! The way she looked at Alyssa... Did she recognize her?

Alyssa replayed the conversation in her head as she pressed the button for deck four. *Hybrid female? Could she be...?*

Alyssa exited the elevator and hurried down the passageway. She slipped into her cabin and fell against the door. Paul jumped up from the chair.

She rushed into the bathroom and turned on the shower.

"Change of plans!" Alyssa whispered breathlessly as Paul entered and closed the door behind him. "We need to get to the server now and get out of here!"

Paul stared at her, bewildered.

"I think I just blew our cover. There was a woman there who may have recognized me from the manor house in Cairo."

"What?" Paul's face dropped. "Who?"

"Doesn't matter. We need to do this now!"

"No, no, no..." Paul whimpered, pacing. "This is not good."

"Paul!" she yelled.

He jerked up. "What about the tracker? Clay said that as soon as it leaves the body, the failsafe gets activated."

"He did say the failsafe is triggered by a decrease in temperature, so we just need to make sure it stays warm," she countered.

"We don't know that! It could be anything. What if it's the pH in your body or salt content that keeps it activated?"

"We have to take a chance. What if we put my arm in warm water and remove it there?"

"Even if you're right, how are we going to take it out?

Alyssa gave Paul a small smile. She reached inside her

pocket and pulled a cloth napkin then unfolded it, revealing a fillet knife. "It's sharp as a scalpel."

"Where did you…?" He shook his head, exasperated. "Never mind. And I suppose you also figured out how we'll know how warm the temperature is."

Alyssa opened the small medicine cabinet. She pulled out a first aid kit. "I checked it earlier," she said and lifted a slim glass thermometer from it.

"Really?" he said.

Alyssa placed the thermometer in the sink and started the water. "The water on this ship is desalinated sea water, so it's relatively sterile." She pointed at the water bottle on the night stand. "We can take out the tracker in the sink and transport it in the water bottle. After we hit the server, we put it back in, take the pills, and get off the ship as planned." She reached into the first aid kit again and pulled out some sterile gauze and tape.

Alyssa checked the thermometer inside of the full sink. "Forty degrees C," she said. She held out the knife to Paul. "Now or never."

"You know this is going to hurt, right?"

She nodded.

"And we have absolutely no guarantee it'll work."

She nodded again.

"Our last getaway to an exotic location got us both shot. Can't wait to see what this luxury cruise will bring…"

"Stop stalling! Are you going to do this, or do I have to cut it out myself?"

"Sorry," Paul said and took the knife. "Here we go."

Alyssa clenched her jaw as Paul tentatively pushed the tip of the blade against her forearm. A bead of blood appeared on her skin before it formed a swirling red ribbon in the clear water.

Paul put the knife down and pressed on either side of the small incision. Alyssa inhaled sharply.

"I'm sorry." Paul winced. "There's the little bugger!" he said as the tiny silver transmitter popped out of her forearm.

He reached for the bottle and submerged it in the sink then guided the transmitter into it with the knife. He took out the bottle and topped it off with hot tap water then slid the thermometer inside. He glanced at the temperature. "Still at forty degrees Celsius."

Alyssa lifted her arm out of the water and dabbed it dry with sterile gauze. She put antibiotic ointment on the incision and pressed the gauze against her arm, securing it in place with tape.

"Contact Clay and let him know the plan. We'll need all the help we can get," she said.

Paul looked at the thermometer again. "We probably have fifteen minutes or so before it cools to below thirty-five."

She gave him a small smile. "No time to waste!"

THE YOUNG GUARD stirred in his chair and faced the array of flat screen monitors suspended on the wall before him. He took another sip from the Styrofoam cup, grimacing as the lukewarm coffee hit his taste buds. His eyes moved to one of the monitors, movement catching his attention. He took a bite from his protein bar to cover up the bitter taste of the coffee and tapped his partner on the shoulder.

"See that? Deck eight, sector five?"

The older man swung his chair around lazily. He scratched his head, making raspy noises on the patchy stubble that matched his scruffy beard. He flicked the small control panel next to him.

The image from the secondary monitor moved to the central display. A young man and woman, both dressed in crew uniforms pranced down the passageway, holding hands.

"What the hell are they doing?" the young guard asked.

"Looks like a couple of crew kids," his partner said.

"Want me to call it in?"

The older man contemplated. "Check their trackers," he said.

The young guard typed a command into his workstation. Two pictures appeared on the screen.

"Jane Morton and James Truman. New arrivals," he read.

"They're just getting to know the ship. Probably looking for a place to spend some quality time between shifts," he chuckled. "As long as they stay away from the restricted areas, cut them some slack."

———

ALYSSA RAN PLAYFULLY along the corridor, holding Paul's hand, ignoring the sting in her forearm and the knot in her stomach. Beneath her playful exterior, she was strung as tight as a violin string, scanning the walls and ceilings for cameras.

The conversation with Clay after their "surgery" didn't exactly fill her with confidence, but true to form, once the initial shock had passed, he cleverly altered the plan, making use of all the resources they had.

As they approached one of the overhead cameras, she shoved Paul playfully against the wall. He reached up as if to steady himself and attached a micro-transmitter beneath the camera. He reached in his pocket and concealed another transmitter in his palm, and they continued along the corridor, repeating the procedure under two more cameras.

Paul's other pocket held the remote trigger for these transmitters. Once activated, they would fire an interference pulse tuned to the frequency of the cameras. Rather than cause the cameras to go offline and possibly create suspicion, the pulse caused the cameras to freeze their transmission, giving them a ten second window before the cameras' software would reset.

Alyssa glanced to the door to her left. *Server room. Bingo.* She considered the location of the cameras. According to Clay, the digital lockpick would take about five seconds to crack the lock. The plan was to find the closest spot out of view of the cameras and activate the transmitters. Once the images were frozen, she would rush to the server room door, unlock it, slip through, and close it. All in under ten seconds, before the cameras went live again. *It's going to be close. Really close.*

She replayed the route in her head that she and Paul had memorized from the ship layout and let Paul nudge her into the port passageway. A few seconds later, they stopped in front of a maintenance closet.

———

DR. CLAUDIA TIBALDI stormed out of the elevator and paced to her cabin, the fiery tempo of her four-inch stilettos warning passersby into giving her a wide berth.

Nothing like spending two hours trapped in a pissing contest with a room full of alphas.

And they were no closer to finding out what had actually happened in Cairo. If the preliminary reports were correct, the situation was even more dire than anybody had suspected. And where the hell was Yuri?

This would have never happened with Will in charge.

With no clear successor, William Drake's sudden death had left a gaping hole in the organization, the members bickering and vying for positions. It was anarchy at its finest. The Society has never been as divided—or as vulnerable.

She frowned. Something else had been nagging at the back of her mind. *The server girl.* She couldn't quite put her finger on it, but something about that girl didn't feel quite right. The hot bath and chilled glass of prosecco waiting in her suite were almost enough to ignore the pesky voice in her head, but she knew she would not have gotten this far without paying attention to her intuition.

She turned on her heel and stepped back to the elevator and pressed the button for the command deck.

———

ALYSSA HUDDLED AGAINST PAUL, feeling the warmth of his body against hers in the tiny supply closet. She untucked her shirt and lifted the water bottle from her waist. She eyed the thermometer before putting the comm in her ear. *Thirty-eight degrees.*

"Clay, are you there?"

"I've had this bloody headset in my ears for eighteen hours straight. You think I'd take it out now?" His voice sounded tense.

She pushed the eyeglasses over the bridge of her nose. "How's the video?" she asked.

"Paul is sweating," Clay replied.

"I take that as 'clear,'" Alyssa said.

"Remember, when you trigger the pulse for the cameras in the hall, we'll be offline for a few moments." Clay swallowed loudly. "You can do this."

Alyssa handed the bottle to Paul. "Ready?" she asked.

He nodded. "You?"

She gave him a tense smile and planted a kiss on his cheek.

"Showtime," she said. Paul pressed the button and activated the transmitter.

Alyssa ripped open the door and rushed out. She tore down the hallway, counting off the seconds in her head, and slid to her knees in front of the server room door.

Three…

She pressed the digital lockpick against the ID scanning panel and started the decoding sequence program on the phone. The display flickered through the number combinations.

Six…

Seven…

Eight…

Now would be good!

The LED light above the panel flashed from red to green, and the door lock clicked open. Alyssa threw her weight against it and flew inside, slamming the door shut behind her with her foot.

That was close.

Brushed aluminum tiles beneath her covered the space wall to wall. Alyssa gave a small shiver at the ten-degree temperature drop and the cool metal against her palms as she propped herself up. Bright overhead lights and polished walls surrounded a ten-foot-tall black tower that loomed before her, perched on a knee-high, circular base in the center of the room. A desk with a three-monitor terminal stood against the far wall.

The soft hum of fans and burble of water was interrupted by

a low whistle in her earpiece as the connection was re-established and Clay soaked in the camera feed.

"Alyssa, meet the D-wave quantum computer. Five thousand qubit of mint processing power. You're looking at one of three in the world. Brill idea to use the ocean as a cooling reservoir, by the way. With that much heat energy coming off—"

"Clay," she interrupted him. "Whenever you're done geeking out—let's do this." She gained her feet and moved to the platform, ready to step up.

"Stop!" Clay called out.

Alyssa froze.

"Give me a closer look of that platform."

Alyssa complied.

"Well, clutch your pearls," he said.

"What's wrong?"

"This beast is sitting on a gyroscopic stabilizer. You have to disable it first before getting up there."

"The what now?"

"The platform it's sitting on is self-stabilizing," Clay explained. "It keeps the tower perfectly upright regardless of the orientation of the ship to keep all the digital bits-and-bobs from swinging about in the waves."

Of course, why wouldn't it have a gyroscopic stabilizer…?

She moved to a panel next to the platform and pointed the camera at it.

"I think this might be the control for it," she said, reading the display. She followed the menus.

"Disengage auto-level?"

"Tickety-boo," Clay said. "What do you need me for?"

"Don't leave quite yet." She pressed the icon, and the platform locked in place with a metallic clang.

"Go to the other side," Clay instructed, "and look for an access door."

Alyssa circled the tower and swung open a tall metal panel. Inside the cylinder, dozens of flat computer modules, lights blinking, were stacked like pancakes, connected with neatly crimped cables.

"Now what?" Alyssa asked.

"See the top module on the left? Pull it out."

"Pull it out? Isn't it going to mess—?"

"This machine is designed with failover redundancy in case of individual component failure or abnormal termination. If any module goes offline, the other ones take over while it runs a self-diagnostic. You just need to get it back online before the diagnostic completes, and it will be reintegrated into the core framework."

Alyssa didn't understand much of what Clay said, but she took confidence from his vocabulary. Still, she held her breath as she unfastened the metal clips and pulled out the top module. She tensed when the lights on it dimmed.

"You're doing great," Clay said. "Now, this is it. Just like I showed you, find an active network port with a cable and plug the remote gateway into the port and then the cable into the gateway."

"Network port," Alyssa recalled. "Like one of those old-style phone plugs, just wider, right?"

"We'll make a computer geek out of you yet."

"Don't count on it." She craned her neck behind the flat box and pointed to a plug with a blinking green light over it.

"That's the one!" Clay confirmed.

She took the remote gateway out of her pocket, unplugged the cable from the network port on the module, and hooked up the device. She slipped the cable into the free port on the gateway.

"Okay, Clay, it's all hooked up!"

"Bees knees," he said. "Now slide it back in."

Alyssa pushed the metal box back in. After a few seconds, the lights on the front flickered, going through a sequence, then continued blinking in synch with the other modules.

"I see the signal!" Clay said. "Establishing remote connection now. Okay, let's see how good these chaps really are. I should be able to—"

The door to the room opened. Alyssa froze.

"Somebody just walked in!" she whispered. Her gaze shot around the room. She spotted an access hatch in the floor behind her.

Too far!

The door closed and footsteps approached. She squeezed her body inside the tower and hunkered down among the hardware and cables, then pulled the panel shut behind her.

She watched through the slats in the metal as a bulky, shaggy-haired man advanced on her hiding place.

———

Alyssa's line went silent.

"Alyssa!" Paul called out.

No answer.

"Clay!"

"I'm here," Clay said, his voice tense. "The interference from the computer is blocking her signal."

Paul glanced at the thermometer. *Almost down to thirty-five.*

"We're running out of time!" He willed the silver column to stop moving down.

"Then you have to buy her more," Clay said.

Paul's mind raced. *Desperate times call for...* He popped the lid and brought the bottle to his mouth. *This is going to be a bit tricky.* He carefully tilted it up and waited for the grain-sized transmitter to touch his mouth, then used his tongue to guide it between his gums and cheek.

———

CLAUDIA TIBALDI STEPPED into the surveillance office. The two guards spun their chairs around. They stood when they recognized her.

"Dr. Tibaldi," the older one said. "What can I do for you?"

"I'd like to see a picture of one our crew members."

"Can you be more specific?"

"A young woman, blonde. Glasses. I have not seen her here before."

The guard typed into the computer and a moment later several headshots appeared on the monitor. Claudia Tibaldi picked out the girl she saw. "That one. What do we know about her?"

"Just a moment, ma'am." The guard's fingers tapped on the keyboard. "Her references are impeccable. It appears that both she and the young man who arrived with her today received recommendations from the highest level."

Claudia Tibaldi skin prickled. "Who did she arrive with?"

The guard pulled up another image. Claudia Tibaldi stepped closer, her heart thudding in her throat as sudden realization rose.

"Where are they now?" she yelled.

The guard reeled back, surprised at the outburst. "They're…" He looked at the younger guard for support, to no avail. "They're in—uh—a maintenance closet on deck eight," he finally muttered.

"What?"

"They looked like a couple of kids, just looking for a place to have some fun."

"Idiots!" she yelled. "Get down there now! And send backup!"

The older guard pushed his partner to the door. "Go!" he bellowed. "I'll call for backup."

The young man stormed out of the room with Claudia Tibaldi on his heels.

———

ALYSSA EVENED OUT HER BREATHING, keeping it shallow and silent as she watched the man continue past her hiding place. He set a tall silver travel mug on the desk and squeezed into a chair before the monitors, slipped in his earbuds, and began typing.

She held her breath as she gently pushed open the panel and slid out, tiptoeing to the door.

"Paul," she whispered. "The cameras."

"Go!" Paul whispered back.

She snuck out, pulling the door closed behind her. Alyssa exhaled and turned—and stared into the eyes of a young man in a guard uniform, his chest heaving with deep breaths.

He drew his pistol. "Don't move! Keep your hands where I can see them!"

Alyssa's pulse hammered in her ears as she stared at the weapon. She spotted the door behind the guard opening. *Paul!* He put a finger to his lips as he stalked toward the young man.

"I'm sorry... Please, this is all a big misunderstanding," Alyssa said, her eyes locked on the guard's. "I... I arrived today and was just exploring the ship."

"Save it!" the guard barked. His face was a mask, a bead of sweat forming on his temple.

"Hey!" Paul's voice rang out behind him. He spun.

Alyssa's hands shot up and reached for the gun. At the same time, Paul rammed into him from the other side, and all three of them tangled to the floor. The guard grunted as he crashed onto his back, his right hand smashing into the hard metal. The pistol slipped from his fingers and slid away.

Paul rolled off him and dove for the weapon as Alyssa pinned him down for the second it took Paul to reach the gun. She groaned as the guard wrestled his hand from her grip and snatched a handful of hair, yanking her head back. She screamed an instant before she heard Paul's voice.

"Stop!"

The guard froze when he spotted Paul's cutting gaze over the muzzle of the pistol. He released her hair, and Alyssa rolled off him, trying to ignore the searing pain in her scalp. She gained her feet and moved beside Paul.

"Stay calm and everything will be fine," she said, trying to sound much braver than she felt. "We don't want to hurt you."

The guard eyed her, anger hardening his young face, but he remained motionless and silent.

She glanced at Paul. His face was twisted in agony.

"Paul! What's wrong?" she asked, concerned.

"I swallowed your transmitter," he said, grimacing.

"Wha—?"

The door at the far end of the corridor burst open, revealing the Italian woman and a guard holding an automatic rifle.

Paul shoved Alyssa ahead of him, away from the pair. They stopped in their tracks when the door at the far end of the hallway flew open, revealing another armed man.

At the same moment, the door to the server room opened up. The shaggy-haired man stepped halfway through it.

"What's all this—?" His jaw dropped when he saw Alyssa and the pistol in Paul's hand. Before he had a chance to react, Alyssa yanked him into the hallway and squeezed through the half-open door, pulling Paul with her. She slammed the door shut behind them.

"Lock the door!" she yelled to Paul.

"What? How?" Paul stammered.

"I don't know! Shoot the control panel or something!"

Paul stared at Alyssa for a second then pointed the pistol at the control panel and squeezed the trigger three times.

The gunshots thundered as the metal walls in the room amplified and reflected the cracks. The three rounds impacted the panel, bursting glass and sending sparks flying. The display on the panel went dark—then the door popped open.

Paul threw himself against it, slamming it shut. He fired a look at Alyssa.

She cringed. "It always worked in the movies!"

"Alyssa, Paul!" Clay's voice rang in her headset. "What's going on?"

"Later, Clay!" Alyssa glanced to the ten-foot tower and at the gyroscopic stabilizer. She rushed to the control panel and flew through the menus.

Manual override. She pressed it.

Calibrate maximum pitch. She crossed her fingers and pressed one of the arrows. The far side of the platform began to rise, tilting the server at the door.

She ran behind the tower, tugging Paul with her.

"What—?" Paul started.

"We'll use it to block the door!" She put her shoulder against the tower and pushed. Comprehension dawned on Paul's face. He threw his body against the tower.

A pained moan echoed through her earbuds. "No! You can't—"

"It's either this or us!" she called out, straining. Beside her, Paul's face twisted. "Come on!" The pitch of Alyssa's voice rose with the edge of the platform.

The upward movement stopped.

"No!" she cried out.

"It's too heavy!" Paul called out between strained breaths.

"Come on Paul!" she yelled, her arms and voice trembling with the effort.

Paul turned and squatted. He dug his heels into the platform and latched onto the bottom edge of the tower, shoving his back against it. A feral grunt escaped him.

The tower budged and sluggishly lifted off the floor.

"This is a really bad—" Clay shouted.

"Not now, Clay!" Alyssa cried.

"But the server controls the uplink!"

"Shut up!" they both howled in unison.

"Listen to me," Clay continued, "if the server goes offline, we're going to lose the—"

With a screech of metal, the server slid down the platform and toppled, wedging itself against the door and sending sparks flying. Clay's voice was replaced by static.

"Clay?" Paul called out. "Clay!" He flicked a glance at Alyssa. "Now what?"

Alyssa allowed herself a moment of triumph, then panic, then forced them both down. They had to get out of there. She rushed to the hatch in the floor and lifted the handle. The seals released with a whoosh, and she pulled up the hatch, revealing a ladder.

Alyssa poked her head into the space below. The deck was barely high enough to stand up and filled with various mechanical components, ducts, and conduits.

She popped back up. "Looks like a maintenance deck."

"Where does it lead?" Paul asked.

"Away!" Alyssa stepped onto the ladder.

Paul didn't follow her.

"Come on!" she urged.

"They can track me," he said. "You have zero chance of making it off the ship with me."

"What are you talking about? We'll cut it out, just like we did mine."

He pointed to his stomach. "What about this one?"

"Paul…" she reached for him.

He squeezed her hand then put the pistol in it. "It will do you more good."

Alyssa clung to the ladder, frozen. A heavy thud rattled the door. Then another.

"Go!" Paul yelled. "They'll be here soon, one way or another!"

"No," she protested. Her eyes darted around the room, to the man's workstation. She spotted the stainless steel mug on the desk. She dashed up and popped the lid.

Soda! With lots of ice!

She shoved the mug in Paul's face. "Drink it—all of it!"

"What?"

"The tracker has to be kept at body temperature, right? Clay said if the temperature drops below that it gets permanently deactivated. If you drink it fast, the cold liquid in your stomach may cool off the tracker long enough to deactivate it!"

Paul stared at her. "This might actually work," he said, shaking his head. "You're a genius!" He lifted the mug and swallowed great gulps of the cold drink.

Alyssa moved to the busted control panel and picked up one of the glass shards. Paul swallowed the last mouthful, grimacing.

"You okay?" she asked.

He stood stock still for a second, his face knotted, then erupted with a savage burp. His expression laxed.

"My throat and stomach feel like icicles. And I'm never drinking Cherry Coke again."

"Good!" She held up the shard. "Ready?"

He clenched his jaw and nodded. Alyssa tried to ignore the

racket from the corridor and keep her hand steady as she pressed the shard against his forearm, cutting into skin. Paul inhaled sharply.

Alyssa winced. "Sorry," she whispered, forcing herself to push the shard even deeper. She pulled it back out and squeezed the incision together. The silver capsule appeared on the skin. Paul lifted it from his forearm and threw it across the room.

Alyssa swung onto the ladder and slid down. Paul followed, securing the hatch over his head. He jumped down the last few rungs.

A wide space stretched before them, as large as a parking garage, save for the ceiling, which was low enough for her to touch without fully extending her arm. Smooth panel flooring lay underfoot, overhead ran rows of fluorescent lights and an open lattice of pipes and utility conduits. Support beams stood at even intervals, giving the place an eerie, grid-like appearance.

Alyssa sensed the weight of Paul's gaze on her, waiting for her assessment.

Static crackled in Alyssa's ear.

"…lyssa… Paul? Do… copy?"

"Clay?" Paul's face lit up with relief. "Clay, we're here," he said. "Can you hear me?"

The static in her headset grew quieter, replaced by Clay's voice.

"Thank God! Are you both okay?"

"How did you—?" Alyssa asked, perplexed. "I thought…"

"I managed to set up a secondary uplink just before you made a dog's dinner of that quantum rig. I had to reroute the connection through…" he paused. "Never mind. What's your status?"

"Could be better," Paul said. "We're on some sort of a maintenance floor." He looked around. "We need to get off this boat."

Clay draw in a sharp breath. "Okay… no faffing about. Good news is we've still got the uplink. Let me see if I can get to the ship's schematics."

A few moments later Clay whistled. "Yeah, baby. Ship's schematics… and security cameras." He paused. "And this will come in handy," he cackled, "their tracking system."

"So, you can see where they are?" Alyssa asked.

"Hoof it!" Clay called out without warning. "Straight ahead, another access hatch in the floor. Get in there, now!"

Alyssa and Paul took off for the hatch and dove inside. Paul secured it behind them.

"Two people just entered this section," Clay said.

Alyssa and Paul huddled in the narrow conduit, motionless, afraid to make a noise. They heard the sounds of footsteps approach then recede.

"Okay, they're gone," Clay said.

"How are we going to get off this bloody boat?" Paul whispered, his voice tense.

"Working on it." The clicking of Clay's fingers typing furiously on his keyboard rang through Alyssa's earpiece. "There is a tender garage all the way aft on deck two," he said after a few moments.

"Tender garage?" Paul asked.

"A space where they keep their smaller boats to get people to shore, along with other toys," Clay explained. "Based on the manifest, there is a speedboat. You get down there, nab that boat, and haul arse as fast and far away from this ship as you can."

"I really like that last part," Alyssa said.

"Deck two?" Paul said. "That's five levels down. We should be able to make it."

"Uh… There is one problem," Clay said. "You also need to make it all the way to the rear of the ship, and they have security cameras in all the passageways. They'll pick you up as soon as you stick your heads out into the corridor."

"Can't you take the cameras offline?" Alyssa asked.

"I could, one or two, but they're going to suspect something is up if I overdo it. I'd rather not give away the one advantage you have."

"Can you get us to the top of the ship?" Alyssa asked.

Paul looked at her quizzically.

"The hangar is aft. Remember the glass elevator?" she explained. "If we can get into the hangar—"

"Brilliant!" Clay exclaimed. "Based on the schematics, the VIP elevator from the hangar takes you directly down to the tender garage."

"Can you open the hangar roof?"

"Let me check. Yes!"

"That's our way out, then!" Alyssa said. "How do we get up there?"

"There's a vertical service shaft that runs from the bottom of the hull to the glass superstructure. It's accessible from the tween decks." Clay paused. "Bugger! It looks like they're stationing guards on all the deck exits."

"Come on, Clay, there's got to be something else," Alyssa pleaded.

Clay's fingers clicked on the keyboard again. "Okay, this could work, but it may get a bit dodgy."

———

SERGEANT TORIN STOOD over the open floor hatch to the maintenance deck, jaw clenched in a vain attempt to control the twitching in his cheek.

"No sign of them down here, Sergeant," one of the guards called up from below.

Claudia Tibaldi stalked up to him, lips compressed into bloodless lines as she surveyed the aftermath in the server room.

"Do you have any idea how troublesome these two have been for the Society?"

One of the guards lifted an object from the floor. "Here's one of their trackers."

"Where are they?" Tibaldi asked.

"It's a huge ship, they could be anywhere," the guard said. "But we have guards stationed on every deck. They—"

Torin's arm shot out and grasped the man by the collar of his shirt. He brought him close to his face, lifting the smaller man to his toes.

"You will sweep the entire ship from bow to stern. Every deck, every cabin," he whispered, barely able to contain his rage.

The man's face turned crimson. "Yes, Sergeant," he croaked.

Torin released the man, and he scampered away, barking orders. Torin faced Claudia Tibaldi.

"We will find them," he said.

"I'm counting on that, Sergeant Torin," she replied. "I have unfinished business with them."

———

ALYSSA'S KNEES and elbows throbbed from grinding against the coarse surface of the ventilation shaft. She tried not to dwell on what critters might call this dank place their home as she crawled through the narrow metal pipe in total darkness. She had turned off her phone flashlight a few minutes ago to save the battery.

"How much farther?" she asked Clay for the tenth time.

"You're more than halfway there," Clay responded patiently.

Paul sighed from behind Alyssa. "That's what you said five minutes ago."

"Just keep going. You've got this, mate. There are a lot of pipes and ducts converging at the vertical shaft. The closer you get to it, the worse the signal will be. But no worries, once you're topside, the signal will come back. I'll crack open the dome, take the hangar camera offline, and you're as good as home." Clay continued talking. Alyssa appreciated his attempt to keep their minds occupied and off their present misery.

As they pressed on, the static in her earpiece grew louder, drowning out some of Clay's words. "That'll probably be enough for them to rea…e that you've got outside… so you'd better… to the tender… and get off this…"

"Clay? Say again," she said. "I didn't get the last bit."

"That... ounds... you go... farther..." Clay's voice cut out completely.

"Clay?"

The static in her headset was the only response. The cramped tunnel seemed to constrict even further, squeezing Alyssa's chest into a tight knot.

"I guess we're on our own," Paul whispered.

They continued snaking through the narrow pipe in silence. After what seemed like an eternity, she reached the opening into the vertical shaft.

Alyssa stuck out her head and inhaled deeply, tasting the salt in the air. She took out her phone and shined the flashlight into the six-foot-wide cylindrical shaft. The beam hit the ladder on the opposite side.

You've gotta be kidding.

She bit back a curse and shined the light down. The gaping hole yawned below her for at least thirty feet, way too high to risk jumping down.

She stretched her hand to the ladder. *Nope.* She shimmied out a bit more and tried again. She extended as far as she could, grunting with the effort, but was still a couple of feet short. She sighed, frustrated, and moved back into the pipe.

"There is a ladder on the far side of the shaft, but I can't reach it."

"How far?" Paul asked.

"About six feet."

"Let me give it a try," he said.

Alyssa flattened herself against the bottom of the pipe while

Paul shimmied to the opening. Her breathing sped up when he moved over her legs, and his face pushed against her body.

"Sorry..." he mumbled awkwardly as he squeezed all the way through.

Well, that could have been exciting, Alyssa thought, *if we both didn't smell like bilge water.*

Paul leaned out. "I see it," he said. She felt him stretch out. "Still short." He slid out a little more. "Hold on to my legs."

Alyssa wrapped her arms around him and wedged her thighs and knees against the inside of the pipe.

Paul leaned out farther. "I think I've almost got it," he said. "Just a little more."

Alyssa felt him slip out of her hold.

"Wait," she tried to adjust her grip.

Paul swung out for the ladder. "I've got it!" he yelled.

His body tensed as he briefly caught hold of a rung, then his hand slipped off and he began sliding out, dragging her with him.

"Pull me back! Pull me back!" he cried.

Alyssa clawed at his clothes. Finally, her fingers locked around his belt. She pressed her thighs and feet into the inside of the pipe hard enough to bruise. Somehow, she managed to stop them both from slipping out.

"Steady now..." Paul voice trembled as his entire upper body dangled out of the pipe.

Alyssa steadied herself and gently slithered back, towing Paul with her, inch after painful inch. As she pulled him all the way in, they both collapsed, her arms still wrapped around his legs, her heart pounding.

"Thank you," he whispered. "We're going to have to try to find another way."

"There may be no other way," Alyssa replied.

She propped herself up and turned on her flashlight again, studying the pipe and shaft over Paul's body.

"If I can manage to stand up on the edge of the pipe, I can jump to the ladder, but I'll need you to hold my legs and keep me balanced until I'm ready to jump."

"After what just almost happened?"

"I'm lighter. It'll be easier for you to hold me. And it's not that far. I can do it once I'm standing."

Paul mulled this over. "Okay," he finally said. He shimmied back down.

"Back for more?" Alyssa asked as his face passed hers.

Their gazes caught and stayed. She grinned, Paul replied with a worried smile.

"Hey," she said. "I trust you. You won't let me fall."

"The only way you're falling down is with my arms wrapped around you," he said.

She melted into him, wanting to kiss him even more than she usually did. *There will be time for this later, when we get out.*

She wrapped her arms tightly around him one more time and moved to the opening.

"Hold on to my belt and feet." She tapped on the flashlight and tucked her phone into her waist. "I'm going to try to scooch out as far as I can then put my feet down and stand up."

Paul nodded and locked his grip around her waistband.

Alyssa's heart raced as she slid out as far as she dared. The air hit her face and stirred her hair. She closed her eyes for one moment, clearing her mind.

"Okay," she said. "Hold my left foot tight, I'm going to get my right foot to the edge."

She maneuvered her right foot under her and pushed up. She stood, her body glued to the side of the vertical shaft. Paul held her legs tightly against him. She peered over her shoulder, gauging the distance to the ladder.

"You ready?" she asked.

"On you," he replied.

"I go on three," she said. "One... Two... Three!"

Paul let go at the exact time she pushed off and twisted. Her fingers found the rung, and she locked her fists around it and clung to the ladder.

"Ace!" Paul called out.

Alyssa waited for her breathing and heartbeat to slow down. "Okay, your turn." She held on with her left to the ladder and extended her right to Paul. "Try to lean out and grab my hand."

Paul shimmied out and reached for her. He missed. Still short.

He leaned out a few more inches and pushed himself out of the pipe, going for it all. Time slowed as she reached for him. An instant later their hands locked. Alyssa strained with the effort, but held on tight.

"We got this," she grunted. "I'll support you as you slide out."

Her muscles strained as he shifted more and more weight onto her arm. The rung dug into her palm, and her left hand began to slip. She groaned.

"Paul, now!"

He wedged one of his legs against the edge of the pipe and pushed off. She swung him across, and he clasped his left hand around a rung. He let go of her and grasped the ladder on the right side, enfolding Alyssa.

They stood on the ladder, his body pressed against hers, trembling and breathing hard. After a few moments, Alyssa glanced up. "It's a long climb," she said and set off.

She counted the rungs subconsciously for the first fifty steps, then stopped. *Better not to think about how high we're going.*

She kept moving, mechanically, one hand over the other. Eventually, her hand reached the top rung.

A large fan idled quietly in the center section of the transparent enclosure above the shaft. A glass access door with a round metal handwheel set in its center was located directly above the ladder.

Almost there.

Alyssa's limbs trembled with exertion and fatigue, her fingers and palms raw from the climb. She hooked her left arm around the top rung and willed her right hand to let go of the ladder and reach up to the handwheel. She gripped it and twisted. The wheel didn't budge.

She collapsed back onto the ladder.

"I can't get it!" she moaned.

Paul climbed up behind Alyssa. He held on to the ladder on either side of her.

"Lean against me and use both hands."

"Are you sure?" Alyssa's stomach churned at the thought. "I know you're just as exhausted—"

"Trust me."

Alyssa leaned into Paul. "I do," she whispered. She inhaled deeply through her nose and exhaled through her mouth, then released the ladder and locked both hands around the wheel. She tugged on it. The wheel budged then rotated.

"Yes!" she hollered. She pushed on the hatch. The ocean air whipped into her as the panel lifted up and swung open. She clambered out and sank onto the glass structure, facedown, inhaling the salty breath of the ocean, tasting it on her cracked lips. Paul collapsed next to her. He groaned and flipped on his back.

"Turn around," he said, his voice choked.

"What?"

"Turn around."

She rolled over. The glass structure of the ship gave way to the night sky. Countless stars dotted the jet-black canvas, the band of the Milky Way bridging the horizons. For an instant, Alyssa was caught between the vastness of sea and space, small and insignificant, yet more connected with the natural world than ever before. She reached for Paul's hand, and his fingers melted into hers. He caressed the back of her hand with his thumb, the simple touch rousing feelings more intimate than any kiss. They lay in the warm breeze and gentle swaying, fingers intertwined, savoring their brief respite.

Her earpiece sizzled to life.

"Alyssa? Paul?" Clay's voice broke through the static. "Do you copy?"

Alyssa reluctantly turned on her stomach, eyes crinkling.

"Want to steal a boat?"

TORIN STOOD in the command center, arms folded across his chest, and followed the progress of the security sweep on the monitors before him. Decks one through eight have been cleared. So far, the two have proven resourceful enough to evade being captured, but it was only a question of time.

It is a big ship, but they will run out of places to hide, eventually.

One of the guards looked up and cleared his throat. "Sergeant?"

"What is it, Dawson?" Torin shot him a glance.

"Is one of our guests departing via helicopter?"

"What?"

"The helipad dome just opened. It looks like—"

"Close it! Now!"

"Yes, Sergeant!"

"Bring up the camera feed."

Dawson tapped on the keyboard then scratched his head, vexed.

"Uh, Sergeant? The camera feed in the hangar seems to be down."

"Get the patrols up there, stat!" Torin stormed out of the security room.

Are they trying to escape on the bird?

He sprinted along the passageway for the elevator to the hangar, his mind racing.

How the hell did they get into the hangar? And how have they been able to avoid all the guards? Unless... He stopped, realization striking.

His hand flew to the communicator.

"Dawson, come in!"

"Yes, Sergeant?"

"Shut down the power to the entire ship!"

"Sergeant, I'm not sure that we—"

"Do it now!"

So, you have somebody on the inside helping you dodge the sweep.

His lips twisted into a cold smile.

Let's see how far you get without them.

———

ALYSSA AND PAUL tore through the hangar as the glass roof above the helipad slid to a close.

"Get to the elevator," Clay's voice rang in her ears. "I will override any stops and send it directly to the tender bay. You are —Wait!" he warned. "Hide!"

They slid to a stop. Alyssa pushed Paul at a group of steel drums. They scrambled behind them.

"Two of them are moving toward the hangar. They're almost—"

Clay's voice went silent at the same instant the entire space plunged into darkness. A second later, the faint glow of emergency lights illuminated the hangar in a faint, eerie glow.

"Clay!" Alyssa whispered. "Clay, do you copy?"

"They figured it out," Paul whispered.

The door to the hangar flew open.

"Come out! We know you're here," a voice barked. "You have no place to go!"

Alyssa scanned the room, weighing their options. "The lights," she whispered.

"What about the lights?"

"Shoot them!"

"We won't be able to see anything!"

"Trust me."

Paul opened his mouth then tightened his lips and nodded. He aimed at the emergency light closest to them. The shot blasted through the hangar and cracked into the ceiling a few inches from the light.

"Damn it!" Paul hissed.

"Hold your fire!" a voice called out.

"You can do this," Alyssa said.

He took aim again and fired. This time the light exploded in a flash of sparks.

"Nice! Now the far one!"

Paul took a breath and exhaled slowly then squeezed the trigger. Another blast then complete darkness.

"I hope you know what you're doing," he said.

Alyssa closed her eyes and took a deep breath. She reached

inside her mind, into the unknown, the part that scared her. Slowly, she became aware of the mechanics of her own body, her breathing, regular and soft. Her hearing more acute.

She opened her eyes. The pitch black was replaced by muted shades of gray. Paul's face radiated with a deep glow in this strange new light that matched his scent. She took his hand.

"Follow me," she whispered.

"I can't see anything!" he whispered back.

"I can see for both of us. Stay close."

Alyssa was aware of her muscles, the way they moved, sleekly, effortlessly, her strides graceful. She didn't stumble, didn't make unnecessary noise. Her feet seemed to find their own placement on the floor beneath her.

A jarring clatter and a curse reverberated through the hangar. One of the men stood next to a toolbox, rubbing his knee, a metal can rolling at his feet. The other man lifted his comm unit.

"Turn on the lights in the hangar!"

The response was soft, but loud enough for Alyssa's hearing. "We did an emergency shutdown. It'll take two minutes for the system to reboot."

"We don't have two minutes!"

Alyssa leaned into Paul, catching a stronger trace of his scent. "Follow me. Tread softly."

They approached the glass elevator. Alyssa looked down the shaft. The elevator cabin was about ten feet below them. There was a gap between the cabin and the glass enclosure for the counterweight. *Wide enough to squeeze through.* She studied the glass enclosure, trying to judge its thickness, then at the pistol in Paul's hand.

"Paul, I'm going to need the pistol," she said.

"For what?"

"I'm going to shoot at the glass enclosure of the elevator to weaken it. The cabin is about ten feet below us. We'll jump down onto the cabin, squeeze past it, and climb down to deck two."

Paul looked at her, stunned. "You want me to jump through a glass pane into a hole I can't see."

"Yes," she said.

Paul handed her the pistol. "Just remember, I'm blind as a badger-mole."

She took the pistol in her right and gripped Paul's hand in her left. "It's about five steps to the elevator shaft. Use your arm to shield your face."

Alyssa pointed the pistol at the glass enclosure.

"Now!" she whispered and took off, pulling Paul with her.

She squeezed the trigger three times. The muzzle flash and crack of each shot assaulted her senses as they tore spiderwebs in the glass.

"Jump!" she yelled to Paul and lifted her arm to shield her face.

They crashed through the glass—and dropped down the shaft. An instant later they landed on the roof of the elevator cabin.

Paul screamed and collapsed, clutching his left ankle, his face twisted in agony.

"Paul!" Alyssa dropped the pistol and grasped Paul's shoulders.

"My leg…" he moaned.

"Can you stand?"

"I... I don't know." He slowly clambered up, leaning heavily on Alyssa, then gently shifted weight to his left leg.

"Ow!" He staggered.

Alyssa caught him. "We're almost there." She studied the gap between the cabin and the glass shaft. She gripped the heavy counterweight cable and guided Paul's hand to it. "We can squeeze between the elevator and the shaft wall. I'll go first."

Paul nodded. He picked up the pistol and slipped it into his waistband as Alyssa shimmied through the narrow space along the cable. She wedged her feet into a narrow ledge.

"I'm through. Come on down."

A few seconds later, Paul's legs appeared beneath the elevator as he made his way down the cable.

"That's it. A few more inches," she said. "There's a ledge."

Paul sighed with relief as he rested his foot on the ledge.

"We have to keep moving," she said.

They descended on the cable, Alyssa leading the way. Paul grunted with exhaustion and pain. Alyssa counted the decks as they worked their way down.

"This is it," she said. She stepped onto another ledge.

The glow of the light from above illuminated the shaft in soft light.

"They must have restored the lights in the hangar!" Paul called out.

"I need you to hold me in place while I try to pry the doors open," Alyssa said.

Paul slid down next to her. He kept hold of the cable with one hand, and balanced Alyssa as she pressed both palms against the door across the shaft, trying to force them open. She strained with the effort, but the doors stuck together as if they had been welded in place.

A rumbling noise filled the shaft and the counterweight cable lurched up, jerking Paul's arm before he could let go. He teetered on the narrow ledge. Alyssa pushed him back against the wall. He stared at her, wide-eyed, then at the cabin barreling down at them.

"Look for an emergency door release. A lever or something like that!" Paul called out.

Alyssa frantically scanned the walls. She spotted a recessed lever just above the door. She twisted it, and the doors twitched with a soft click.

Alyssa pressed her hands against the doors and pushed them apart. The panels slid open. They jumped through, seconds before the elevator zoomed past.

Alyssa pushed to her feet, panting. At any other time, she would have been happy to spend a week exploring all the toys packed in this gymnasium-sized billionaire playground, dimly lit by the emergency lights. A sixty-foot mahogany tender boat sat in a drydock in the middle of this aquatic garage. A dozen Jet Skis, motorcycles, and all-terrain vehicles lined up along the far wall.

"Looks like we're in the right place." Paul pointed at a cylindrical vessel that hung suspended by steel cables against a wall lined with diving gear. "Is that a bloody submarine?"

Alyssa ignored the sub and raced to a black, arrow-shaped boat stationed in a nook. She eyed the stern and the wide twin nozzles below the water line.

"It's a jet boat!"

"Blinding! But we still have to get it into the water!" He

hobbled over to the control of the tender door and examined it. "It looks like the door pivots down and makes a dock." He pressed the button. Nothing. He pressed again.

"Doesn't work on emergency power! I'm going to look for a manual override."

"No time," Alyssa countered. She glanced at the rails along the ceiling and cranes hanging from them. *And no time to hook up the boat, either, even if we had power.*

She spotted an SUV-sized amphibious vehicle parked across the drydock then eyed the door again.

If I can get it going fast enough...

"Find a rope!" she yelled to Paul and took off for the vehicle. "A thick one!"

"What?"

"Just do it!"

She rushed to the amphibious vehicle and climbed inside. An array of switches and levers confronted her.

It's just a car that floats, right?

She spotted a button marked "Start" and pressed it. The engine roared to life. She swung the vehicle around the drydock and came to a screeching halt next to the jet boat.

Paul speed-limped to her, an armful of coiled nylon line in his hands.

She snatched the rope and fastened one end to the tow hook of the vehicle. She threw him the other end.

"Oh no..." he muttered as realization struck.

"Tie it to the jet boat—" she pointed at the two cleats on the bow—"then get in! We'll use the vehicle to ram the door open, and it'll pull us out behind it in the jet boat!"

Alyssa raced to the wall with the scuba equipment and

picked up an oxygen tank. She lugged it back and threw it on the passenger seat.

"Clear!" Paul yelled from the back. She pulled forward slowly, cringing as the jet boat scraped along the floor.

She lined up the amphibious car with the tender door.

"Ready?" she glanced at Paul.

"You're crazy," he replied, then his lips curved into a grin despite the pain that burned in his eyes. "And I wouldn't have it any other way."

She threw the gear shift into neutral and jammed the scuba tank between the throttle and the seat. The engine growled under full acceleration.

Let's hope this thing is as strong as it looks... She popped it into gear. As the vehicle careened forward, tires squealing, she leaped onto the back seat then the rear deck and launched herself into the jet boat. The rope tightened, and the jet boat lurched forward.

Alyssa and Paul were thrown against the seats as the boat screamed across the floor, sending sparks flying. They beelined for the center of the ten-foot-wide door. Alyssa squeezed Paul's hand. Then the vehicle veered off to the left.

"Nonono!" Alyssa yelled an instant before the deafening crash.

The amphibious SUV barreled into the edge of the tender door, bursting it open, but the impact lodged the vehicle into the corner instead of catapulting it out into the water and pulling the boat with it.

The jet boat screeched across the floor, slowing down. Alyssa's heart raced as it skidded for the water before coming to a stop, its front half hanging off the ledge two feet above the water.

Before she had a chance to react, Paul leaped out and hobbled behind the boat, then strained against it, pushing it forward.

"Get those lines off!" he yelled, grunting.

She jumped on the bow and worked the cleats, untying the boat from the other vehicle. She felt the boat inch forward and teeter down.

"Come on," Paul grunted. "Only a couple more—"

A door crashed open. Torin stormed into the garage an instant before the boat tilted and slipped into the water.

Torin rushed forward as the boat slowly drifted away from the ship. Too slowly.

"Come on, Paul!" Alyssa yelled.

"Get out of here!" Paul called out then turned and faced Torin, shielding the boat as it drifted away.

"No!" Alyssa screamed.

Paul rushed Torin. The big man did not attempt to step aside. He took Paul's attack head-on without flinching. He locked Paul into a chokehold. Paul raked at Torin's arm, but the big man continued crushing his neck.

Alyssa screamed in horror as Paul collapsed to the deck, unconscious.

Torin stalked to the boat. He spotted the line still attached to the bow. His lips curved into a smile as he plucked it from the deck and tugged on it.

Alyssa stared at him, frozen in terror, bile burning in the back of her throat, as more security guards flooded into the room while he reeled in Alyssa and the boat like a prized deep-sea catch.

Paul twitched. His eyes fluttered open. He shook his head, as if trying to clear it. He staggered to his feet and pulled out the pistol.

"Stop!" Paul yelled, pointing the weapon at Torin.

The big man turned. "Even if you shoot me, she won't get away," he said. "You can't win."

"I've heard that before," Paul replied. He gazed at Alyssa with a strange look in his eyes. His eyes shifted to the oxygen tank next to the amphibious vehicle.

Alyssa's heart stopped.

No.

He shifted the pistol then found her eyes one more time. He smiled. His lips mouthed three words. They sounded in her head as clearly as if Paul had whispered them into her ear.

I love you.

Alyssa's scream tore through the night as Torin rushed Paul.

Paul fired the weapon.

The blast cut off her scream. Alyssa flew onto the deck of the speedboat as the blast hurled bodies from the ship and pushed the boat into open water. A wall of blue flame rolled over her, blast-furnace hot.

"Paul!" Alyssa screamed, tasting blood.

Dazed, she lifted her head. The entire tender dock was engulfed in flames, the boats and other vehicles blazing. A second blast erupted as a fuel tank exploded, hurtling debris into the open water.

Alyssa collapsed on the deck, eyes scanning the water.

"Paul!" she called out, sobbing.

The ship illuminated as its power was restored. Moments later, the fire alarm claxon wailed into the night.

Her headset crackled. Alyssa forgot it was still in her ear.

"Alyssa!" Clay's voice rang in her earpiece. "Alyssa, are you there?"

"Paul…" Alyssa cried. "The blast…" Her voice gave out.

"Where are you? What happened?"

"I'm in the water. On the speedboat… but Paul… the explosion." The words came between sobs. "He blew up the… so I could…" She moaned. "God… I think he…"

Clay inhaled sharply. "You have to get out of there."

"I can't! Not without Paul!"

"You only have a few seconds before they spot you. You won't be able to outrun the chopper once it's airborne. You have to move now!"

"No!"

"Ally, please listen to me," Clay said, his voice shaking. "If they get you, Paul sacrificed himself for nothing."

She sobbed, scanning the water near the ship one last time, straining her eyes for any sign of movement.

I'm sorry, Paul… I'm so sorry…

Her mind and body were numb as she fired up the boat and gunned the throttle forward, speeding away from the ship.

PART 2

CONVERGENCE

Yuri Korzo's skin tingled as he studied the brick-shaped object on the display. He admired the form for what it was, for what it was capable of, for what it had already achieved. Nature's ultimate evolution of lethality.

Variola major. Smallpox.

One of the most virulent and deadliest diseases known to humanity, the virus was responsible for taking half a billion lives in the twentieth century alone. It was also the only human disease ever that, through massive global vaccination efforts, was completely eradicated from naturally occurring on the planet. Eradicating the disease eliminated the need for further vaccinations. And no vaccinations meant no immunity.

Because of this, only a handful of sites around the world were authorized to store the virus, under tightest protocols and security. Fortunately, his foresight had allowed him to acquire and stock away several strains before any possession of the virus was strictly outlawed and regulated by the world's governments.

Yuri had no idea whether the Hybrid woman was aware of his personal stockpile when she contacted him or whether it was just happenstance. No matter what brought them together, he had the tools and the knowledge to give her what she needed.

He scrutinized the dumbbell-shaped viral core that contained the smallpox DNA. His first step was to deactivate it. Throughout his career, he did many things that were of questionable ethics, but he wasn't about to reintroduce smallpox into the world. For now, to satisfy the woman's directive, he only required the virus envelope and its unrivaled ability to infect anything with which it came into contact. It would provide the perfect delivery vehicle for the even more lethal cargo that he was about to place inside it.

Yuri activated the molecular manipulator, a marvel of technology that translated the movements of his hand and fingers into the microscopic environment, allowing him to directly handle the virus. With practiced, steady movements, he maneuvered the articulating arm toward the pathogen. He held his breath when he made contact with the outside of the viral envelope then pressed through it and removed the DNA core.

He exhaled. The first part was completed. The next would be trickier.

Yuri moved the manipulator arm to the pod containing the ancient bioweapon, admiring the capsule surrounding it with a self-satisfied smile. The capsule was a molecular timer, his own creation of an assembly of proteins that decayed at a precise and predetermined rate, functioning like a molecular countdown. The combination of the highly infectious smallpox delivery vehicle and his own molecular timer would allow the smallpox-enveloped ancient bioweapon to spread through an entire population and lie dormant until the molecular count-down reached zero, triggering the bioweapon at exactly the same instant in all infected individuals.

He took out a handkerchief and dabbed his head, allowing himself a moment of triumph before moving the merged virus into the replicator.

It was time to make history.

———

ALYSSA STOOD in her second-story bedroom of the Renley estate, a faraway gaze passing through the open window into the garden below. Raindrops fell against her skin as she fought back the tears.

It's all my fault.

The door behind her opened, the sudden draft stirring her hair. Footsteps approached. *Clay.* A moment later she felt his hand on her arm. She turned, wordlessly, and buried her head in his shoulder. The tears came again. He wrapped his arms around her.

"I'm so sorry…" she sobbed.

"It's not your fault," Clay said.

"I should have never let him come with me."

"You could not have kept him from going with you, you know that."

"I—" her voice cracked and her words died. She stood for several moments before swallowing to gain her speech. She gently pulled back. "Were you able to find anything?"

"I was able to recover some of the data, but," he hesitated, studying her face, "perhaps we should wait—"

"No," Alyssa said. She wiped her eyes with her sleeve.

Clay nodded softly. "Lord Renley is waiting in the library."

Alyssa followed Clay down the marble staircase and into the spacious room. George Renley glanced up from a computer terminal, and their gazes met. Just like when she arrived at the estate a couple of hours ago, his eyes shone warmly, lacking the cool superiority to which she had grown accustomed. He nodded wordlessly. Alyssa appreciated the silence. There was nothing left to say that hadn't been said when she arrived. She owed him her life. The GPS in the boat had led her to the harbor in Tenerife. An hour later she was on the jet that brought her back to England. It was impossible to imagine that only eight hours ago she was on the *Valediction* with Paul. She swallowed around the lump in her throat. There would be time to grieve later.

"What have you learned?" she asked.

"Not a great deal as of yet, unfortunately," Renley replied.

Clay moved to the workstation. "We were only able to obtain disjointed fragments of the database before we lost connection. On top of that, the data stream became corrupted when the server went down. And if that's not enough, what we did manage to retrieve is encrypted." He sighed. "It's like trying to untangle a well-digested digital hairball."

Clay plopped down onto the chair. He pointed to the monitor. "I'm running a recovery algorithm to put together the pieces."

"Are you able to do a keyword search on the data we do

have?" Alyssa asked, trying to make sense of the jumbled display.

"We can give it a shot, but don't expect too much right now. Most of the data hasn't been indexed properly." He switched to another screen and opened up a console window.

"Can you run a search for 'Hybrid female' or 'Hybrid woman'?"

"Hybrid woman?" Clay asked, drawing his eyebrows together.

"Perhaps it might be helpful if you shared with us what you heard at the meeting," Renley offered.

Alyssa stretched her memory. "It all happened so quickly. They're confused and on edge about what happened in Cairo, and they're worried about potential implications. They bickered, then one of them mentioned something about genes from a Hybrid female."

"I can run a query on the term." Clay's fingers tapped on the keyboard. A few moments later, several files came up.

Alyssa studied the display. "What's that?" she asked, pointing at a series of image icons.

"Looks like image files." Clay typed in another command. "Interesting. They all appear to have been taken on the same day."

"Perhaps an event?" Renley offered.

"Or surveillance," Alyssa said. She clicked on one of the files, and a scrambled image filled the screen. It appeared to show two individuals, perhaps a man and a woman, but the photograph was too jumbled to make out any details. She clicked through the other files with the same results.

"Is this it?" she asked.

"Hang on." Clay brought up a Google map. "Looks like the images are geo-tagged."

"Geo-tagged? To where?"

"Nepal," Clay replied and zoomed in. "Cambay, to be exact."

"Cambay?" Alyssa gasped. "That's where my mom traveled right before we lost her." A cold shiver ran down her spine. "My God, what if somehow, this Hybrid woman is... my mom, and..."

"And she's alive and involved with the Society?" Clay cocked an eyebrow, leaving the implication hanging.

"Why would she not have attempted to reach out to you," Renley interjected, "or your father?"

Alyssa's mind swam. It raced through a dozen scenarios, her gaze flashing from Clay to Renley.

"The Society wants Hybrid blood above anything else. What if she's trying to protect me and my dad? Or they are holding her captive? Maybe that's why she hasn't been able to contact us."

Clay glanced at Renley.

Alyssa caught the exchange and bristled. "You think I'm crazy, trying to hold on to hope that my mom might still be alive."

Clay shook his head. "That's not it," he said. "It's just, we are all gutted about what happened to Paul." His face caved at his own words. "I think we're all looking for something to hold on to. I just don't want you to be disappointed."

Renley put a calming hand on her arm. "We should keep our minds open to any and all possibilities—however improbable they may seem."

Alyssa pressed her hands to her eyes. The pain threatened to surface. She breathed in deeply, pushing it back down. Deeper.

Renley pulled up a chair, and she sank into it, rubbing her temples, trying to control her emotions. She stared at the pin in the center of the satellite image.

"They talked about this woman like she was still alive. Even if it's not my mom, it's the best lead I've had since starting this. I need to go to Cambay. Perhaps I can find information that will lead me to Hybrids."

Renley deliberated for several moments before speaking. "Miss Morgan, I have learned that once you have made up your mind, any attempt to dissuade you is futile, so I shall spare us all that particular exercise." He gave a small bow. "My resources are at your disposal."

"Thank you, Lord Renley," Alyssa said.

He studied the monitor. "The location is remote. It may not be in your best interest to travel alone." He glanced to Clay.

Clay lifted his hands. "Oh, no… I'm not cut out for this field agent stuff. I'm more of an idea guy."

Renley smiled. "I believe Mr. Obono's assessment of his strength is accurate. Regrettably, I believe my own company on this journey would prove more of a liability to you than an asset." He hesitated and studied Alyssa with a curious expression.

What's that about?

A long pause stretched, as if he was weighing what to say. When he spoke, his words were carefully measured. "I have a suggestion for a travel companion, but I'm not certain my choice will meet with your approval."

"At this point I'll work with anybody who can help me get to the bottom of this," Alyssa said.

Renley stood. "I'm glad you feel this way. Please follow me."

They exited the house into the courtyard and entered the stables. Alyssa spotted a woman, her back to them, grooming a horse.

"I have been looking for an appropriate time to reacquaint the two of you," Renley said.

The young woman turned at his voice. Alyssa froze and gaped into her violet eyes. Her head spun.

"I thought you were—"

"Dead?" Tasha asked.

————

YURI KORZO RAN his hands through his hair, his gaze fixed to the screen displaying the countdown sequence and the vital signs for both of his subjects. He peered through the two-way mirror into the adjoining room, scrutinizing the two men who lay sedated and strapped to the bed.

The countdown gave a soft chirp as it reached zero. Yuri leaned forward.

Slowly, the steady beeping of the heart rate monitor increased for one of the subjects, and the temperature reading rose. The man stirred and moaned.

The door opened behind Yuri. He let an annoyed sigh escape his nostrils. "I said not to be disturbed," he grunted, keeping his eyes on the monitors.

"The girl has surfaced."

Yuri's irritation evaporated at the sound of the voice. He took a moment to collect himself before swiveling the chair and rising.

"I am pleased that your plan is working as you had predicted," he responded, striving to keep his voice even.

The woman approached the two-way mirror. "Your progress has been encouraging," she said. "But can you guarantee that my men will be safe?"

Yuri swallowed then pointed to the subjects. The man on the right maintained his steady breathing, and his vital sign monitor continued displaying readings in the normal range. The other man moaned again and gave a wheezing cough. His monitor gave a warning chirp as his temperature and heart rate kept rising.

"Both men have been injected with the ancient bioweapon that was encased inside the smallpox envelope," Yuri explained. "However, prior to the injections, I administered the smallpox vaccine to the subject on the right, but not to the other one."

Nephthys stepped closer to the two-way mirror.

Yuri pulled in a deep breath. "Because the ancient weapon is completely enveloped by the smallpox virus, the smallpox vaccine protected the vaccinated subject. The other, unvaccinated subject is susceptible to smallpox, and hence afflicted by the ancient weapon."

Nephthys studied the two men. "Fascinating," she said. "And the timing of the onset of the symptoms?"

"The molecular timer is working as expected," Yuri replied. "The ancient bioweapon remains encapsulated and inactive until the countdown reaches zero, at which point it is released into the bloodstream."

The woman nodded, satisfied.

Yuri hesitated. "We still need to ensure it spreads between individuals as expected. I need additional... volunteers." He swallowed again. "If not calibrated—"

"You shall have additional volunteers," the woman interrupted, her voice cold. "There must be no missteps. And remember, no harm must come to the girl." She moved to the door and glanced back over her shoulder. "I shall hold you personally responsible for any losses."

———

TASHA STUDIED the other girl and George. Alyssa's face was pale and stricken. She stood still as a statue at the entrance to the stable, glaring.

The filly tossed her head, sensing the tension, and Tasha offered a calming pat on the animal's neck. She had known this meeting was inevitable, but it didn't make it any easier.

"I was as good as dead," she finally said. "If it wasn't for George, I would have never made it out of the hall alive."

Alyssa turned as if to bolt out then stopped and glared at George. "She shot Paul!" Her head snapped to Tasha, nostrils flaring. "He's dead, anyway, but what do you care!"

Tasha's chest tightened. "I'm truly sorry for what I did. And I can't tell you how sorry I am for what happened to Paul on the ship."

"Whatever!" Alyssa spat. She pointed her finger at George. "You are unbelievable, you know that, right?"

"I have already apologized for my lapse in judgment, Miss Morgan," he replied calmly. "And be that as it may, Tasha is the best resource we currently have for following this particular lead."

Tasha stepped forward. "We got caught up in the Society's scheme, and things just spiraled out of control."

Alyssa scrubbed her hands over her face, as if to wash away the frustration. "That's the best you can do? Things spiraled out of control?"

"Miss Morgan," George said. "I do not believe the current conversation is to anyone's advantage. I understand your anger, but the ultimate question remains, are you willing to accept Tasha's help?"

"How can I ever trust you? Either of you?"

"I will not deceive you again," Tasha said, her eyes locked on Alyssa's.

Alyssa's shoulders slumped. "Do I even have a choice?" she asked, dejected.

"Why don't we take some time to process all this," Renley offered. "In the meantime, I shall make several calls."

Alyssa nodded and stormed out. Tasha glanced to George.

"Well, that went better than expected," he said.

"She hates me."

"She will come around."

"She still doesn't know that I…" she trailed off.

"Shot her with a sniper rifle in the back?" he asked.

"Yes."

"No, she does not. And it appears to be in your best interest that she never finds out."

THE MIDDAY SUN hung high in an achingly blue sky when Alyssa stepped out of the Tribhuvan Airport arrivals terminal. She stretched the kinks in her neck and inhaled deeply, savoring the crisp air. The view of the snowcapped mountain ranges glistening in the distance and the smell of fresh pine almost made her forget the twelve-hour flight. She shaded her eyes against the sun's glare and surveyed the sidewalk across the terminal building.

A middle-aged man holding a sign for "A. Morgan" waved at them. His sunburnt face was a tangled web of deep wrinkles, but his smile sparked with youthful vigor.

"*Namaste.* You must be Miss Alyssa and Miss Tasha. Welcome to Nepal," he said in heavily accented English as he offered a leathery handshake. He gave them a grin that revealed a gap in his front teeth. "I am Maansa. I have had the pleasure of serving as Sherpa for Lord Renley during his numerous visits."

"Thank you," Alyssa said. She found it easy to return the

smile. Tasha appraised the man, who either didn't notice or didn't mind the probing look. Instead, he pointed to their small backpacks, his grin fading.

"The rest of your luggage? It got lost in travel?"

Alyssa shook her head. "That's all we have."

"We like to travel light," Tasha added. "Were you able to arrange for the equipment we requested?"

Maansa nodded. "The time was short, but with Lord Renley's resources, we obtained all items necessary for your excursion," he replied. "The car is nearby." He motioned them to follow him.

They arrived at a gray Mercedes Geländewagen. Alyssa scrutinized the imposing SUV and its huge off-road tires. *Leave it to Renley.*

Maansa led them to the rear of the vehicle and opened the tailgate. The interior was loaded with three deep aluminum shell containers. He pointed to the one on the left.

"This bin for your equipment." He lifted the lid and pointed at two portable GPS units. "Satellite navigation in the car, plus two portable GPS with three battery packs each. Enough for one week. Also, headlamps with spare batteries, medical provisions, Diamox for altitude sickness."

He lifted the lid of the middle container. "This bin for expedition gear."

Alyssa picked up one of the thermal jackets and tried it on. It was a bit loose, but would do. She looked at the sleeping bags and tent then examined the step-in crampons and rest of the climbing gear. She nodded in approval.

Maansa pointed at the container on the right. "And water and food rations for one week."

"What about the special requisition?" Tasha asked.

"Ah, yes," Maansa lowered his voice and leaned over the left container. He pointed at two pairs of night vision goggles, a pair of high-powered binoculars, and military-spec communications equipment. "Lord Renley's money is welcome at Nepalese military." He flipped open a hidden compartment in the box. "Two Ruger pistols with one hundred rounds ammunition each." He reached into his pocket and handed her two documents. "Weapon permits in your names. Very important. Do not lose. Penalty for carrying weapon with no license in Nepal is very big."

Tasha smiled approvingly. Alyssa shot her a glance. She seemed as comfortable with these transactions as she was buying a Coke from a vending machine.

"You will be fine without guide?" Maansa asked. "The terrain is difficult, unpredictable, especially in monsoon season."

Alyssa smiled at him. "We have a lot of experience."

"Many dangers on road," he said.

"That is why I travel with a personal bodyguard."

"Oh," Maansa said, pressing his hand to his heart. "I did not see." He glanced around. "Where is he?"

"*She* is already here," Alyssa said, pointing at Tasha.

Maansa opened his mouth and blinked several times. Tasha met his gaze calmly. He scratched at his temple then shook his head and closed the tailgate.

He handed the keys to Alyssa and extended his hand. "Please do be careful."

"Thank you for your help, Maansa," Alyssa said.

"My number in satellite phone," Maansa added. "Call if you

need anything."

Alyssa nodded and climbed into the driver's seat. She glanced around the dashboard, familiarizing herself with the car as Tasha exchanged goodbyes with Maansa. Alyssa pressed the starter, and the powerful engine growled to life.

"Ah, the sweet sound of a V8 twin turbo," Alyssa said as Tasha hopped in.

Tasha shot her a glance. "Personal bodyguard, huh?"

"The poor man seemed concerned," Alyssa said innocently, waving at Maansa as they rolled out of the parking lot. "I was just trying to put his mind at ease." She paused for a moment before they both cracked a smile.

———

MAANSA WATCHED the two girls exit the parking lot and take the east road into the mountains. He whistled contently as he cut across the parking lot to the trail that would take him home. If he was careful with the money, the latest payment from Lord Renley should last him through the end of the year. The expedite bonus alone was more than he usually made in three months. It was a good day.

He spotted the tall man across the street, and his merry tune withered. The stranger was dressed in a dark coat with the hood over his face. Maansa's skin prickled. He sped up. The man increased his pace to keep up. Maansa darted into the next alley and zigzagged through the narrow back streets before ducking behind a garbage bin. He held his breath, his heart pounding. He crouched motionlessly for several minutes, listening for any noises, then lifted his head. Maansa breathed a sigh of relief when he saw the alleyway empty. He stood and turned.

He staggered and crumpled to the ground at the sight looming before him.

Lakhey.

Though never seen, he knew the truth.

Mountain demon.

He crabbed backward, fear robbing him of his voice, until his back hit the rough wall behind him. He gasped for air as the *Lakhey* moved forward. Maansa closed his eyes and screamed.

————

ALYSSA FOLLOWED the main highway out of the city for thirty minutes before turning off and continuing on an unpaved road that led them into the highlands. Tasha reached into her backpack and pulled out the laptop. She hooked it up to the satellite phone and dialed out. A few moments later Renley's face appeared on the screen.

"How are you?" he asked.

"So far, so good," Tasha replied. "We picked up the car and are on our way."

"Thanks for the ride," Alyssa chimed in. "Nice touch."

"I'm glad it is to your liking," Renley said.

Clay squeezed into the frame next to Renley. "It is just over one hundred miles to Kodari. Most of the ride will be dirt road, but there may be some tough spots."

"How long from Kodari to our destination?" Alyssa asked.

"After you reach the village, it's a seven-mile trek."

"That doesn't sound so bad," Alyssa said.

"That doesn't include the six-thousand-foot vertical ascent," Clay continued. "I grabbed the latest geospatial data and mapped out the safest route. Sending you the route and GPS markers now."

Alyssa shot a quick glance at the screen as a red line superimposed on the map.

"In this terrain, you're looking at about an eight-hour hike," Clay continued. "You'll be trekking through the forest for most of the way. Once you get above the tree line, you should be right on top of the site. The satellite images show a large clearing before a mountain face. There seem to be some regular structures that could be man-made, but the resolution isn't high enough for any details. The good news is that you seemed to have lucked out with the weather. The next couple of days are forecasted to be clear."

Alyssa processed the information. "Anything else you were able to find out from the data?" she asked.

"Nothing yet. The software is still cranking."

"Thanks, Clay," Alyssa said. "For everything."

Clay gave her a small smile in reply.

"Do take care of yourselves," George Renley added.

Tasha nodded and ended the connection. They sat in silence for a few minutes while Alyssa navigated the beachball-sized divots in the road.

"Why don't you try to get some shut-eye while you can?" Alyssa suggested. "May as well get some rest before we get trekking. I'll wake you up when we're halfway."

Tasha stretched. "Good plan. Wake me if anything exciting happens," she said and nestled into the seat.

Alyssa followed the GPS over the next hour, taking a series

of narrow dirt lanes leading them higher into the mountains. Despite her best efforts, the car pitched and rolled, seeming to hit every pit and pothole in the road.

Alyssa zigzagged around a two-foot fissure in the path, the last maneuver getting her uncomfortably close to the steep drop on the left. She wished for the hundredth time for a guardrail as she continued navigating the winding road.

A sweeping crack of lightning split the sky ahead. A few seconds later the clouds opened up, and water pelted the windshield like she had just driven into a carwash.

"What was it Clay said about the weather?" Tasha mumbled, yawning. She rubbed her eyes as the rain hammered on the roof like a hundred drumsticks.

"At least we're not trekking yet." Alyssa flipped on the windshield wipers. "Try to go back to sleep."

"No chance with this racket. Besides, looks like you could use an extra set of eyes."

Alyssa sighed. "I suppose you're right. It's starting to get dark." Alyssa eyed the path ahead. Puddles of water welled into fledgling streams that flowed across the narrow road.

The windshield wipers worked overtime as they continued for a tense quarter hour. It seemed impossible for clouds to hold that much water. By now the dirt road had given way to a broken escarpment of steep cliffs and hills. As the torrent continued, the streams grew into small rivers snaking their way down the mountain road.

Alyssa spotted a large log rolling into their path. Tasha inhaled sharply when the current caught it and sent it careening straight for them.

Alyssa jerked the steering wheel to the right, putting the

right front tire onto the steep cliff. Her maneuver saved them from a head-on collision, but the tail end of the log swung around in the water and caught them, vaulting them off their seats.

Alyssa gunned the engine. The wheels spun in the air as the car inched backward.

"The log is wedged under the car!" Alyssa cried.

"Try reversing then moving forward," Tasha said, her voice strangely calm.

Alyssa threw the car in reverse and squeezed the throttle. The car budged back a few inches as one of the wheels made contact with the ground. She popped it back into drive. The car rocked forward, but didn't clear the log.

Without warning, a tree exploded in a brilliant flash of light and ear-splitting noise. A firebolt surged for the car and enveloped them.

Alyssa and Tasha screamed, then it was over, gone as suddenly as it had appeared.

"Did we just get hit by—?" Alyssa started.

A creaking noise above the vehicle ended in a deafening thud when a massive branch landed a few feet in front of them. An instant later it slipped and rolled down the path. Alyssa gripped the steering wheel. It crashed into them, jolting the SUV backward to the edge of the cliff. Alyssa hit the accelerator, but the car continued to slide back.

"We're still stuck!" Alyssa yelled. "I can't control it."

Tasha pointed to the charred tree a few car lengths ahead, jutting out from the cliff side about ten feet up.

"Release the winch!" she yelled and tore the door open.

"Are you crazy?" Alyssa yelled. "You can't go out there! Did you see what just happened?"

"Lightning is not supposed to strike twice in the same place!"

"I don't think that's really true!"

"We're going to get washed off this cliff!" Tasha jumped out.

Alyssa grunted, looking through the series of switches for the winch controls. She flipped up the red case that covered the rocker switch and toggled it to 'out.' Tasha rounded the fender and disappeared in front of the hood. A moment later she popped up, holding a hook attached to a steel cable. She yanked on it and trudged through the water for the tree.

The car jerked back, yanking on the cable and throwing Tasha off her feet. It continued to inch back to the ravine.

Alyssa threw open the driver's side door and jumped out. It was like stepping into a shower. She was instantly soaked from head to toe. Another bolt of lightning flashed above her. An instant later an ear-splitting blast shook the ground.

Alyssa waded behind the SUV and leaned into the car, pushing against the current, trying to slow the backward slide. She threw a glance back. They were about twenty feet from the edge of the cliff.

"Hurry!" she yelled to Tasha, grunting with the effort.

"Thanks!" Tasha yelled back. "I've been taking my time!"

Tasha scaled the cliff under the tree. As she swung her arm back to flip the hook around the trunk, she lost her footing and slid, spitting a loud curse.

"Hold on!" Alyssa ducked out from behind the car and rushed to Tasha. "I'll give you a—"

The lightning raced across the sky again. Another crack of thunder followed.

The images in Alyssa's head echoed the flash in the sky, her mind jangling through a rapid-fire series of visions.

The rain whips my face...

My bare feet pound the mud...

The towering shape knocks me to the ground...

Alyssa staggered and fell.

"Come on!" Tasha called.

Alyssa lay on the ground, cold sweat mixing with the rain.

"Alyssa, now!" Tasha yelled, feverishly.

Alyssa lifted her head, struggling to focus. The slack from the steel cable was almost completely gone. She glanced back. The SUV was only a few feet from the edge of the cliff.

Alyssa took a deep breath and gained her feet. She staggered to Tasha.

"Let's do this!" She dug her feet into the ground and made a basket with her hands. "Climb on top of me."

Tasha stepped into Alyssa's hands and climbed onto the wall. She swung her arm back and lobbed the hook at the tree.

"Yeah!" she cheered when it looped around the trunk. She caught it and secured it to the cable. A few seconds later, the cable stretched tight with a twang. Alyssa stared in horror as the SUV teetered on the edge of the cliff.

"Back to the car, now!" Tasha skipped down and rushed for the SUV.

Alyssa stumbled to the car after her. She toppled into the driver's seat just as Tasha triggered the winch. The motor whirred, and the car lurched forward, inching them away from the edge of the cliff. The car jerked and cleared the log with a screech. Alyssa glanced in the side mirror, watching it roll down and tumble over the edge. They crept forward against the current for a few more feet before Tasha flipped the switch to stop the winch.

"You okay?" She glanced at Alyssa. "What happened out there?"

Alyssa hugged her shoulders wordlessly. She shivered, a sudden chill hitting her to the bone.

"You're completely soaked." Tasha hopped into the back seat and reached for Alyssa's gear. She shuffled through Alyssa's backpack and the bin with the clothes. A few moments later she laid out a small towel and dry clothes on the passenger seat.

"I pulled socks and underwear from your backpack, and got your expedition clothes from the supplies. Get changed."

"Thank you," Alyssa managed.

She stripped off her wet clothes as Tasha did the same in the back seat. She toweled off and slipped into the dry clothes then spread out the wet ones across the dash.

Alyssa turned at the metallic clicking behind her. Tasha rested on the back seat in a pair of sweatpants and a sports bra, the Luger pistol on her lap, loading the magazine.

She glanced up. "If we're going to spend the night here, I want to be prepared."

Alyssa's eyes moved to the pale scar on Tasha's stomach.

"Does it still hurt?"

Tasha blinked. "Every now and then."

Alyssa lifted her shirt and pointed to the gunshot scar in her side. "Mine gets achy when it's cold." She gave a rueful smile. "We've got quite the conversation starters, huh?"

A strange expression crossed Tasha's face. "I'd rather not talk about any of it." She frowned and turned away.

"I'm sorry, I didn't mean to—"

"We should get some rest while we can," Tasha said. She perched herself against the rear passenger door and stretched out her feet on the seat behind Alyssa. "Lock the doors."

Alyssa wrinkled her brow, but faced forward and flipped the lock. She reclined her seat and leaned into the headrest.

The scars we can see aren't the worst we bear, are they?

————

ALYSSA WOKE with an eerie sense of disconnection, not remembering when she fell asleep. She looked at the clock on the dash. 8:47. The sun stood a couple of hand breadths above the horizon, bathing the valley below in a warm tangerine glow. Absolute stillness surrounded her.

"Welcome to the land of the living," Tasha said.

Alyssa turned. Tasha chilled in the back seat, looking infuriatingly posh in her matching tight-fitting black thermals.

Was that a special requisition, too, along with the night vision goggles and guns? Alyssa felt only a small stab of guilt at the thought.

Tasha gave her a small smile, blissfully oblivious to Alyssa's inner monologue. She held up a protein bar and a bottle of water. "Hungry?"

Alyssa accepted both gratefully, all fashion envy disappearing with the first bite of the chocolate-flavored bar. She took a sip of water and looked at the road before them. The rivulets of surface water had all but disappeared, leaving behind a mucky trail. The SUV was still tethered to the trunk above them.

"Looks like a fun drive ahead," Tasha said.

"If the suspension of this beast is as reliable as the winch, she'll get us there," Alyssa replied. She fired up the engine and positioned the SUV under the tree. Tasha opened the sunroof and climbed out then unhooked the cable from the trunk of the tree. She hopped onto the hood and guided the cable back in as Alyssa retracted the winch.

"Well, that was a lot easier than last night," Tasha said, sticking her head in through the sunroof. She wrinkled her nose. "Eww… smells like a guy's locker room in here."

"Note to Maansa for next Nepal expedition: one large can of Febreze," Alyssa said, a serious expression on her face.

Tasha gave her a look then cackled. She slipped back into the car.

"But seriously, open the windows," she said.

They set out and continued along the path for a few minutes when the ring of the satellite phone interrupted the silence. Tasha answered and connected the phone to the laptop. Clay's face appeared on the screen.

"Oh, look, it's our head meteorologist," she said dryly.

The vexed look in Clay's face made Alyssa snort.

"What—?" he started.

"Never mind," Tasha replied.

"Any news on the images?" Alyssa asked, trying to keep her face serious.

"Not yet," Clay replied. "It's slow going, but we'll get there. How is the trip?"

They updated him on their progress, sparing the details of

last night's adventure. "Looks like we should get to Kodari in about three hours." Tasha said.

"Sounds good," Clay said. "Be careful and keep us posted."

Tasha nodded and disconnected the call.

The next three hours were mercifully uneventful. Tasha switched into the driver's seat midway through the drive, and Alyssa prepped her rucksack and checked in again with Renley and Clay.

They arrived in Kodari around noon. The village was little more than a collection of ramshackle structures, none of them larger than a small camper. The main street appeared to be made of tramped down manure. A flock of goats inside a fenced enclosure lifted their heads as the vehicle passed by, but quickly lost interest and returned to munching on the clumps of grass surrounding the huts.

Tasha maneuvered the wide vehicle between a jumble of carts and barrels littering the narrow path. Before they knew it, they were joined by a handful of children who gave chase after the SUV, yelling and whooping. Tasha pulled up as close to the rocky terrain as she dared without risking them getting stuck and shut off the engine.

"That's it," she said, exhaling deeply. "Looks like we're legging it from here."

They clambered free of the vehicle. Alyssa took a deep breath, relishing the mountain air and stretching circulation back into her stiff limbs. She took in the surroundings. The midday sun reflected off the snowcapped peaks to the north. It was beautiful, pristine.

"Timi yaham kina ho?" A thin voice called out behind her.

Alyssa turned. A young boy, no older than seven, gave her a grin. She shook her head. "I'm sorry, I don't understand."

The boy didn't seem to mind. The sound of Alyssa's voice speaking to him in English made him giggle. His friends joined in. Alyssa winked at them, which only made them laugh louder, as she stepped around the SUV and lifted the back gate. She pulled out her gray rucksack and slipped it on. Tasha eyed the backpack.

"What's up?" Alyssa said, the hair in the back of her neck tingling.

Tasha shook her head. "Sorry, nothing, just lost in thought." She reached for her own pack and lifted her hand to close the tailgate. She hesitated and instead opened the supplies container and pulled out a dozen chocolate protein bars. She dealt them out to the kids, producing shrieks of delight.

Alyssa eyed her with a smirk.

"The Siberian ice princess has a heart."

"Maansa did say we had a week's worth of supplies," Tasha replied. "I'm not planning on being here that long." She raised an eyebrow. "And I'm from St. Petersburg."

Tasha's gaze moved over Alyssa's shoulder, and her face tightened. An elderly man from the village approached them. Though he looked to be at least eighty, he strode briskly, stopping several paces short of them. He gave a lighthearted smile, revealing dull brown teeth, but his eyes shone with ageless ardor. A nose the size of a small potato was planted in his round, leathery face, and a sheaf of gray hair peaked out from his colorful *Topi* hat. He pressed his hands together and gave a slight bow.

"Namaste," he said.

Alyssa and Tasha mirrored his gesture. *"Namaste,"* they said in unison.

"English?" the man asked.

Alyssa nodded. "May we leave the car here?" she asked, pointing at the car.

The man studied the car and the children pressing their noses against the windows. He nodded. "Yes, yes." He scratched his head. "Where you go?"

"We're trekkers." Alyssa pointed at the path leading into the woods and the mountains beyond. She held up two fingers. "Two days."

"Ah! Trekking! You need guide? Sherpa?" he asked with an air of readiness.

"No, thank you," Tasha replied. "Thank you very much." She put her hands together and bowed. "We go alone."

"No," he shook his head, and his face darkened. "Not good for you." He shook his head again. *"Lakhey."* The kids stopped playing when they heard the word.

"Lakhey?" Alyssa repeated.

He scrunched his windburned face, as if trying to remember the word. "Mountain beasts."

Alyssa bowed. "Thank you. We will be very careful." Alyssa reached into her pocket and pulled out five hundred Nepalese rupee, the equivalent of five dollars.

The man put his hands up defensively. "No, no."

"Please," Alyssa said. "To keep the car safe." She pointed at the SUV. "Yes?"

The man eyed the money then relaxed and took it from her hand.

"Dhanyabad," he said, pressing his hands together and bowing.

"Thank you," Alyssa said.

"Namaste," the man said, bowing again.

"Namaste," Alyssa and Tasha replied. They waved to the kids and set off into the forest.

They trekked for several hours, following the GPS. Tasha led the way with the skill of a mountain goat as they carved their path through the maze of boulders and trees, climbing higher and higher.

The frigid air cut through Alyssa's thermal top. She stopped and zipped up the parka and pulled the collar over her ears. She took a long sip from her water bottle, savoring the fresh taste before handing it to Tasha. A fine sheen of perspiration made Tasha's cheeks glow, but she didn't seem winded despite the thin air.

Alyssa rubbed her hands together, trying to warm them. She continued to rub her palm, distracted, her thumb fingering the scar on the inside of her right palm.

Tasha handed the bottle back. "Is that where Will…?"

Alyssa winced at the memory of the searing pain as Drake's blade slashed through the glove of her biosuit, slicing into her flesh.

Alyssa nodded. She stowed the water bottle and stood, lost in the memory. It seemed like a lifetime ago. "You and Drake…" she started, then stopped, not sure how to continue. "Was it all an act, or…?"

"You mean did I actually have feelings for him?" A bitter expression hardened Tasha's face. "Are you asking because you're concerned or because you want to make yourself feel better about the fact that you killed my lover?"

Alyssa reeled back at the sting in Tasha's words. "He was a lunatic, Tasha, he tried to kill us. Not to mention his utter disregard for the safety of thousands of people who could have been infected."

"Many thought he had a vision and were willing to follow him to the very end. That's more than you can say about most people."

"A vision? Building a spaceship to go to Mars is a vision. Creating a super-race cult is insane. That's meddling with the natural order of things."

"Oh, really? Have you sequenced your genes lately?"

"I didn't ask for this!"

"We've used genetic engineering to create cures that would have naturally killed people. So why not use genes to make people smarter and stronger?"

"That's completely different," Alyssa countered.

"Is it? How so?"

"Well, for one, people who work on genetic engineering to cure diseases don't kill anybody."

"Sometimes things aren't as simple as they seem," Tasha said. "I'm not certain Will intended for it to go as far as it did. He—"

"I can't believe you're defending him!" Alyssa burst out. She threw up her hands and trotted off. After a few steps she stopped and turned. "Look, I..." she trailed off.

"I had known Will since he was a boy," Tasha said. "George Renley and William's father were close friends. Will was different when I first met him… an idealist… a dreamer, always protecting me." A distant memory seemed to cross her eyes. "I was hopelessly in love with him—for a twelve-year-old," she chuckled. "He was my prince, and I was going to marry him one day."

"What happened?" Alyssa asked, drawing closer.

"His father sent him away to college. I was devastated, of course, but Will insisted on obeying his father's wishes. I hated him for leaving me. We didn't speak again until after his father's death. When we met at his father's funeral, he was a different person." She gave a heavy sigh. "We both were."

"I didn't know…" Alyssa reached out and put her hand on Tasha's arm. "I'm sorry," she said.

Tasha flinched when Alyssa touched her, and she pulled her arm away. She wiped her eyes with the sleeve of her parka and inhaled sharply. "I don't need your sympathy. I'm here because George asked me to help you." She adjusted her backpack. "We should keep moving," she said and set off.

Alyssa stood for several moments then followed in her footsteps. They treaded in brooding silence for several minutes when Tasha stopped abruptly. As Alyssa reached her, she spotted the reason for Tasha's sudden halt. A twelve-foot-wide fissure separated their side of the cliff from the path forward. Alyssa exhaled, glad to focus on something else.

This I can handle.

Alyssa glanced at the GPS unit as Tasha crept up to the edge and peered down.

"Can't see the bottom," she said. "Clay must have missed this one when he mapped our route."

"Or it could be new," Alyssa offered, remembering the devastating earthquake that left the country reeling a couple of years ago. "This area is a hotbed of geological activity, sitting right on top of where the Indian Plate is diving underneath the Eurasian Plate." She swept her gaze from left to right. The rift went on as far as she could see. "Looks like we'll have to map out an alternate route."

Tasha studied the far side of the fissure then cleared off the loose pebbles from the edge. She stomped on it a couple of times.

"Seems pretty solid here and looks the same on the other side," she said. "I go first. Then you throw me our backpacks and follow me."

Alyssa stepped up to the edge and looked down. She glanced at Tasha with newfound respect.

Tasha met her gaze straight on. "What?"

"Nothing," Alyssa replied. "It's just that usually I'm the one with the wacky ideas. You sure about this?"

"Believe me, I'd prefer a zipline, too. You're not afraid of heights, are you?"

Alyssa bit back a retort as Tasha backed up a few steps. She slipped off her backpack and crouched, bending one leg and keeping the other one straight, then shifted her weight to the other leg, stretching her hamstrings. She rose and took a deep breath through her nose and out her mouth.

"Here we go." She took a couple slow steps before accelerating and sprinting for the crevasse. She pushed off the edge and launched into the air. A second later she landed on the other side. She turned around with a grin.

"See? Nothing to it. Your turn."

Alyssa tossed their packs to Tasha then backed up, willing herself not to think about the bottomless pit she was about to cross. Her heart thudded in her chest, and a sudden rush of adrenaline surged through her body. *It's just a twelve-foot jump, nothing to it.*

She raced to the edge at full speed and pushed off. She sailed eight feet past Tasha, landing softly. She turned. Tasha's mouth fell open, her gaze bouncing between the crevasse and Alyssa.

"I think you just broke the Olympic long jump record," Tasha said.

Alyssa stared back at her, a fluttery feeling in her stomach. "I guess fear does give you wings, after all."

"The ceremony will have to wait." Tasha cracked a grin and threw Alyssa's backpack at her. "Let's move."

They continued trekking through the forest for another hour. Soon the thin air made every breath a struggle. A rustle behind Alyssa made her stop in her tracks. She turned, her body tense.

"Wait," she said.

"What is it?" Tasha asked.

"I thought I heard something."

Tasha squinted, scanning the trees behind them. "I don't see anything," she said after a few moments. "Do you?"

Alyssa's skin prickled, but she shook her head. "Probably just some local wildlife."

Tasha checked the GPS. "We're getting close to the coordinates. Just beyond the tree line there."

After several minutes, the dense trees parted. Alyssa stopped. The mountain sunlight streamed through a break in the clouds in great watery shafts of gold, glinting off Imja glacier and lighting the unmistakable shape of Mount Everest, surrounded by its sister peaks.

The magnificent view in the distance did nothing to diminish the ethereal sight directly before her. Set in a valley beneath them, a sloping courtyard stretched for over a hundred yards. It funneled into a natural stone bridge that led to a thirty-foot-high gateway carved into the mountainside.

Alyssa rubbed her eyes.

"Is this it?" she asked, her voice trembling.

Tasha took in the view for another ten seconds before glancing at the GPS. She nodded, unwilling to break the spell of the sight with words. She dropped her backpack and fished out a set of high-powered binoculars. She pointed them at the courtyard.

"The only way in seems to be across that bridge," she said. "We should wait until nightfall, in case anybody is watching it."

Alyssa glanced at the setting sun and nodded. "Makes sense. Besides, I could use a break." She slipped off her backpack and rested it next to Tasha's.

———

THIRTY MINUTES LATER, they huddled together, nibbling on protein bars. Alyssa soaked in the warmth of the battery-heated parka as the air around her grew colder by the minute. She took a deep breath.

"About what I said earlier. I'm sorry."

"I told you before, I'm not asking for your pity," Tasha replied.

"I'm not offering you my pity," Alyssa countered. "A few months ago, you told me I had no right to judge you. You were right."

Tasha looked out in a pensive gaze, lips pressed together. She was silent for so long Alyssa didn't think she was going to say anything. Finally, she spoke. "When I met William again, after his father died... he was different... he scared me, but George insisted..."

"You got together with Drake because George Renley wanted you to?" Alyssa felt a burning in her throat.

"After they took my mom, I didn't have anybody. George saved me. He plucked me from the streets and gave me a life. I wanted to make him happy, show him my gratitude for everything he has done for me."

Alyssa shook her head.

"I thought I would be able to just play the role, do what George wanted, but after spending time with William... He made me feel like I was everything to him. I was his princess again." She looked at Alyssa, tears glistening in her eyes. "I thought I was strong enough not to fall in love with him again."

Alyssa met Tasha's gaze. "I'm so sorry."

"I know you had no choice," Tasha whispered. "I didn't want to hate you for what you did, but—"

Alyssa's ears picked up an unusual sound, and she put a hand on Tasha's arm, silencing her.

"What is it?"

Alyssa shushed her. The sound grew louder, into the unmistakable chop-chop-chop of the blades of a helicopter.

"A helicopter."

"I don't hear anything," Tasha said.

Alyssa grabbed her pack and rushed for the trees. "Hide, now!" she yelled. Tasha followed closely behind.

A few moments later the noise from the rotors grew louder.

Alyssa watched through the branches as a large chopper flew above them and descended on the clearing. She waited for it to touch down then crept closer and hid behind a stony outcrop. Tasha crept up to her a moment later.

The helicopter door opened, revealing a man dressed in a tan jumpsuit. Alyssa's heart quickened when she spotted a second man exiting the carved gateway and pacing across the bridge. The men met at the helicopter. They didn't shake hands but exchanged words.

Tasha fumbled through the backpack and lifted the binoculars to her eyes. She inhaled sharply.

"What is it?" Alyssa whispered. She knew it was silly, there is no way the people at the helicopter could ever hear her.

"That guy who just stepped out of the temple," Tasha said. "That's Dr. Yuri Korzo!"

Yuri Korzo? Where did she hear—? Memory hit. "They mentioned his name in the meeting on the ship!"

"Dr. Korzo took over the Society's bioengineering program after Baxter's death."

"I knew it! So, the Society..." Alyssa trailed off when she spotted several figures exiting the helicopter. Something seemed odd about the way they moved.

"What's going on?" she asked.

Tasha handed her the binoculars wordlessly. Alyssa pointed the glasses at the scene below. Her skin prickled. The people were bound and hooded. Two armed men exited the chopper and pushed them into a line.

The scientist approached them. He seemed to appraise them, then nodded approvingly and motioned the armed men to usher them inside.

Alyssa lowered the binoculars. "Do you think they're using these people…" She shivered, not from the cold, but from the implication. She swallowed to ease the burning in her throat. "What if my mother is still alive, and what if the Society is using her, too?"

"Alyssa, you don't know that," Tasha said.

"We need to get inside," Alyssa said.

"Did you see those guns?" Tasha asked. "I'm pretty sure there are a lot more of those inside whatever hides beyond this entrance. We'll never make it past that bridge."

Alyssa clenched her jaw, knowing that Tasha was right. She sat up.

"What?" Tasha asked.

"So, this Yuri guy is continuing Baxter's work, right?"

"That's right," Tasha replied.

"Which means he's still looking for Hybrid blood."

Tasha nodded wearily. "Where are you going with this?"

"Let's give them what they want."

Tasha stared at her, perplexed.

Alyssa leaned forward. "As far as the Society is concerned, you are George Renley's daughter and have been loyal to the Society and William Drake. Nobody would question your continued commitment to them. You could deliver me to them as your captive and set me free once we're inside."

Tasha stared at Alyssa, unblinking. She opened her mouth, then closed it again. She finally found her voice.

"Absolutely not," she said.

"If you had a chance to see your mother again, wouldn't you do anything in your power to make it happen?" Alyssa pleaded. "What if they've kept my mom alive all those years? I have to know!"

Tasha pinched the bridge of her nose and shook her head with a sigh. "You are completely insane, Alyssa."

"I've been told before," Alyssa replied. "We have to figure out how to remove any doubt from their minds that you're on their side."

A hard smile crossed Tasha's lips. "I might have an idea about that, but you won't like it."

ALYSSA STUMBLED down the path blindly. She tripped and almost fell, but Tasha grabbed her and yanked her upright.

"Try to keep it together," she said.

"Easy for you to say," Alyssa shot back. "You're not the one trying to walk down a mountain with a hood on your face and hands tied behind your back." Her cheek throbbed where Tasha had hit her to make the "capture" seem more believable. She knew it would sting, but—*damn*—did that girl pack a punch. Her head was still ringing from it.

Tasha pulled her to a stop. "We're here," she said.

"Now what?" Alyssa asked.

"Now we wait."

A minute later Alyssa heard footsteps approaching them. *Two men?*

"Namas—" she heard one of them say.

"Let's skip this," Tasha interrupted. "I need to talk to the person in charge."

"You must leave immediately," the man said.

Tasha inhaled sharply. "I am George Renley's daughter. I'm here to see Dr. Yuri Korzo."

A stunned silence followed.

"Is he expecting you?" one of the men finally said.

"No," Tasha replied, "but you can tell him that I brought him a present."

She removed Alyssa's hood. Alyssa squinted in the fading light at the two men in gray coveralls.

"Tell Dr. Korzo I brought him ten pints of fresh Hybrid blood," Tasha said.

———

Dr. Yuri Korzo was a short man, his eyes level with Alyssa's. He had a round face with a craggy nose and thick, fleshy lips. His receding hairline was emphasized even more by a pair of black-rimmed eyeglasses that rested on top of his head as if forgotten there.

"Alyssa Morgan," he said, appraising her. The animosity in his voice stirred and lifted the small hairs on her arms. "I have waited a long time to meet you in person."

Alyssa swallowed. *Perhaps this wasn't such a good idea after all.* She flicked a glance at Tasha. If she shared any of Alyssa's distress, she was hiding it adeptly beneath her well-practiced Mona Lisa smile.

Korzo brought his face closer to Alyssa's. She tried backing away, but the two guards held her in place by her bound arms. He cupped her chin and tilted her head, examining the bruise on her right cheek. Alyssa hoped the scrutiny the bruise brought to the right side of her face would take away the attention from her left side where a small comm unit hid in her ear, concealed by her hair.

"Your work, Miss Renley?" he glanced over his shoulder to Tasha.

"She wasn't cooperating," Tasha replied lazily.

Korzo curled his lip. "How unrefined," he quipped before turning and heading for the stone bridge. "Bring her along," he said over his shoulder.

They crossed the stone bridge and approached the entrance into the mountain. The remaining rays of the sun cast a diffuse light, beaming it through the pillared entryway. The intricate detail carved into the mountain was apparent even though the once smooth rock was left pitted and scarred.

As they passed through the entrance, Alyssa's sense of awe and reverie only deepened. A vast natural cavern stretched before them, its rough stone and jagged peaks transformed into a majestic temple. Arching ceilings rose fifty feet above her, and smooth walls were lined with intricately carved, life-sized statues.

Alyssa's knees buckled when she recognized the subjects of the carvings. Ganesh, the man with the elephant head. Nure-onna, the snake with the head of a woman. Chu Pa-chieh, half man, half sow. Alyssa stared at the falcon-headed man.

"Wh-what is this place?" she stammered.

Korzo ignored her question.

"Keep moving," one of his guards said, pushing her on.

Alyssa continued through the temple as if in a trance, past rows of statues representing hybrid entities from religions and folklore from around the world. She swept her gaze through the cavern, looking for anybody else, but other than Korzo and his two guards, the temple was empty, with no sign of the others who had arrived earlier by helicopter.

They stopped in front of a carved wall. One of the guards spoke into his comm, and the wall lifted, revealing a gate of polished metal. The gate parted before them. Alyssa blinked as she stared into the cabin of a modern elevator. She followed Korzo and Tasha inside, flanked by the guards.

"The Society built this?" Tasha asked. Her voice betrayed her wonder.

Korzo stabbed the button for the lowest floor. He studied Tasha, an amused expression in his eyes. "The Society?" he chortled, shaking his head as if she had made a joke.

Tasha's face tensed for an instant before returning to her usual dispassionate expression.

Alyssa watched the digital display showing the floor numbers as they descended. Every floor that flashed by had her heart thudding faster, louder. She chewed at her bottom lip, taking slow, deep breaths, questioning her wisdom once again.

What did I get myself into this time?

The elevator stopped, and they exited into a corridor. The sparse, narrow hallway lined with metal cell doors and a low ceiling bore a striking contrast to the airy, sacred structure above their heads.

So this is where you do your dirty work. Fear curled up inside her and clung to her ribs as a sudden shiver chilled her spine.

They moved through the corridor and stopped at one of the countless cells. One of the guards unlocked the steel-barred door and shoved her inside.

Korzo appraised Alyssa through the open door, the resentment for her spilling from his eyes. "I look forward to getting closer acquainted with you, Miss Morgan," he said in a tone that made her flesh crawl.

The guard moved to close the cell door. Tasha lifted her hand.

"Wait," she said and approached Alyssa. She grasped Alyssa's hair and yanked her head to the side then took the miniature comm unit out of her ear. She handed it to the guard.

"You didn't really think I'd go along with your ridiculous plan, did you?" she asked.

Alyssa gaped at her, frozen, when Tasha stepped back and opened Alyssa's backpack. She emptied the contents on the ground and picked out the box with the crystal.

"Here is a little bonus for the Society," Tasha said, and handed it to Korzo. She turned to Alyssa. "I will never forgive you for killing William," she said, "but seeing what they will do to you will help ease my pain."

She clasped her hand around the back of Alyssa's neck and pulled her close, her lips almost touching Alyssa's ear as she whispered, "Paul wasn't the only person I shot in Cairo." She pressed her fingers into the scar in Alyssa's side, making her wince. "This one is on me, too."

She backed away, a self-satisfied smirk on her absurdly beautiful face.

Alyssa's brain took a few additional snaps of its synapses to make sense of what she just heard. She lunged at Tasha, her nostrils flaring. "You two-faced—!"

Tasha slammed the cell door in her face.

Alyssa's shoulders sagged. "How could you?"

Tasha turned. "Some people never learn," she said.

Korzo's cold smile matched Tasha's icy expression. "I want the subject in the procedure room in five minutes," he said before he and Tasha strode away, leaving the guards at the cell.

Alyssa sank to the floor, sobbing. *Tasha shot me?*

She took a minute to calm down then slowly lifted her gaze. She kept an eye on the guards from beneath her hair as she untucked the back of her thermal jersey from her pants.

So far, their plan had worked perfectly. Before their—mostly—staged squabble at the cell door, Tasha had concealed a small pocket knife in her own palm. When Tasha had put her hand around Alyssa's neck, she dropped the knife down the back of Alyssa's jersey.

Alyssa wiggled the knife into her hand. She allowed herself a small victory smile before she flipped it open and began working on the rope. The guards had checked her bonds and searched her before Korzo arrived, just as she and Tasha had anticipated, so Tasha made sure to tie the rope tight to prevent any suspicion. *But couldn't she have made it just a little looser?*

Alyssa grimaced when she nicked her wrist.

Come on. Concentrate.

One of the guards turned and opened the cell door just as the knife sliced through the rope.

Alyssa folded the knife and slipped it in her waistband. She pushed her wrists together, squeezing the rope between them. She glanced up at the guard in the doorway. He was as wiry as a starved Terrier, his brown coveralls only boosting the resemblance.

The man lifted up a menacing, two-foot-long stun baton. "This is Fred." He pointed at the baton in the other guard's hand. "And that's Barney. Aptly named because they'll have you babbling like a caveman for a solid hour. So, here's the deal. You be a good girl, and Fred and Barney won't have to make your acquaintance." He paused for effect. "Understood?"

What kind of sickos name their stun rods after the Flint-stones? Alyssa thought and nodded as meekly as she could manage.

"Outstanding." The guard lowered the rod named Fred. "Get up slowly and come out. Nice and easy."

Alyssa complied. They led her through the corridor until they reached another metal door. "Barney" knocked. A moment later the door opened, and Korzo's face appeared. He stepped aside as the guards brought her in and closed the door.

The laboratory was every shade of gray from faded concrete to a pale slate. Black-top laboratory tables and a myriad of equipment and electronics lined the walls. A metal examination table with straps stood in the middle. Tasha lingered in the far corner, looking bored.

Alyssa's eyes flickered to the box with the crystal perched next to her. *It's still here.*

"Secure her to the table," Korzo said, and he turned to a keyboard.

Alyssa wiggled out of the guards' grips. "No!" she cried. She backed against the door and stood, keeping her hands behind her.

Korzo swung the chair around, an amused expression on his face.

"I thought we had a deal," the guard said, and lifted Fred. "You will end up strapped to that table. Whether you're coherent or drooling is up to you."

Alyssa willed herself to stand still. Time seemed to slow as the guards advanced, stun rods at the ready.

"Say hello to Fred," the man spat, lashing out with the baton.

Alyssa waited until the last moment then yanked the other guard into the path of the charge. The man's expression curdled to shock as his baton struck his partner, causing him to twitch uncontrollably and slump to the floor.

Alyssa snatched Barney from the limp guard's grasp and swung it at the other's legs, sweeping him off his feet. She flipped the baton in her wrist and drove it hard into his chest, activating it. The guard seized for several seconds before his body went limp.

Alyssa rose slowly and lifted her head.

"Yabadabadoo," she said.

Yuri Korzo cowered in the chair, his face pale. His gaze flashed from Alyssa to Tasha, who stood looking as bored as she did when Alyssa was brought in.

Tasha gave him a shrug. "Don't look at me. She's *crazy*."

Yuri Korzo bounced out of the chair and dashed for a door across the room. Alyssa hurtled the baton at his feet, tripping him. He plunged face-first into a metal cart, toppling it and spilling its contents.

Alyssa snatched a guard's pistol from his holster and lobbed it to Tasha.

Yuri Korzo groaned as he labored onto his back. He glared at them, a thin line of blood forming from a gash on his forehead.

"I look forward to getting closer acquainted with you, Dr. Korzo," Alyssa said as Tasha raised the gun at him.

"Screw you!" he spat.

Tasha fired, and a piece of black metal equipment near his foot burst into a shower of sparks. He tucked in his leg.

"You bitch!"

"That looked important," Tasha said. She turned to Alyssa. "Did that look important to you, too? Because it looked pretty important to me."

"Trust me, she's very good with weapons," Alyssa said, touching her side.

Tasha's face turned crimson. "About that…"

"Later," Alyssa replied. *Hell of a way to get a real reaction out of me.*

"What do you want?" Korzo's voice shook like a badly balanced centrifuge.

"Answers," Alyssa said. "Let's start with the Hybrid woman."

"The who?" Korzo said. Tasha fired again, bursting a bottle of clear fluid near him. He covered his head with his arms, cowering down as pieces of glass and liquid rained down on him.

"Oops," Tasha said. "Was that important, too?"

"Probably not as important as his leg," Alyssa said, her tone ice cold.

Tasha took aim.

"Stop!" Korzo pleaded, petrified. "Please!"

Tasha lowered the weapon. "That's better," she said. "Answer the question."

"She provided the blood."

"Is she… alive?" Alyssa asked.

Korzo looked at her, confused. "She was when I saw her this morning."

"She's here?" Alyssa's breath bottled up in her chest.

Korzo nodded.

"Take us to her, now." Alyssa said. She cut across the room and picked up the box with the crystal.

Tasha motioned to Korzo with the pistol. "Let's go." As he passed by her, she added, "And please know that, at the slightest provocation, I will shoot you in such a way that you will still remain able to point us in the right direction."

"You're both insane," he blurted.

Tasha smiled a cold smile. "Another reason for you to play nice."

They exited the room and entered the elevator. Korzo pressed the button for the top floor. Alyssa shared a look with Tasha. *Not where I was expecting us to go.*

The elevator stopped, and the doors parted into a spacious chamber. The elegant furnishings and floor-to-ceiling glass window on the far end stood in striking contrast to its rough stone walls. Alyssa squinted to adjust her eyes to the dim light offered by the wall sconces.

A white-clad figure sat in an ornate, high-backed chair, flanked by four armed guards dressed in black.

Photo-flashes of memory cracked across Alyssa's vision.

A shape in the night, wearing white.

Eyes gazing down at me, spilling unconditional love.

Alyssa's heartbeat throbbed in her ears. Her vision swam. She opened her mouth, unable to speak. Finally, a single word came out, like a whisper of hope.

"Mom?"

CLAY BOLTED up at the soft ding from the computer. *Finally!*

He had been on pins and needles for the last five hours, waiting for the final iteration of his image recovery routine. The computational resources at Renley's estate were nothing to sneeze at, but the job would have been done in half the time on his server at the WHO. *Or in a few minutes on the Society's quantum computing rig.* He still cringed at the fate of that digital marvel.

Let's see what we've got.

He navigated to the recovery folder and clicked on the first image. A photograph of a woman filled the screen. Elegant features and stunning golden eyes peered at him from the monitor. He brought up a picture of Alyssa's mom next to it.

He frowned.

Bollocks.

He studied both photographs, scratching the stubble on his chin. He could see a resemblance to Alyssa in both women.

What does that mean?

He transferred the picture to his phone and headed for the door, looking for George Renley.

———

ALYSSA STARED at the stranger before her. The woman's face and high, arching cheekbones looked carved out of marble. She studied Alyssa with a sense of bemused curiosity through almond-shaped eyes that glinted with a golden hue, the irises catching every bit of the dim light.

The woman flicked her hand, and the four guards surrounded them. Tasha put up her hands and didn't resist when one of the guards disarmed her. Alyssa didn't feel another man plucking the box from her limp grip. The guards placed the weapon and box on the table before the woman.

"And so we meet," the woman said. "Sit down. We have much to discuss."

Alyssa was numb with disappointment. Numb and furious for allowing herself to hope. A feeling of self-pity swept over her. She looked to Tasha whose face was a blank mask as she stared at the yellow-eyed woman.

The woman opened the box. Her eyes widened ever so slightly when she glimpsed the crystal inside it. She lifted it, her eyes focusing deep inside as if seeking a lost memory. Then she peered at Alyssa, who flinched at the intensity in her eyes. The woman's gaze was hypnotic, both irresistible and impossible to hold.

Alyssa couldn't shake the feeling that she had met her before. No, not only met, that she had known her. The odd sense of familiarity nagged at the back of her mind.

"Why was I not informed that the girl was here?" the woman addressed Korzo.

"I… I thought the tests—" he stammered.

"You may be a brilliant scientist," she interrupted, "but you are still an imbecile. Get out of my sight."

Korzo tensed and opened his mouth then closed it with a snap and turned on his heel.

The woman turned to the armed guards. "Leave us," she said.

Alyssa shared a surprised glance with Tasha as the guards withdrew. Only now did she note their appearance. They were tall, muscles bulging beneath tight, black outfits. Alyssa struggled to place their features, their dark skin in contrast with their piercing blue eyes. She kept her gaze on them until they exited.

The woman perched the crystal on the table and rose. She was a sculpture of elegance and power, soft curves and hard muscle. She approached Alyssa with leonine grace, her white dress fluttering, tracing her fluid movements. She was the most striking person Alyssa had ever encountered.

"I'm afraid we have gotten off on the wrong foot," the woman said, her expression softening. "My name is Nephthys."

Alyssa's skin tingled at the sound of the name. Again, the sense of familiarity.

"Are you a… Hybrid?" Alyssa asked.

A strange flicker crossed the woman's eyes. She gave a small smile.

"Now what would make you ask a question like that?"

"I feel like I know you," Alyssa replied. "And… your eyes."

The woman approached and lifted her palm. Alyssa wanted

to pull back, but could not bring herself to drop the mesmeric gaze. Nephthys grazed her cheek. Her skin was smooth, and her touch made Alyssa's skin tingle beneath the woman's fingers.

"I have so much to teach you," Nephthys whispered, almost to herself.

Alyssa spotted Tasha's eyes dart to the pistol on the table. She balanced on the edge of the chair behind the woman's back.

"Are there more of you?" Alyssa asked, trying to keep the woman's attention. "And how do you know—"

Tasha leaped out of the chair. She reached for the gun—and flew against the wall as Nephthys pinned her to it with one hand. Alyssa barely noticed the woman's lightning quick movement.

"Stop!" she yelled and vaulted up.

"Don't move," Nephthys warned. "I don't want to hurt either one of you. But I do need your attention."

"Please, I'll listen," Alyssa lifted her hands. "Just don't hurt her."

"Of course," Nephthys said and gently released Tasha.

"I wish to speak with Alyssa alone," Nephthys said.

"And if I say no?" Tasha glared at the woman, rubbing her neck.

Nephthys's lips curved into a cold smile. "I would insist."

"It's okay," Alyssa said. "I'll be all right."

"You sure?" Tasha asked.

Alyssa nodded. Tasha shot Nephthys another glare then moved to the door.

Alyssa waited for her to leave. "What do you want?" she asked.

Nephthys studied her for several moments, as if contemplating the question, then smiled. "I suppose the more appropriate question is, what can I offer you?"

Alyssa blinked in confusion.

"Your visions, dreams," Nephthys said, "they come unbidden. They are becoming stronger, more intense. At times you cannot tell where the vision ends and reality begins."

Alyssa sank into the chair, slack-mouthed.

"I told you, I have much to teach you."

"What is happening to me?" Alyssa asked.

"You are becoming a true Hybrid," Nephthys replied.

A Hybrid?

"You are already noticing the changes." Nephthys continued. "You are becoming faster, stronger. You can sense things." She moved closer. "But your mind is confused, unable to deal with it. Hence the visions, the daydreams."

"How... how can you know?" Alyssa stammered.

"As ingenious as the device was that your friend constructed to allow you a glimpse into the crystal, it opened a floodgate of knowledge that was thrust into your mind. The parts you remember are but a fraction of all the memories your subconscious holds. Now, the buried thoughts are rising to the surface, merging with reality."

Alyssa blinked, struggling to absorb Nephthys's words.

The woman eased into the chair beside Alyssa. "If I don't help you, the memories will eventually overwhelm you."

"Are there more like me? Like my mother?"

Nephthys's face darkened. "We are the last two of our race."

"Who are you?"

"Somebody who understands what you are going through."

"How?"

"Because, a long time ago, I went through it myself."

Alyssa rubbed her temples, trying to clear her mind.

"Who are you?" she repeated.

The woman rose. "I am Nephthys, direct descendant of the Queen and Sovereign Ruler of the Island Kingdom of Atlantis."

Alyssa's head spun, her mind unable to process the information.

"Are you part of the Society?"

"The Society?" Nephthys gave a small laugh. "The Society is nothing but a pawn."

"Did you have anything to do with the break-in at the genetics institute?"

Nephthys leaned closer. "You know as well as I do that the institute was not fit to safeguard Thoth's weapon. The Society had the resources to take possession of it before someone else did, so I enticed them to secure it."

"*Enticed* them? You mean by offering them your blood? Your genes?"

The ghost of a smile edged Nephthys's lips. "They never knew about me. They believed Korzo's story that he success-fully synthesized the ancient genes from the data. Convincing them that the virus was required to finalize their transformation guaranteed their full commitment."

"Then you killed them!"

"Alyssa, the Society had plans to use the virus to engineer an advanced bioweapon. Eliminating them was the only way to ensure it couldn't happen."

"How...?" Alyssa started, then realization struck. "You convinced Yuri Korzo to betray them."

"Regrettably, it was the only way to stop their efforts."

"Why kill them?" Alyssa bristled. "You already had Korzo."

"You are naïve, Alyssa. There are dozens of Yuri Korzos. They would have found somebody else to continue his work."

Alyssa inhaled deeply in a vain attempt to make sense of it all.

"Why do you want to help me?"

Nephthys moved to the table and lifted the crystal again. She held it against the light.

"Your father was wise in giving you the sacred stone. He knew it was not safe at the Museum. But even he does not know the true value hidden within."

Nephthys lifted the crystal to Alyssa reverently. "This stone does not hold the memories of just one Hybrid, Alyssa. It holds memories of an entire race. You can help me bring them back. But to do so, you must allow me to unlock your mind. Only then will I be able to revive my race. Our race."

She fixed her gaze on Alyssa. "Together, we can awaken the Hybrids."

———

THE ICY DRAFT cut through Tasha's red parka as she stood on a stone terrace, brooding. She hoped the frigid air and views of the snowcapped peaks glistening in the moonlight would cool off her temper and soothe her nerves. She rubbed her neck where the woman's hand had pinned her against the wall. *That's gonna leave a bruise.*

She was still reflecting on several objectionable ways of

getting even with the woman when the satellite phone rang. Glad for the distraction, she answered.

"Tasha?" Clay piped out. "I've been trying to reach you!"

"It's been… eventful," Tasha said.

"Are you both all right?" George's voice sounded equally concerned.

"Yes," she replied. *For now.*

"Where are you?"

"Well," Tasha started. "It's a bit of a story."

"Tasha, the first photograph was restored," Clay said. "I'm sending it to you now."

"Wait… don't tell me. The woman in the picture isn't Alyssa's mother."

"Uh, how did you—?"

"Your intelligence report is impeccable, if not as timely as we would have liked," she replied dryly. She glanced at the picture Clay sent her, her suspicion confirmed.

George cut in. "What do you know?"

"The woman's name is Nephthys," Tasha said. "She seems to be in charge of this temple, or research facility, or whatever it is." She apprised them of the situation.

A long pause followed. "Well, that is certainly unexpected," Renley said after he found his voice.

"Oh, and she's a Hybrid," Tasha added.

"Wh-what?" Clay stammered.

"Yeah, and if she's an indication of what our girl is turning into…" Tasha rubbed her neck again. "We'd better watch out."

"What do you mean?"

Tasha closed her mouth when the heavy door opened, revealing Alyssa.

"Well, speak of the devil," Tasha said.

Alyssa stepped up to Tasha, cringing. "There you are." She reached out. "How are you?"

"My ego somewhat worse than my neck," Tasha replied. "Clay and George are on the line." She put the phone on speaker.

Alyssa filled them in on her conversation with Nephthys.

Tasha crossed her arms. "I can't believe you're even thinking about it! We just met her, not to mention your first introduction to this place landed you in a cell. Now you're thinking about letting this woman inside your head?"

"She said my mind will continue to fall apart. That I will eventually… go mad."

"Tasha does have a point, Alyssa," Clay chimed in. "You don't know if you can trust that woman."

"But she's a Hybrid," Alyssa appealed. "A real Hybrid. She knows what I'm going through and wants to help me."

Tasha's face twisted. "I understand your need to believe her. I know what it's like to feel like you don't belong and needing something to hold on to, but I have a really bad feeling about this."

"For whatever reason, the Society has been trying to keep tabs on her," Clay said. "I'm not sure why they have those surveillance pictures of her. Maybe we'll find out more when the other ones are repaired. Now that the algorithm completed the first one, restoring the other ones shouldn't take as long."

"If anything, the fact that the Society doesn't trust her gives us even more reason to do so," Alyssa said. "She prevented them from building a bioweapon."

"I have never known the Society to be involved in something so overtly aggressive," George countered. "Using Hybrid blood to extend their lifespan is one thing, but meddling in bioweapons…"

"We'll never know if I don't take this chance," Alyssa said. "Clay, why don't you continue working on the other pictures. I'm going to see Nephthys." She ended the connection before he had a chance to reply.

"Don't do this—" Tasha started. She reached out and clasped Alyssa's arm.

Alyssa stood still, her teeth gnawing at her lower lip. "I'm losing it, Tasha. It's getting worse every day." She gently removed Tasha's hand and held it. "If there is a chance she can help me, I have to take it."

"No, you don't. We'll figure out another way."

"I'm doing this, Tasha." Alyssa turned and stepped back inside.

Tasha unzipped her parka and took a deep breath of the icy air.

Not cold enough.

CLAY THREW up his arms in frustration.

"Why does she always have to be so... so..." he stammered, unable to find the right word.

"Impetuous?" Renley offered.

"Precisely!" he exclaimed. "Impetuous!"

Renley's lips curved into a small smile. He put a hand on Clay's shoulder. "My dear Mr. Obono, it is the dictum of youth that it cannot restrain its own impetuosity."

"Well, that must mean I'm an old geezer," Clay said.

Renley chuckled as Clay turned back to the computer. "I'm going to see if we're getting anywhere with the other images."

"That sounds like an excellent idea," Renley said. "And this old geezer here shall retire for the evening. Do not hesitate to wake me if you learn anything."

Clay plopped down in front of the monitor as Renley left the room. He opened the folder with the images. A couple more icons appeared.

Progress!

He clicked on the first new image. He stared at the display. It looked like the woman, Nephthys, and...

Is that...?

He tapped to the next picture, drumming his fingers on the keyboard as it loaded.

Come on, come on...

Clay inhaled sharply as the image filled the monitor.

No, no, no...

"Lord Renley!" Clay yelled as he reached for the phone.

———

TASHA PICKED UP THE PHONE. *Clay again?*

"Where is Alyssa?" Clay's voice was breathless.

"She went to see Nephthys," Tasha replied. "What's going on?"

"You need to find her before she gets to Nephthys!"

"Why? What is it?"

Tasha glanced at the new picture Clay sent her. She paused for an instant then bounded out of the room and sprinted down the corridor to the elevator. She pressed the button, sighed, then turned heel and made for the stairway. She raced up the stairs, taking three steps at a time.

———

NEPHTHYS LINGERED IN HER CHAIR, four black-clad guards flanking her, their piercing blue gazes following Alyssa as the elevator doors parted and she stepped closer.

Alyssa eyed the guards' hard, dark-skinned faces and chiseled features. *If these guys had been guarding me instead of the Flintstone fans...* She shivered at the thought and pushed it out of her head.

Nephthys rose when Alyssa stopped a few paces in front of the chair.

"I want you to help me," Alyssa said.

"And I shall," Nephthys replied. She closed the gap and held out her hand. Alyssa hesitated, but accepted it and let the woman guide her across the chamber to a spiral staircase carved into the stone.

Nephthys turned to the guards.

"We must not be disturbed," she said before she and Alyssa ascended the staircase.

Alyssa followed Nephthys, holding her hand, her nose picking up the scent of incense as they continued their climb. A minute later, the spiral staircase opened into a small round room that stood completely empty, save for a thick rug decorating its stone floor. Alyssa pivoted three hundred and sixty degrees, following the seamless view of the mountains through the room's single curved window and domed glass ceiling. Alyssa realized she was in a glass-enclosed turret at the top of the mountain.

"This is breathtaking," Alyssa said.

Nephthys stepped on the rug, pulling Alyssa gently behind her. She knelt and motioned Alyssa to do the same.

"Are you ready?" Nephthys asked.

Alyssa nodded. Her breath quickened when Nephthys lifted her hands and placed her palms on Alyssa's forehead, forming a triangle between her thumbs and forefingers.

"Close your eyes," Nephthys commanded.

Alyssa obeyed. Her skin tingled and warmed under the woman's touch.

"Open your mind to me," Nephthys whispered.

———

TASHA STORMED into Nephthys's chamber. A pair of guards stood at her empty chair.

"Where is Alyssa?" she grunted between heavy breaths.

"She is with Nephthys," one of them replied.

"Take me to her."

"Nephthys commanded not to be disturbed."

Tasha spotted a second pair of guards covering the base of a circular staircase in the far corner. She darted across the chamber. The two guards at the staircase stepped in her way.

"I'm going up there, one way or the other," Tasha threatened.

"You will leave now." The guard motioned to the other pair. They stalked up, surrounding her.

Four on one. This ought to be interesting.

"You guys really don't want to do this," Tasha said, relaxing her body and centering her stance.

The guard behind Tasha reached for her. She stepped aside and whirled, kicking the back of his leg. It was like kicking a tree trunk, but he staggered and dropped to one knee.

A second guard charged her. She ducked under his grasp and lunged for the stairs.

She barely felt the pinprick in her back an instant before her muscles caught fire. She writhed in pain, wanting to scream, but no sound came out. She collapsed to the floor, her body twitching uncontrollably. Straining to focus, she glimpsed a black-clad figure holstering a Taser gun before her vision closed in.

———

ALYSSA DREAMED AGAIN. Only this time, she knew it was no dream. She knew she was reliving a shard of memory. She braced herself for the vision to engulf her mind, to smother her. Instead, the shard drifted into its own place, completing another piece of the puzzle.

She opened her eyes, not remembering falling asleep. Nephthys knelt next to her on the thick rug.

"How are you feeling?" she asked.

"Better," Alyssa replied. "I think."

Nephthys rose and offered a hand to Alyssa.

As she stood, a wave of vertigo caused her to stagger. Her knees buckled. Nephthys caught her before she could fall.

"Easy," the woman said. "This will pass. Now you must rest."

They descended the circular staircase. Alyssa stopped when she saw Tasha sitting against the wall, her arms and legs bound, surrounded by Nephthys's guards.

She rushed to her. "What did you do to her?" she glowered at the guards.

"I'm okay," Tasha said.

Alyssa whirled and faced Nephthys.

"We could not risk any disruption—" Nephthys started.

"Save it," Tasha interrupted. "We know that you conspired with William Drake."

Alyssa's chest tightened, unable to take a breath. Disbelief rang through her.

"That's right," Tasha continued. "Clay found surveillance pictures of her and William on the Society's server."

"Is that true?" Alyssa seethed.

Nephthys gazed at her for a few moments then laughed, startling her.

"This could have been so much easier on you," she said. "It's too bad your friends had to meddle in this."

A cold wave swept through Alyssa, freezing her to the floor. "What?"

"People are so predictable," Nephthys said. "William craved power above everything." She turned her back on them as she crossed the room to the table. "I gave him the location of the Hall of Records, and he passed the information to George Renley... and to your father."

She lifted the crystal from the table, studying it.

"William's father must have become suspicious and placed him under surveillance. William told me his father learned of the plan and confronted him. He thought it was too dangerous, too much of a risk for collateral damage. But William's obsession with the ancient power made him blind. Once he secured enough support from the most zealous members of the Society, he... eliminated the obstacle."

Tasha gasped in disbelief. "William killed his own father?"

"It was his dream to control the Society," Nephthys said. "This was the perfect opportunity. With his father out of the way, nobody else dared oppose him."

Alyssa's throat tightened, hardly able to produce a sound. Still, heat fired through her words, realizing the depth of the betrayal. "You've played them all... Drake, Renley... my father." Her stomach roiled as she spoke the next words, afraid of the answer. "What about my mother?"

"She meddled in affairs she didn't understand," Nephthys replied, setting the crystal back on the table. "And paid with her life."

Alyssa screamed and charged at Nephthys. The woman slipped aside and flung Alyssa to the floor.

Alyssa sprang up. The guards moved to seize her. Nephthys held up her hand, and they froze.

"Do not challenge me, girl," she warned, her tone matching the icy glint of her golden irises.

Alyssa snarled and lunged at Nephthys again. The woman stirred, the thin scepter in her hand seemed to appear out of thin air. Alyssa's body spun through the air, limbs flailing, before slamming into the table, neck pinned beneath the scepter. She thrashed, wheezing, fighting for breath, but the woman did not relent. Alyssa's vision closed in, every fiber in her body screaming for air. Just before complete darkness surrounded her, the crushing pressure relented. Alyssa gulped great breaths of air as Nephthys shoved her at the guards.

They seized her, twisting her arms behind her back. She glared at Nephthys, panting, then fixed her gaze at the crystal perched on the table.

"I will never help you," she spat, the words burning her bruised throat.

Nephthys followed Alyssa's eyes to the crystal.

"Do you think that's what this is all about?" She let a thin laugh escape her lips. "I told you, you had so much to learn."

Time slowed as Nephthys lifted the scepter and slammed it into the crystal, shattering it into a hundred fragments.

Alyssa froze, her mind refusing to believe what she had just witnessed.

Nephthys's eyes burned into Alyssa.

"My plans for you are much greater, girl," she breathed.

PART 3

TRANSCENDENCE

THE MAN WOKE UP, gasping for air.

Where am I? Who am I?

The fiery blast.

The cold water.

Strong, rough hands grasping my body, pulling me out.

Paul. My name is Paul Matthews.

He opened his eyes and winced. The dim overhead lamp sliced into his head like a floodlight. He lifted his hand to shield his eyes. The leather cuff strapped to his wrist jerked it back. He froze.

The Valediction… Alyssa!

Slowly, the memories returned, and he put the pieces into place. They must have captured him after he fell into the water. They didn't let him die. That meant he was more valuable to them alive than dead. Or they thought he had information that could be useful. He swallowed.

He closed his eyes. No swaying. No humming from the

engines. Was he still aboard the *Valediction*? *How long have I been out?*

The sound of a door lock unlatching snapped him back. He held his breath and squinted at the bright light as the door opened, revealing a looming figure. Paul swallowed again.

Oh, man... I'm royally buggered. I only hope Alyssa is faring better.

———

ALYSSA STRAINED against the leather tresses that bound her arms and legs to the metal examination table. Yuri Korzo approached her, holding a needle and an empty vial. She cowered back as far as the restraints would allow.

"Don't you touch me, you creep!" she screamed, her voice sounding much braver than she felt.

"The more you struggle, the more this is going to hurt," Korzo said, grasping her forearm. Alyssa flailed.

"Stop it!" he barked.

"Screw you!" she fired back.

Yuri sighed then waved to Nephthys's black-clad guard at the door. The huge man moved to the table.

"This is your last warning," Korzo said.

Alyssa glared at him but stopped moving. She clenched her jaw as Yuri cleaned her vein with an antiseptic and inserted the needle. Alyssa watched her blood flow into the plastic vial then looked up at his face, again surprised at the bitterness spilling from his eyes.

"Why do you hate me?" she asked.

Korzo remained silent, his face as cold as the metal table beneath her.

"Please. At least tell me the reason."

"My son is dead because of you."

"What?"

"You showed up in Cairo with that damn VR gadget. My son volunteered to use it. He wanted to impress Drake, make his mark in the Society. It cost him his life."

Alyssa's head spun from the needle in her arm and Korzo's words. "It—it wasn't my fault," she stammered. "The Society captured us—"

"If you and your friends hadn't built it, my son would still be alive," he spat.

"I'm so sorry about your son," Alyssa whispered. "But please understand, we never wished to harm anybody. I only wanted to save my father."

Korzo lifted his gaze, a crack in the bitter façade. "Your father?"

"He and his team were dying. I was trying to find a cure for him."

He pressed a piece of gauze on the puncture site and pulled out the needle. He held the gauze against her skin for a few seconds, wordlessly.

"I can't imagine how you feel," Alyssa continued, "but this isn't going to bring him back."

Korzo pursed his lips, his expression shifting for an instant. "Perhaps if—"

The door opened, and Nephthys entered, shadowed by two of her guards. Korzo's face hardened again.

Alyssa glared at the woman.

"I have her blood sample," Korzo said.

"Very well, let us see how special she really is," Nephthys said.

Alyssa's glance darted between them. "What do you mean?"

Korzo moved the vial to a glass cabinet and injected fluid from another tube into her blood. He inserted the sample into a device and activated it, scrutinizing the data for several moments.

He turned to Nephthys. "It is as you suspected."

Nephthys drew closer, her eyes gleaming. "You are certain?"

"The DNA sequences remain stable," he replied. "Her blood is resistant to the modified strain."

"*Modified* strain?" Alyssa cried. "You altered the virus!" She remembered the woman in the Cairo hospital. "That's why the cure didn't work on her." She paused. "But she had ancient genes. She shouldn't have been infected in the first place."

"Dr. Korzo's modifications circumvented the genetic markers that provide immunity to it," Nephthys replied.

"Why would you want to do that?" Alyssa glared at her. "And why is my blood resistant?"

Nephthys remained silent.

Alyssa stared at Korzo. "Tell me!"

Nephthys ignored her and turned to Korzo. "We need to ensure the latest modification still has the desired effect on others," she said. "Bring her friend," she ordered the guards, who left the room.

"Desired effect? You mean kill people." A cold wash swept through Alyssa.

Korzo glanced at Nephthys. His face tightened, drawing his brows together. "George Renley's daughter may be too valuable. May I suggest an alternate—"

Nephthys silenced him with a look. He kept her gaze for several moments, then cast his eyes down.

"As you wish," he said.

"No!" Alyssa cried. "You can't—"

The door swung open, and the guards led Tasha into the room. Her arms were bound behind her back.

"Alyssa!" Tasha lunged for her, but the guards hauled her back and secured her into restraints on a second table.

"Please don't do this," Alyssa pleaded with Nephthys. "I'll do anything you want."

"Don't do what?" Tasha bucked in the restraints. "What are you going to do?" She stared at Alyssa. "What are they going to do?"

"Get away from her!" Alyssa's cry mixed with Tasha's screams as Korzo attached vital sign monitors to her body.

"When will you know the results?" Nephthys asked.

"We will have confirmation of the effect in thirty minutes," Korzo replied, shifting uncomfortably.

"Report to me when you are finished." She eyed Alyssa. "You may wish to convey any final words to your friend," she said before leaving.

Alyssa stared at Korzo, every muscle in her body taut with despair. "I beg you, don't do this."

Korzo ignored her and moved to a cabinet, drawing his lips into a tight line.

"Do you think this is what your son would want?"

Korzo's expression shifted. He removed his glasses, his face sagging. "It's too late now. I have made my choice." He pulled open a drawer.

"It's never too late," Alyssa said.

Korzo paused. His eyes shifted to the guard at the door as his hand hovered over the drawer. He swallowed and lifted a syringe. He approached Tasha.

"Don't!" Alyssa cried.

Yuri ignored their duet of obscenities and injected Tasha's arm. Her body tensed. A few seconds later, the lights on the display flared red, and Tasha's body lifted up in a backbreaking arc, spittle flowing from her lips as her limbs contorted into a full-blown seizure.

Alyssa screamed.

"She's having an adverse reaction to the anesthetic," Korzo barked. He turned to the guard. "Get the crash cart from lab three!"

The guard hesitated. "Nephthys told me to stay—"

"We need her alive for the experiment!"

The guard's face twisted, betraying his internal battle.

"Now!" Korzo yelled. "Before it's too late!"

The guard shot Korzo a final look and stormed out.

Before the door fell shut, Korzo rushed to a drawer and pulled out another syringe. He injected Tasha's arm and grasped her head between his palms. A moment later her body sagged. He moved to Alyssa and loosened her restrains.

She lunged for his neck. "You bastard!" she snarled, squeezing her hands around his throat.

"Stop…" he groaned. "There isn't time."

"What did you do to her?"

"She will… be fine… I induced a chemical seizure… to

distract the guard… get him to leave," he spat between gasping breaths.

Alyssa looked at Tasha. Her eyes fluttered open.

"Alyssa?" she breathed.

Alyssa released Korzo and rushed to Tasha. She pulled her into a tight hug then freed her from the table.

Korzo scurried to a computer terminal.

"There isn't much time," he said. "I forced a reboot of the surveillance system, but it will be online in one minute." He took off his ID badge and held it out. "At the end of the corridor. There is an emergency exit into a tunnel that will lead you outside."

"Why?" Alyssa asked.

"I have my reasons," he replied.

"What about you? Are you going to be—?"

"You have to go, now!" Korzo helped Tasha off the table and pushed them to the door. "I will try to distract them for as long as I can."

"Thank you," Alyssa breathed then hooked an arm under Tasha and rushed out.

They staggered to the end of the corridor. Alyssa waved Korzo's badge at the panel next to the door, and the electrical lock released. They slipped into the tunnel.

She blinked, her eyes adjusting to the dimly lit passageway, shored up by massive wooden beams.

That'll have to do!

They raced ahead. Alyssa spotted a faint point ahead of them, growing larger as they tore through the shaft.

"I see the exit!" she called out. "We're almost there!"

They flew out onto a rocky plateau, panting. Alyssa pointed

to a ridge. "Head for the trees!" Her heart pounded in her ears as they raced across the rough terrain. They hit the rocky slope leading to the trees at full speed, scampering up.

The commotion behind them forced her to slow and risk a quick glance back. A dozen armed men swarmed out of the tunnel and raced across the plateau in pursuit.

Tasha shot past her. "Eyes front!" she yelled.

Alyssa was back to full speed in an instant.

A moment later the sound of helicopter blades spinning up reached her ears. Its spotlight flared up and swept the sloping rocks.

Tasha scrambled up the last few yards. "Get to the trees! We'll lose them in the forest!"

A gunshot rang out.

"Stop!" a voice commanded.

"Keep moving!" Tasha called out. She had cleared the edge and dashed for the trees.

"Stop or he dies!"

Alyssa stopped in her tracks and swung around. Yuri Korzo knelt on the ground, his hands laced behind his head. One of the guards loomed over him, a pistol pointed at his temple.

"Keep going!" Alyssa called to Tasha. "They want me."

Alyssa lifted her arms. A moment later Tasha slid down and appeared beside her.

"No, Tasha!" Alyssa cried. "Why…?"

A rueful expression crossed Tasha's face. "And let you have all the fun by yourself?"

The spotlight from the chopper lit them up, blinding Alyssa. The men rushed up the slope and surrounded them.

"On your knees, now!" one of them barked, pushing her

down. Alyssa's heartbeat throbbed in her throat as the rough rocks bit into her skin. She raised her arms, eyes growing wet, vision blurring.

One of the men shoved Korzo forward.

"Don't hurt him," Alyssa cried. "I'll do what you—"

The explosion rang out into the night, tearing across the sky. Alyssa's eyes shot up to the chopper. Fire spewed from its cabin, leaving a spiral of smoke as it spun like an amusement park ride. It plunged into the rocks, exploding in a fireball. An instant later the sound of automatic gunfire erupted. The men surrounding them dropped to the ground.

"Get down!" Tasha screamed. She dove on top of Alyssa, driving her into the ground.

Alyssa stared as five figures emerged from the forest, firing at the men surrounding them. The surprise didn't last long. Nephthys's men fell into an organized retreat, pulling Korzo with them.

The group of newcomers reached Alyssa and Tasha. Their black outfits blended into the night, the wraith-like look completed by headgear and tinted visors.

"Come with us, now!" one of them ordered, his voice muffled through the helmet.

Three other figures stepped in front of Alyssa and Tasha, forming a shield with their bodies. One of them took a hit and recoiled, but continued firing, keeping his position.

Body armor.

They pulled back next to a rock, retreating to the tree line beyond. Without warning, shots in ragged bursts peppered them from the side. Stone fragments from the rocks ricocheted and whizzed by Alyssa. They dropped to the ground. A group of

Nephthys's men had reached the top of the plateau and pinned them down with gunfire, cutting off their retreat into the forest.

They flattened against the rocky outcrop, taking what little cover it provided. The two groups of Nephthys's men advanced on their position.

The man next to her flicked a wide bracelet on his left forearm. Alyssa stared at the holographic display that appeared above it. He selected a triangular symbol.

"Stay down," he said.

"Who are you?" Alyssa asked.

Instead of his answer, a faint whooshing noise reached her ears. A few seconds later it grew louder, heading right for them. She lifted her head to the source. Her mouth fell open when she spotted a delta-shaped jet hovering about sixty feet off the ground. A moment later, heavy automatic gunfire blazed from beneath its wings, blasting into Nephthys's men.

The organized retreat she witnessed earlier erupted into chaos as their attackers fell back, seeking out what cover they could find.

The man pushed Alyssa to her feet. "Get up!"

Five ropes fell to the ground. He clipped into one and pulled Alyssa to him by her waist, grasping the rope with his other hand.

"My name is Dharr," he said. "Hold tight."

Alyssa threw her arms around him an instant before they lifted off amid the gunfire. She saw Tasha clinging to another rescuer as the plane ascended sharply, reeling them in.

The wind whipped into her, chilling her to the bone. She tightened her grip, then she was inside the plane, and the floor beneath her slid shut.

Alyssa stared at the interior of the spacious cabin as their five rescuers unclipped from the lines.

"You can let go now," Dharr said.

Alyssa released him and took a step back. "Who are you?"

Dharr moved to the side of the plane and secured his rifle to the wall, among a dozen others. He turned around then unbuckled his helmet and lifted it off his head.

Alyssa's jaw dropped.

Completely hairless, bronze scales covered his face, his irises two green emeralds with thin vertical pupils. A prominent jaw curved gracefully around his neck.

In a daze, Alyssa shifted her eyes to the figure next to him, the tight black outfit hugging the slender curves of her body. She took off her helmet and shook out a dazzling set of cascading champagne curls. When the girl lifted her head, Alyssa stared into the most striking feline eyes. Her irises were a caramel brown, rimmed with a thin line of gold.

Alyssa's gaze swept through the other three as each of them removed their helmets. A second girl with scaly, reptilian skin rubbed her right shoulder where the bullet had struck her armor. In contrast with Dharr's dark and rough-textured scales, hers were smooth and shimmered in a rainbow of colors, reflecting the light in the cabin. The last two looked like twins, with canine features and strong jowls. Their matching, boyish grins sparkled from their chestnut eyes, set deep into shaggy, bearded faces.

Alyssa's head spun. "You're... you're all..." words failed her.

"Rathadi," Dharr said.

"Hybrids," Alyssa whispered.

"Well, not *all*..." Alyssa froze at the sound of the voice behind her. She whipped around—and stared at Paul, standing at the bulkhead.

Alyssa's knees buckled. "H-how?" she stammered.

He moved to her, and she collapsed into him, burying her head in his shoulder. She felt the shudder of his relief, matched by her own.

"I thought I lost you..." she whispered between sobs, holding him tight. Without thinking, she grasped his head in her hands and pulled his mouth to hers. She kissed him, hungrily, blissfully oblivious to the others around them.

Paul froze when her mouth pressed against his, then his lips parted, and he returned her kiss. His hands cradled her back as hers wrapped around his neck. She felt as if the outside had faded away, and the universe had shrunk to just the two of them.

After an eternity, she let go, savoring the tingling on her lips and the taste of his sweet breath that remained in her mouth.

"They saved my life," Paul said. "Pulled me out of the water."

Alyssa faced Dharr. She moved to him wordlessly and put her arms around him. Her throat unwilling to produce a sound, she hugged him, not in the terrified death grip from a few moments ago, but with all the gratitude and relief that she was able to convey.

"We have been following the Society for years," Dharr said when she stepped back. "Since the death of William Drake's father, they have become unpredictable."

Alyssa shook her head. "So, while they have been looking for you for decades, you were right under their noses."

"Following the events in Cairo four months ago, we increased our surveillance." He chuckled. "I have to admit, we did not anticipate something quite as spectacular as the explosion you caused—"

"Or having to play fishermen in the Atlantic Ocean," said the girl with the lizard skin, smirking. Her eyes sparkled with a stunning deep amber.

"We were able to follow your trail here." Dharr said. "Though I am afraid your contact at the airport may have suffered a bit of a scare, but time did not allow for subtleties."

"Maansa?" Alyssa asked. "Is he okay?"

"Yes," Dharr said. "He will be fine."

Alyssa looked at each of them in turn. "I have so many questions."

"There will be time for all of them," Dharr replied. "It has been a long day for all. We should get some rest. We have much to discuss when we land."

A part of Alyssa wanted to argue, but she felt the adrenaline ebb out of her body. Her legs barely managed to keep her upright.

"Where are we going?"

"Hong Kong," Dharr replied.

"Hong Kong? But—"

"Rest now." Dharr lifted his hand. "We will talk again soon." He turned and exited the cabin, followed by the others.

Alyssa glanced at Tasha, who stood in the corner of the cabin, hands tucked behind her elbows, eyes distant. Alyssa reached out and wrapped her arms around the other girl. Tasha stood still for a moment, then she relaxed and returned the embrace.

"You could have left me down there, but you didn't," Alyssa whispered. "Even though you knew what they were going to do to you." Her voice broke. "I don't care that you shot me."

A shiver went through Tasha's body, and she sagged against Alyssa. When she let go, Tasha's eyes were wet.

Paul stared at them, a quizzical expression on his face.

"Well, things between you two sure have warmed up since last... Wait—" he said as he processed Alyssa's last words —"she shot you, too?"

Alyssa took his hand and nestled into a seat. She drew him next to her and rested her head against his shoulder. She remembered the taste of his lips, and melting into him at the touch of his hands on her back. Her body and mind drained, she ached with exhaustion, but for the first time in weeks, she felt safe.

———

YURI HOWLED as Nephthys's guards twisted his arms behind his back and wrenched him to her chamber. They pushed him to his knees in front of her.

Nephthys rose out of her chair. She lifted the thin scepter from the table and approached him.

"Leave us," she said. The guards nodded and obeyed.

She loomed over Yuri, studying him. Finally, she spoke.

"You did well." She reached down.

Yuri accepted her hand and shuffled to his feet. "You are risking a great deal by allowing her to leave," he said.

"The reward will be worth the risk," she said. "The virus?"

"Renley's daughter will remain free of any symptoms for twenty-four hours," Yuri replied. "The virus will lay dormant in everyone she infects until it activates." He hesitated before asking the question, "And the mind directive? Was the procedure successful?"

Nephthys sank into her chair and leaned back. "Alyssa Morgan will do as I wish, when I wish it," she said.

ALYSSA LAZED in the spacious seat, enveloped in a vibrant duet of muffled jet noise and resonant snoring. Paul stirred beside her, and his head drooped on her shoulder. His chest rose and fell rhythmically, his features softer in sleep, the worry lines in his forehead all but melted. Her fingers tingled when she moved a strand of hair from his face, and he shifted again, mumbling in his dream.

This is not a dream. We are both alive. Saved by Hybrids… Rathadi.

The five Rathadi had been holed up in the front cabin for most of the flight. Alyssa had been champing at the bit to pepper them with more questions, but beyond giving their names, Dharr had made it clear that they were going to debrief her, and get her story, after they had arrived at their home.

A Hybrid home… There are others.

She glanced out of the small window. They were approaching Hong Kong's sprawling skyline. She could make out the tallest buildings, rising like spears above the horizon.

Almost there... The anticipation tingled through her like electrical sparks on their way to the ground, gathering in her toes.

Her thoughts were interrupted when Dharr entered the cabin. He had changed from the black body armor into a pair of ripped faded jeans and a short-sleeved, black button-down shirt that he wore open, revealing more of his scaly skin.

"We'll be landing in a few minutes," he said.

Alyssa pointed at the wide cuff bracelet that still encircled his left arm. "What is that?"

He lifted it to Alyssa. "It's like a smartphone—only smarter."

She reached out to touch it then pulled her hand back.

"Go ahead," Dharr encouraged her.

Alyssa tapped it. A shimmering three-dimensional display appeared above it.

"Are you serious?" She laughed, her hand flying to her mouth. She leaned forward and studied the display and symbols. "During the fight, you used it to summon the plane."

Dharr touched the glowing triangular icon, and a series of other symbols appeared. "This brings up the controls for the plane."

"So, you control it remotely? And the guns, too?"

"We can, but the AI does a better job." He pointed at a symbol.

"Artificial intelligence? So the plane flies itself? And shoots?"

Dharr nodded. He tapped the bracelet, and the shimmering image disappeared. "There'll be time later. Let's get ready." He tagged Paul on his shoulder.

Paul groaned.

"Did you see that?" Alyssa asked him as Dharr left the cabin.

"See what?" Paul asked, groggy.

"What?" Tasha opened her eyes from the seat across.

Alyssa shook her head. "Never mind." *Clay would so geek out over this.*

She looked out of the window again. They advanced on a skyscraper that soared above others. A glass dome capped its peak, encircled by seven towers interconnected with transparent skywalks along the perimeter. One tower stood taller than the other six, and a gold spire rose from its center.

Are we going to—?

The jet decelerated rapidly. Alyssa squeezed the arm rests at the sudden loss of speed. For an instant, her stomach clenched, her body expecting her to plummet, before she realized the jet was hovering. They descended slowly until the wheels made contact. Then the jets began to wind down.

Paul glanced out. "Are we here?"

Alyssa laughed softly. "You can sleep through anything, can't you?"

"Hey, I'm still recovering from a near-drowning," he replied. "Some sympathy and patience, please?"

Dharr came in again, followed by the other Rathadi, minus the combat gear. Nel had braided her long curls into pigtails and donned a crop top and short skirt straight from the eighties. Tef, the girl with the reptilian skin, stretched against the bulkhead in a leather jumpsuit that earned a raised eyebrow from Tasha. The twins, Jawad and Vol, sported surfer-style baggy shorts and tees. Alyssa watched their cheerful banter. They looked like a bunch of kids planning to hit the town, not the team of soldiers that had rescued her and Tasha in a firefight just a few hours ago.

A ramp at the rear of the plane tilted down, and they exited onto the landing pad on the tower. The wind whipped Alyssa's hair as she spun, taking in the breathtaking view amid the sea of high-rises below them. The spired tower, tallest among the seven, stood to the south of them, across the glass dome below. Beyond it, lush green mountain ranges crested the island, topped by Victoria Peak. To the north, across the harbor, thousands more skyscrapers spread through Hong Kong's Kowloon district.

A door slid open, and a young man rushed out of the interior of the tower. Alyssa smiled, her belly buzzing with anticipation. He stopped in front of Dharr and spoke rapidly. The language was foreign, with Middle Eastern inflection, but more melodic with strange, guttural undertones. She didn't need to understand the words to interpret his mood. Alyssa's smile wilted when he stopped talking to Dharr and faced her.

"You should not be here," he said, switching to flawless English, curling his pale, thin lips. His face was strong and defined, with a sharp jaw, slender nose, and prominent cheekbones. His light brown eyes sloped downward in a serious expression. He pointed at Paul and Tasha. "None of you."

Before any of them had a chance to muster a reply, Dharr intervened. "Please forgive Heru-pa. It appears he has forgotten his manners—" he drew his eyebrows together—"and place."

Heru-pa's jaw twitched, but he remained silent. Dharr motioned them inside. "Come, we have much to discuss."

They entered the building. *Well, that's not quite the welcome I expected,* Alyssa thought as they moved to a glass elevator.

Paul stopped.

"What's wrong?" Dharr asked.

Paul grimaced. "Not a fan of glass elevators. Well, actually glass elevator shafts…"

Dharr gave him a blank look.

Alyssa squeezed Paul's hand. "Come on," she said pulling him in.

As the elevator descended, Alyssa watched the other six towers that surrounded the glass dome beneath them. They passed the level of the glass dome, and Alyssa gasped. Below them, a massive pyramid stood in the center of a twenty-story-tall atrium, surrounded by what appeared to be an indoor park. Above the pyramid, a ten-foot-wide golden disk hung suspended by a pair of wires, its brilliant polish reflecting the sunlight streaming in through the atrium.

The elevator stopped on the bottom floor of the atrium. Dharr and Tef exited. Alyssa followed with Paul and Tasha behind. Alyssa turned when she realized that Nel and the twins stayed put.

"You're not coming?" she asked.

"No way," Jawad said. *Or was it Vol?* "We'll leave the talking to Dharr. You kids have fun." He shot her a coy smile as the doors closed. "But do let us know when you're going out again."

They entered a spacious conference room and gathered around a twelve-foot-long gray slate table. Alyssa was flanked by Paul and Tasha, with Dharr and Tef taking seats facing them. Alyssa tensed when Heru-pa entered the room a few moments later and occupied the seat at the head. Dharr shot him a withering glance, not attempting to hide it.

"Who are the Rathadi?" Alyssa blurted out, not being able to contain herself a second longer.

Heru-pa's lips, already thin, compressed into bloodless lines. Dharr took a breath and leaned forward. "We are the descendants of Ra, our first ancestor."

Alyssa took a minute to let the words sink in.

"But... how?" she stammered. "I thought they... you... all died... killed by the Pureans."

"The war between the Rathadi and the Pure Ones cost countless lives, but not all perished," Dharr replied.

Alyssa swallowed, allowing her brain to catch up and consider the implications.

"And the Pureans? Did some of them survive, as well?"

Dharr nodded. "Horus destroyed Atlantis and all lives on the island, but the Pureans were a race of seafarers. Those at sea found strength in their hatred for Horus—and the Hybrids. They vowed revenge." His face darkened. "And so the war has waged on for millennia. The Pureans, united under Nephthys—"

"Nephthys?" Alyssa interrupted. "As in, the Nephthys in Nepal?"

Dharr drummed his chin with his fingers for several moments before speaking. "The Nephthys you met is a direct descendant of the Hybrid woman who unified the Pureans," he said. "They follow her in their cause to destroy us."

"But she's a Hybrid!" Alyssa exclaimed. "The Pureans are led by a Hybrid?"

A painful expression crossed Dharr's face. He opened his mouth when Heru-pa cleared his throat and leaned forward.

Both elbows on the table, he steepled his fingers and faced Dharr.

"I think our guests have had enough of a history lesson for now," he said.

"But I have so many more questions!" Alyssa pleaded. "What about the temple in Nepal?"

"All in due time," Heru-pa said. "Perhaps it may be best if—"

"The outbreak four months ago," Alyssa interrupted, "you knew about it. Why didn't you help? Your blood could have been used to create a cure."

"It is not our world," Heru-pa said. "Not our problem."

"It is now!" Alyssa fired back. "Nephthys has altered the virus so it's lethal to Hybrids."

"That is impossible," Heru-pa replied.

"Tell that to the people who died in Cairo," Alyssa pushed.

"As you said," Heru-pa said coldly, "they were *people*, not Rathadi."

"They had Hybrid genes," Alyssa said.

"What?" Dharr cut in.

Heru-pa's look betrayed his own surprise.

"I was there when the last of them died," Alyssa said. "The doctor who constructed the cure for the virus four months ago confirmed it."

Dharr scratched his neck. "How is that possible?"

"I'm not sure," Alyssa said, "but I think Nephthys shared her blood with them, allowing them to fuse her DNA into theirs."

Heru-pa snorted. "These individuals were not Rathadi. They were abominations. Our blood will protect us."

"If what Alyssa says is true, these are grim tidings," Dharr countered. "We cannot risk ignoring these reports."

"And the cure?" Tef asked. "The one manufactured from your blood for the epidemic?"

"It didn't work," Alyssa said.

Heru-pa crossed his arms and sat back defiantly. "How did one of them just happen to escape and get to the hospital?"

Dharr tapped his fingers on the table. "Unless…"

"Unless Nephthys wanted her to survive and get to the hospital," Alyssa said, sudden realization striking.

At this, Heru-pa nodded, a flicker of respect showing, along with an insulting amount of surprise.

"Why would she do that?" Tef asked.

"To confirm that the cure no longer worked." Dharr said.

"Because she is planning to use the virus," Alyssa whispered.

A ripple of unease passed through the room, followed by a long stretch of silence.

Dharr placed his palms on the table. "These reports are too serious to ignore," he said. "If any of it is true, we may be in significant danger." He rose. "Is there anything else you can tell us?"

Alyssa reflected, then shook her head.

"Thank you," Dharr said and opened the door. "Please allow us some time to evaluate the new information."

"But—" Alyssa started.

"You have given us a great deal of valuable and potentially troubling news. We must pass it on. Decisions will have to be made." He touched her arm. "I know you must have many questions. Perhaps we can all meet for our evening meal together?"

Alyssa sighed, resigned. "I understand." She gave a small smile. "Evening meal sounds great."

Paul nudged Alyssa after they left the room. "Did you just make a date with him? I thought you and I are—"

"Going steady?" Alyssa teased. "He is pretty dashing, you know. I've always had a thing for bald and scaly."

"I can shave my head," Paul offered.

"What about the scales?" Alyssa asked, stepping closer.

"I suppose it's hard to compete with a descendant of an Egyptian god." His shoulders slumped. "There's got to be a joke there somewhere."

Alyssa grasped his head in her hands. "I thought I already lost you once. I'm not going to risk it again." She leaned in and kissed him. "Not even for bald and scaly." She moved in and kissed him again, first on the cheeks, then more deeply on his lips, heat rising in—

"What's wrong with bald and scaly?" Tef's voice rang from behind Alyssa. She whirled, staring at the Hybrid girl's multi-colored skin shimmering in the sunlight.

"Are we interrupting something?" Tasha asked, sheepishly.

"Uh, I was just…" Alyssa stammered.

Tef winked, and Alyssa let out a huge breath. She fired a glance at Tasha. "And, yes, as a matter of fact you were."

Alyssa studied Tef's skin. She swallowed and reached out. "May I?"

Tef nodded and held out her arm.

Alyssa caressed it, running her fingers along the skin. It was velvety and pliant, but its strength unmistakable. The small ridges between the scales were barely perceptible.

"It's so… beautiful," Alyssa whispered, mesmerized. "Your whole body is like that?"

Tef stepped back. "Now that's getting a bit personal, no?"

Alyssa jerked her hand back, heat rising in her cheeks. "I'm sorry, I didn't mean to—"

Tef laughed. "Just teasing. But you did have it coming for making fun of bald and scaly. And, yes, those of us who have been chosen by the serpent sentinel go through the morphing after the Rite of Transcendence."

"Sentinel, morphing, transcendence," Alyssa repeated, "Rathadi…" She rubbed her face. "I feel like I'm in a dream. There's so much I want to see, learn…"

"Would you like me to show you?" Tef asked.

Alyssa perked up then eyed Paul. "I would love to, but Paul and I—"

"Go on," Paul said. "I'm not going anywhere."

"You sure?" she asked, her eyes crinkling.

"Better go before I change my mind," he grinned.

"Thank you!" Alyssa beamed. She gave him another kiss.

"Dharr said we could check in with Clay and George," Tasha said.

"I'll go with you," Paul said. He turned to Alyssa. "I'll see you soon."

"Come," Tef said. "There are many Rathadi who would like to meet you."

They walked back through the corridor and stepped into the atrium. Dozens of Rathadi strolled around the walkways or lazed on benches under green trees, watching children play on the manicured lawns, surrounded by vibrant flower beds, streams, and small ponds. The subtle concentric design of the walkways and the ponds drew the eye to the pyramid, no matter where Alyssa looked.

"What is this place?"

"It is our place of repose and play, but it also serves as a sacred place for our ceremonies."

"It's magnificent. It feels so open, almost like we're outside."

"It is difficult for some of us to spend much time among non-Rathadi." A brief shadow crossed Tef's face. "This building is our home."

Alyssa reached out and touched Tef's arm. "How many of you are here?" she asked.

"Almost seven hundred," Tef replied.

Seven hundred Hybrids? Alyssa's mind reeled. "Does Nephthys know where you are?"

Tef nodded.

"Aren't you worried she'll attack you?"

"She would never risk a full-out attack. She knows our strength," Tef replied. "Still, we are prepared to defend our home—or to evacuate it—at a moment's notice. It is something for which we train from the time we are born." She sighed wryly. "This war is part of who we are."

They crossed onto a bridge overlooking the glass pyramid and the large golden disk suspended above it. The light reflected from the disk and beamed down onto the glass, bathing the entire atrium in a soft orange glow. Alyssa studied the stairs leading to the top of the structure, stirring memories within memories.

"How did you survive?" Alyssa asked.

"Few Hybrids lived to see Horus free them from Set's

prison. Fewer yet survived the voyage to Egypt. By the time the ships reached land, only a small group of our Ancestors remained. Faced with the extinction of our race, we turned to science to ensure our survival."

"What do you mean?"

"Ever wondered why Egyptian mythology is full of incest?" She cocked an eyebrow, leaving the implication hanging.

Alyssa kept a stunned silence.

"Don't worry. Turns out it's only half-true. The more accurate description would be cloning."

"Cloning?" Alyssa's mouth dropped.

"Our ancestors used the genetic materials from siblings to create their offspring. Genes from our animal sentinels provided the genetic diversity needed to sustain us. So, from a few individuals, our race was reborn."

Alyssa tried to process everything that Tef told her when somebody poked her from behind. Alyssa turned. A small boy stared at her with huge eyes. His face was round with a smattering of pale freckles dotting his nose and cheeks. His expression was curious and eager, like a boy who'd just walked into a bakery full of pastries.

"Are you Alyssa?" he asked.

"It appears you're a bit of a celebrity," Tef pointed at a group of children who had gathered behind them. Alyssa had been so engrossed in the conversation she hadn't noticed them before. The children stood, staring at her. She smiled at the boy and motioned the kids closer.

"Yes, I am," she said. "What's your name?"

"Wen," the boy replied.

"That's a nice name," she said. He beamed.

"Is it true what they say about you?"

"I don't know," Alyssa replied. "What do they say about me?"

"That you found the Hall of Records?"

"Well, my dad found it, actually. But I did get to go inside."

"What was it like?" he asked, leaning in.

"Magical," Alyssa said, lost in a memory.

His eyes grew even bigger. The other children nudged closer.

"Tell me more," Wen said. "Did you see the sacred monument?"

"The sacred monument?" Alyssa blinked. "Oh, the pyramid! How do you know about it?"

"We hear stories from the elders," a girl said. She looked to be a few years older than Wen. Her skin shimmered in the golden light like Tef's, but seemed unfledged, lacking the radiance of the older girl's.

I'm talking to the descendants of an Egyptian god...

Wen scooted closer and tugged on her hand. She flinched at the strange touch of his skin.

"Well, did you see it?" he asked.

"What? Right! Yes. Yes, I did," Alyssa said absentmindedly.

She turned over Wen's hand and studied it. Fine white fur covered his skin. "What is your—" she searched for the right words—"animal sentinel?"

The boy looked at her proudly. "The hare," he said. "Swift and clever."

"Swift to run from chores and studies," the girl said. The other children giggled, and Wen's face turned crimson.

"And yours must be the serpent," Alyssa said to the girl with the shimmering skin.

"Yup," she said. She poked Wen and licked her lips. "And we do adore hares."

"One does not talk about one's food in front of guests, Kara," Tef admonished the girl.

Alyssa's gaze flew from the children to Tef. "Your… food?"

Tef tried to keep a straight face before she cracked up. The children joined in, laughing gleefully.

"Really?" Alyssa called out in mock exasperation before joining in. "You know you can tell me anything!"

"And what is you animal sentinel?" Wen asked Alyssa.

Alyssa stopped mid-laugh, turning serious, reflecting. "I… I'm not sure," she finally said.

"You don't know?" Kara scrunched her brow. "But you're —" she pinched her lips, looking for the right words—"so old!"

Alyssa gaped at her open-mouthed before she laughed out loud again.

Tef stepped in. "Alyssa didn't know she was a Hybrid until just a few months ago."

The children's mouths dropped into a collective wow.

"You mean you haven't entered the Rite of Transcendence?" Wen asked.

"How about the Ceremony of Awakening?" Kara asked.

"Or even learned about the Celebration of Legacy?" another girl chimed in.

Alyssa shook her head. "I'm sorry, I don't know what any of those are."

"They are the Nine Sacred Liturgies," Wen said. He counted out on his fingers. "Awakening, Reflection, Revelation, Valediction, Convergence, Transcendence, Discord, Sacrifice, and Legacy." He beamed at her proudly, holding up nine fingers. The other children nodded their agreement enthusiastically.

"I... I'm sorry," she said. "I would love to learn all I can about every single one."

Wen opened his mouth, but Kara beat him to it. "The Ceremony of Awakening occurs on the seventh day after your birth and is the first of—"

Tef held up her hand, silencing the girl. "I think Alyssa will have plenty of time to learn about our traditions—just not right now."

The children gave a disheartened sigh.

Alyssa smiled. "Thank you, Wen and Kara. And all of you. I can't wait to talk to all of you again," she said. "Then you can tell me all about the nine rites."

"Nine *Liturgies*!" Wen corrected.

"Right, sorry, Nine Liturgies!" Alyssa laughed.

The pain in her head was as sudden as it was blinding. She fell backward, her limbs rubbery and limp. Her world collapsed to a tight agonized knot. Then, darkness.

"Whoa, mate, that's too close!" Paul leaned back as far as the chair allowed. "I can count your nose hair."

"Sorry about that." Clay moved back from the camera, grinning, allowing room for George Renley's face to be displayed alongside his on the massive flat screen hanging on the wall. "Not used to having my mug broadcast on a movie screen."

"With your looks, it's just a matter of time," Tasha snickered.

"Thank you, kind lady. But despite my devilishly good looks, I shall continue to rely on my brain for my future fame and fortune."

"Speaking of that brain," Paul said, "you're sure about the virus?"

Clay's face turned serious again. "Kamal said that the virus and Alyssa's blood showed similar mutations. Like she's linked to it, somehow."

"What does that even mean?" Paul asked, mystified.

"I've contacted my collaborators at the WHO, and we are

running some additional tests," Clay offered. "We should be able to—"

Tef burst through the door. "You must come now!"

Paul whipped about, almost falling out of the chair. "What is it?"

"Alyssa!" she said and stormed off.

"We'll call you back." Paul disconnected the call and raced after Tef, white-faced, with Tasha at his heels.

———

GRIEF.

Anger.

Rage.

I stand over the small body. If not for the paleness of his face, he could be sleeping. Horemheb's steady breathing echoes behind me. He has been there, motionless, a silent shadow for the countless hours I have held vigil over my son's lifeless body.

I was too late. Perhaps if we had left sooner, sailed swifter…

I am beyond grief. I am beyond anger and rage.

I fall to my knees. Empty.

I am sorry, Hathor, my beloved, for I have failed you.

I did not save our son.

———

I HAVE FAILED YOU.

Alyssa woke with a shudder, at the edge of a scream. She wept. She wept for her lost love. Her lost heir. Her lost life.

She opened her eyes slowly and blinked the tears away. Paul's face was a mask of concern as he lingered on the bed, cradling her hand. Dharr and Tef stood at her feet with Tasha. The look in their eyes echoed Paul's worry.

"How long has this been going on?" Tef asked.

"I… I'm not sure," Alyssa answered, still dazed.

"It started after the events in the Hall," Paul jumped in. "The episodes have been similar to what she experienced with the crystal and VR gear, except now they're spontaneous—and random." He squeezed her hand. "And they seem to be getting worse."

The door opened, and a figure entered the room. Dharr and Tef stepped aside, revealing an ancient-looking Hybrid wearing a cobalt-blue robe. His skin was like Dharr's, but its scaly texture appeared even more burred and leathery. The spark in his gray eyes was muted by the passage of time, but they shone with wisdom and kindness. Dharr bowed to him. The old man placed his palms on Dharr's head in the traditional greeting.

"This is Bes, our First Kah," Dharr said. "He leads the council of Elders."

Bes approached the bed. His hands moved to Alyssa's head.

Alyssa recoiled.

Dharr tensed. "Alyssa?"

Alyssa bristled. "Nephthys," she breathed. "That's what she did."

Bes lowered his arms, his gray eyes soothing. "You are safe here, my child. We do not wish you harm."

Alyssa took a shuddering breath and nodded.

He drew near once again and placed his palms on her head.

Alyssa flinched. A stab of pain. A flashbulb memory.

His hands, rough on my head, unlike my mother's.

Her back arched, sending a spasm through her body.

"Alyssa!" Paul cried out.

Bes pulled back as Alyssa lay on the bed, panting. He lifted his head and faced the others. "Please leave," he said.

Alyssa clung to Paul's hand.

"You may stay," Bes said, before Paul could protest.

Bes waited until everybody stepped out.

"Horus's memories," he said. "They confuse your mind. They are bonding with your Rathadi entity."

"How…? How can you know?" Alyssa asked.

"I sense the struggle inside you, child."

"It is consuming me," Alyssa whispered, "every thought, sensation. I feel it growing."

"What happened to you in the Hall, it began the process of Transcendence. Thoth's ancient weapon is accelerating it. You are becoming a Hybrid, yet your body is resisting it."

"Why?" Alyssa asked.

"Your Hybrid consciousness seeks your animal sentinel. To transcend is to join with another life. Only then can you become a true Rathadi."

"That is what Nephthys said. She said she could help me."

"She fed you half-truths to earn your trust, so you would believe her lies. No single Rathadi can help you. Only you can help yourself. You must undergo the Rite of Transcendence."

"What?" Goosebumps slid along the back of Alyssa's neck. "You mean like Horus and the falcon?" Her mind flashed back to the first memory. Horus, the boy, ascending the sacred pyramid.

"Like Horus and countless Rathadi before him, and countless who have followed in his footsteps," Bes said.

Alyssa took a moment to let it sink in.

"The process of Transcendence allows your animal sentinel to bring balance to your mind, your body," Bes continued.

"The children spoke of other… liturgies."

Bes nodded slowly. "There are nine Sacred Liturgies, five that precede Transcendence."

"Shouldn't Alyssa go through them first?" Paul jumped in.

Bes's gaze shifted to Paul then back to Alyssa. "Your mind cannot wait that long."

"What do you mean?" she asked, swallowing.

"You are losing control. Without transcending, your mind will slip into darkness."

"How long do I have?" she asked, her voice frosted with dread.

Bes's ancient face darkened. "A few days, at most."

Alyssa's brain refused to believe what she heard. A wave of nausea swept over her.

Days?

"But I don't even have a… sentinel," she stammered. "Even if I decide to go through with it, where would I find one?"

"The Rathadi liturgies may be rooted in eons-old traditions, but we have evolved with the times," Bes said. "We have preserved the DNA of the sentinels, to fuse with our own. I will guide you through your journey, so your sentinel can find you and reveal itself to you."

Reveal itself to me?

Another memory took shape in Alyssa's mind. Unlike the others, this one filled her with a warmth that radiated through her chest, spreading to her limbs.

The magnificent bird on her small arm, its talons pricking her soft skin.

It cocks its head, its golden eyes studying her curiously.

She is weightless, soaring.

"The falcon," Alyssa said, her body tingling. "It is the Lanner falcon."

———

ALYSSA LAY ON THE BED, her mind racing, locked in a battle long after Bes had left the room. Paul's hand slipped into her fingers. With just his touch, the tightness inside her eased a little. She squeezed his hand, a silent note of gratitude.

"If we... if *you* can't trust them, who can you trust?" he asked, huddled on the bed beside her. "They want to help you."

Alyssa snorted. "Like the woman helped me?"

"They aren't like Nephthys," he replied gently.

"I trusted Nephthys, too," Alyssa said, her voice growing rough. "She also said she was going to help me. Then she betrayed me."

"Tasha told me," Paul said.

"It's not only the betrayal," Alyssa continued. "I wanted to —*needed to*—trust her."

"I understand," he said.

"Do you?" she asked. "Do you know how much I want to trust them? To believe that they can help me?" Her body shook. Paul placed her hand between his palms.

"The changes, these… daydreams… *nightmares*… I'm scared. I'm scared of what is happening to you." His lips trembled. "Of what you're becoming. You're not yourself. If there is a chance that this can help…"

"Of course I'm not myself!" Alyssa cried, letting a thin, desperate laugh escape her lips. "I've got ancient friggin' genes and some death bug wreaking havoc with my body and mind! Now I'm learning I have *days* left?" She pressed her mouth into a thin line. "I never wanted this, Paul."

"I know." He squeezed her hand. "Please, I'm asking you to trust them."

Alyssa sensed the weight of his gaze on her, waiting for her answer. She held it for a long moment before finally nodding.

Paul sighed with relief and stood. "I'll let Dharr and Bes know. They will prepare the ceremony."

Alyssa squeezed his hand, pulling him to her. "One condition."

"Anything."

"I want you with me. The whole time."

"I told you I'm not leaving you again."

———

"Get out, Paul!" Alyssa yelled, chucking a towel at the door.

She stood, naked and shivering, in the shallow tub in the small, windowless room.

Did I really sign up for this?

She flinched when a warm, gooey sponge touched her right shoulder blade. A creamy trail of milk and honey oozed down her back and leg, tingling her skin. Another sponge was dipped into the tub and the process repeated on the left side.

When in Atlantis…

Alyssa closed her eyes as the two old Rathadi women on either side of the copper tub continued the ceremonial bath. With her eyes closed, the sickly-sweet scent of honey and milk invaded her nostrils and filled her throat. She took short, shallow breaths and waited for the syrupy bath to end while the women clucked contently in the strange Rathadi tongue.

Soon enough, the milky residue was washed away with warm water, and she was wrapped in a soft towel and dried as if she were a child. The women toweled her enthusiastically until her skin developed a pink tinge. Only then did they allow her to step out of the tub.

A third woman drew near, a white robe draped across her arms. The other two lifted the linen as the third slipped it over Alyssa's head. The feathery cloth fell smoothly against her naked skin, enfolding her in a faint scent reminiscent of cinnamon. They arranged the delicate garment with practiced movements and cinched it around her waist with a finely woven, jeweled belt. They stepped back and appraised her with self-satisfied smiles.

Oh, my God. It's the three fairy godmothers… What's next? Glass slippers?

She put on her most innocent smile as they motioned her to a chair, and she sank into it. One of the women applied fine chalk powder to her face while another used what looked to be extract from rose petals as rouge on her cheekbones, then mixed beeswax and red dye and rubbed it on her lips. The third woman applied a golden shadow to her eyelids.

They picked up three hairbrushes and began pulling it through Alyssa's long hair, humming a soft melody. They hummed and weaved her hair into narrow braids, twisting in gold strings and capping each braid with a blue stone.

Alyssa closed her eyes again, losing herself in the strange tune. Her mind relaxed and wandered. When she agreed to participate in the Rite of Transcendence, she had no idea what it entailed. Upon the announcement, all activities came to a grinding halt. Tef informed her that, by tradition, the ceremony is witnessed by all the Rathadi as they gather around their sacred pyramid. The Rathadi girl had spent the last hour before Alyssa's ceremonial cleansing with her, teaching her the protocols and proper responses for the ceremony.

As if I don't already have enough to worry about…

The absence of the melody startled her. She cracked one eye as one of the women stood and moved to the door, opening it. Tef entered. She stifled a squeal of delight and grinned widely.

"You look magnificent!"

Alyssa rose.

"Not so fast." Tef pushed her back down gently. "One final step."

She lifted a stick of black kohl from a silver tray.

"Don't move," Tef said. "This is the most important part."

Alyssa held still as Tef gently lined her eyes with the black powder. She continued drawing under her left eye, tracing out a symbol.

"There," she said, taking a step back and appraising her work. She nodded, satisfied. "Now you're ready."

She handed Alyssa a polished silver mirror.

Alyssa hardly recognized the person looking back at her

from behind the smoky, almond-shaped eyes. The makeup brought out her dark complexion and made her features appear exotic, emphasizing her fine lines and high cheekbones.

The breath caught in her throat when she looked beneath her left eye, recognizing the symbol traced out with the black kohl. A symbol of protection and force, representing the female counterpart to the sun god.

The Eye of Ra.

———

PAUL BOUNCED on his toes as he stood between Tef and Tasha in the front row, among hundreds of Hybrids who crowded the space around the pyramid. He unfastened the top button of his shirt and ran his hand through his hair.

Tasha elbowed him. "You're gonna make it through this?"

A flush crept across his cheeks. "Sorry," he said, wiping his palms on his pants and forcing himself to stand still. He looked over his shoulder and scanned the faces in the huge atrium. Nel and the twins shot him a grin, standing a couple rows back. None of them mirrored his own anxiety. He spotted Heru-pa, standing by himself at the back of the chamber. He seemed to be the only one in the crowd wearing a sour expression. The Hybrid gave him a glum look when their gazes met.

What's the guy's problem? He leaned to Tasha and opened his mouth when a small murmur rose through the space, and the crowd parted, creating a path for the approaching figure.

Paul's heart seemed to freeze, then pound when he glimpsed Alyssa. She slowly moved through the ranks. The contours of her naked body were unmistakable beneath the white robe, shifting the fabric gently as she strode barefoot to the pyramid.

She stopped beside him and smiled. The twilight reflected from the golden disk, resting gently on her face as if the rays of the sun desired to touch her as much as he did. For just a moment, his body felt untethered, a mere fragment of a dream floating above the earth. His heartbeat fluttered in his wrists, in his chest, in his belly.

She looked… *divine.*

Alyssa faced the pyramid and Bes, who stood at the peak dressed in a long, gray robe, a hood covering his scaly head. With her first step on the glass, a soft chanting from hundreds of Rathadi throats ensued. The chanting crescendoed as Alyssa ascended, the voices rising both in pitch and volume only to stop abruptly when Alyssa reached the top. She knelt before Bes and bowed her head. He placed his palms on her forehead.

"Are you prepared?" he asked.

"I am," Alyssa replied.

"Who comes before me?"

"Alyssa, daughter of Kaden and Anja," she replied.

Bes lifted his arms. "Alyssa, daughter of Kaden and Anja," he called out, "this day marks the last day of your life as a child. From this day forth, you shall live your life as a woman, blessed with the gift of your sentinel."

Paul's skin prickled at the words.

"Have you chosen?" Bes continued.

"I have," Alyssa answered.

"What is to be your sentinel?"

Alyssa's body twitched. She remained silent.

Bes waited for several moments before he asked again, "What is to be your sentinel?"

Paul felt a shiver run down his back.

Without warning, Alyssa collapsed to the ground, writhing. Paul's brain seized for an instant, then he screamed and leaped up the stairs, taking three steps at a time.

"Paul!" Tef called out and raced after him.

Paul reached Alyssa and dropped to the ground beside her.

"What did you do to her?" he screamed at Bes.

Tef knelt by her other side. She pressed her fingers against Alyssa's neck.

"We need to get her to a hospital!" Paul yelled.

Bes bent down and placed his palms on Alyssa's head.

"A hospital will not be able to help her," he said.

Alyssa's eyelids began to flutter erratically.

"We're losing her," Tef said, her voice trembling.

"No, we are not!" Paul slid his arms under Alyssa, ready to lift her up.

He froze and turned at the murmur behind him. The Hybrids below the pyramid parted and knelt reverently before a tall, hooded figure. The man moved swiftly up the stairs.

"Who are—?" Paul rose and placed himself between Alyssa and the approaching figure.

Tef put a hand on his shoulder and pulled him back. "Be still, Paul!" she commanded, her tone leaving no room for dissent. She sank to one knee and bowed her head. The man moved to Alyssa.

"What are you going…?" Paul started.

The man removed his hood and faced Paul, a single eye

burning bright amber, deep lines lining his face. Paul fell silent under his gaze and bowed his head.

The man knelt next to Alyssa and placed his palms on her forehead. Alyssa's body was still, her chest unmoving.

———

THE DARKNESS IS COMPLETE, and I am content.

Then it begins to lift.

I beg for it to stay, but it does not obey me. I shiver, not from the cold, but from the knowledge that this is wrong. This should not be.

Sand pours into my body and courses through my veins. It pushes against me from the inside until I fear my skin will break. I try to scream, but sand fills my throat.

The grinding sound of stone on stone reaches my ears, chilling me to the core. My senses are overwhelmed, hyper-aware. I struggle to open my eye, but even that simple task is beyond me as my body fails me, defying my command. My eyelid is a metal plate, fused shut with fire.

I try again.

And again.

Finally, my body relents, and my eye opens. A flash of light assails my brain. The veil of a shadow. A face. A woman.

Nephthys.

Her lips move close as if to bestow a lover's kiss, but her face is cold, her eyes even colder.

"I have missed you—brother," she whispers and presses the dagger against my throat.

———

ALYSSA GASPED. Paul cried out, dizzy with relief. Alyssa twitched, her eyelids fluttered. Her chest rose and fell in shallow breaths.

"Alyssa!" Paul leaped to her. He fell to his knees and grasped Alyssa's head.

She opened her eyes and moved them from Paul to the figure standing above him. Recognition flooded her face.

"How...?"

NEPHTHYS STOOD on the summit of Victoria Peak, overlooking Hong Kong island. The high collar and long sleeves of her black dress held back the chill of the wind. The countless high-rises on the island blended into their counterparts across Causeway Bay, forming a sea of lights. A single building rose above them. Nephthys's body filled with an electricity she hadn't felt in decades. Even at this distance his presence was unmistakable.

"The ancient bioweapon will activate in five minutes time," Yuri Korzo said, interrupting her thoughts, his voice filled with the tremor of pride.

Nephthys nodded, her thoughts far away. *Ancient bioweapon… Horus virus… Thoth's curse…* Her jaw tightened. No matter the name, tonight, there would be retribution. Their own weapon, Thoth's lethal creation that had ravaged so many Pure Ones, would be used against the Rathadi. Using the knowledge she bestowed on him, Korzo altered it, bypassing the natural immunity the Rathadi blood offered against it. But his true genius, and what would bring her victory tonight, lay in how they had delivered it to the Rathadi.

Her lips curved into a smile as she imagined the bodies of the Rathadi, ravaged by their own weapon, wrapped in a biological Trojan horse designed by Korzo. It was brought inside by the girl he infected and lay dormant as it spread, only to activate in every one of them at exactly the same time.

Yuri continued his nervous rambling. "They will be most vulnerable during the initial phase of the active infection. Their bodies will be overwhelmed as they try to mount an immune response against the pathogen."

She nodded silently, not chastising him for the nervous chatter.

Most importantly, Alyssa Morgan continued to be immune to it. Nephthys did not want to risk damaging her spoils. Not when she was so close to her goal. Tonight, she would celebrate two victories. She would defeat the Rathadi and secure her prize.

Behind her, four military transport helicopters stood in formation, her men on board, awaiting her command for liftoff. Nephthys's connection within the Chinese government facilitated the introduction between her and the top brass of the People's Liberation Army. But it was Yuri Korzo's biologically synthesized timer that captured their interest and convinced them to grant her the use of the choppers and freedom to operate in their airspace in exchange for his technology.

She raised her hand and watched three of the helicopters lift off. She and Yuri entered the fourth one as its blades spun up.

"It is time for a family reunion," she said as the helicopter rose into the air and set course for the building.

———

ALYSSA GAZED out of the tall window. On any other night, the view of the cityscape from the tallest of the seven Rathadi towers would be the most spectacular sight she could hope to behold. Tonight, it was a distant second. She shifted her focus to the reflection of the figure standing behind her. Even though she had never laid eyes on his face, she knew it was him. He held himself with a stillness that reminded her of carved stone.

She turned.

"Are you a god?"

He held her gaze for several moments, the yellow iris in his single eye reflecting thousands of distant pinpoints of light. His mouth twitched, the first crack in his perfect, sculpted face, then he gave her a small, amused laugh.

"What makes a god?" he asked, his voice low, almost hypnotic. "I have been worshiped as one. Temples have been built to idolize me. Wars have been waged and more lives lost in my name than even I can count." He paused. "But if you are asking whether I am immortal or omnipotent—" he fixed his gaze on Alyssa—"I fear my answer shall leave you disillusioned."

"Then how… how can you be alive? After so many years? I saw you. I *was* you. And now, thousands of years later…?"

"We are blessed with long life," he said, "but not that long."

"Then you're not Horus?"

"I am Horus," he said.

Alyssa blinked. "I don't understand."

He took a deep breath, as if searching for a place to begin.

He was silent for so long Alyssa thought he would never answer the question.

Finally, he spoke. "My consciousness has been passed down through generations. I am the direct bloodline of Horus. His descendent."

"Your consciousness?" Alyssa asked. "The crystal?"

"The sacred stone is but a window into our minds. It holds memories and thoughts, but cannot be used to pass down a full consciousness." He approached her. "That feat can only be accomplished by linking two living minds."

A wave of heat rushed through Alyssa. So many questions splintered her mind that she couldn't keep them straight.

"When I am ready to cross over, my son shall take my place," Horus continued. "Just as I did two centuries ago, when I myself ceased to be Heru-pa and became Horus."

"Heru-pa?" Alyssa managed to ask, finally finding her voice. "The Rathadi I met? He is your son?"

"Heru-pa-kaat—Horus the Child—is as much a name as it is a title for Horus's vessel. As countless generations before him and before me, Heru-pa has been groomed from before the day he was born to serve as Horus's vessel. His birthright and his duty are to carry forward the legacy of our people, and the legacy of our first ancestor."

"Ra," Alyssa whispered.

Horus nodded. "Once he takes my place, Heru-pa's transcendence shall be complete."

She brought a shaky hand to her temple, rubbing it. She focused on the one thing she thought she understood.

"I thought that to transcend meant to join with your sentinel," she said.

"All Rathadi join with their sentinel during the Rite of Transcendence, the most sacred of our liturgies. I—the first Horus—transcended millennia ago when I joined with my falcon. Herupa must remain free of a sentinel until my consciousness is passed down to him. It is but one price we all must pay to serve as Horus's vessel." His hand drifted to the ornate eyepatch.

Alyssa moved to a black leather armchair and sagged into it, absorbing what she heard.

"What happened four months ago? Did you know the Hall would be opened?"

Horus stared at her. "Nephthys," he said.

"The woman I met in Nepal?"

Horus nodded.

"Nephthys... she is your—"

"Sister," Horus completed. "Half-sister, actually." He took a deep, steadying breath. "She has suffered greatly. At the hands of the Pureans... and the Rathadi." A pained expression crossed his face. "I did not know she existed until it was too late..."

"I thought your family..."

"The night my grandfather and I escaped the island, my mother was captured. Young Set saved her life."

"Set? The same Set you killed?"

Horus's gaze turned inward, as if reliving that night. "We grew up as brothers," he said. "Set, Prince of the Pureans. I, Prince of the Hybrids. Had we been able to produce offspring, we would have been married to seal the peace between our people. I loved him like my own brother, my mother loved him like her own son."

"But the Pureans were your enemies!"

"It was not always that way. The attack on our people was

as stunning to him as it was to the Hybrids. When the Pureans captured my mother, she was to follow my father into death. Young Set begged for her life until his father relented and allowed her to live."

"What happened to her?"

"My mother... became pregnant in captivity. Her daughter, my half-sister, Nephthys, was raised among the Pureans. Set's love for my mother spilled over to Nephthys. He felt responsible for her, protected her. They fell in love. It was a forbidden love, full of danger. When it was discovered, she was forced to join with a sentinel and forced to leave the island." Horus's mouth twisted. "An abomination of the cruelest kind..."

"That is horrible," Alyssa whispered.

"When Nephthys returned and learned that I had killed Set and destroyed the only home she had ever known, she vowed to make me suffer as I had made her suffer."

"So all these years of fighting..."

"It is a war fueled by revenge—and pain," Horus completed her thought. "Pain that I inflicted."

Alyssa stood in sullen silence. "Nephthys, is she like you? I mean, her consciousness and memories?"

"Her life among the Pureans has diluted her Rathadi bloodline, weakened it." Horus stepped closer. "You are important to her. More important than you could—"

The door to the room burst open. Dharr rushed in, pale and breathless, clutching a bundle in his arms.

"We were betrayed," he uttered between heavy gasps.

Alyssa stared at the bundle, her brain slowly registering it as a child. *No.* She willed it not to be, but the face was one she knew. *Wen.* A thin trickle of blood flowed from his right eye down his cheek, like a red tear.

"The infection," Dharr said, "it is here." He staggered.

Horus rushed to him and caught him before he and Wen could fall to the ground. He eased them down gently then turned to Alyssa.

An icy terror blossomed in her chest, expanding like a tumor.

The crushing pressure was there before she realized Horus had moved across the room and lifted her up by her throat like a rag doll.

"Did you know?" he growled, his face contorted in a snarl.

Alyssa struggled to breathe. She tried to pry his fingers away from her throat, but his grip was like a vise, sucking the air in the room from her lungs.

"No," she cried. "I would never…" She gasped for breath, her vision closing in.

Horus fixed his eye on Alyssa, burning through her, as if probing her soul. Two unimaginably long heartbeats later, he lowered her to the ground. She collapsed, sobbing, heaving in great gulps of air.

Horus's face twisted with sudden realization. He faced Dharr.

"Go on high alert. Activate the—"

Bursting glass. Short thumping sounds. Alyssa screamed as everything around her exploded at once.

———

PAUL STAGGERED along the corridor past the elevator, the alarm blaring in his ears, the air thick with smoke. His vision swam, and his head threatened to explode. Without warning, the body appeared in his path. He crashed into it, grunting. Before he knew what happened, he was flat on his back, staring into a muzzle, a knee grinding his gut into the hard floor. Tasha's feral eyes glared at him from behind the pistol.

"Paul!" she cried. "I'm sorry!" She lowered the weapon.

She sprang up and held out her hand, helping him to his feet. He winced while the organs in his gut rearranged themselves into their anatomically correct positions. A hundred words surged through his mind, but he kept his mouth shut. *She still has the gun.*

"What's happening?" he asked.

"We're under attack!"

"Who?"

"Does it matter?" She looked around. "Where is Alyssa?"

"She was with... Horus." He shook his head, still in disbelief at his own words. "We need to find them!" He turned, ready to take off, and staggered.

Tasha caught him. "Are you okay?"

"Yeah... I think so." *It's just the smoke.*

Tasha grasped his shoulder and handed him the pistol. "Do you know how to use it?"

Paul took the weapon and nodded. He looked at her empty hand. "What about you?"

"I'll manage," she said and took off down the corridor.

No doubt, Paul thought, rubbing his gut as he staggered after her, trying to keep up.

———

My ears ring as I lie face down, stunned and blinded. I shake my head, trying to see through the haze.

Slowly my vision returns. I roll to my side. The men who guarded my left flank are gone, their mangled bodies strewn across the marble grounds of the palace courtyard. Their shields and bodies protected me from the force of the explosion.

Black powder? But Thoth—

Alyssa snapped back as strong hands lifted her to her feet. Horus's face was marred with dirt and blood, his eye fierce.

"Are you injured?" he asked.

She shook her head.

Horus moved to Dharr. His body lay on the ground, covering Wen and shielding him from the blast. Dharr stirred when Horus touched him. He slowly gained his feet. Horus knelt next to Wen and placed a palm on his head.

Horus tapped his bracelet, and a three-dimensional diagram of the building appeared above it. He studied it for several seconds. He tapped it again, and a shimmering image of Heru-pa's face replaced the building.

"She is here," Horus said.

"The link has been disabled!" Heru-pa cried.

Horus's jaw tightened. "I shall restore the transmitter. Be ready to send the signal."

"Let me go, instead," Heru-pa pleaded. "You cannot risk—"

"Do not question me!" Horus warned, his voice tense. "They waited until we were vulnerable," Horus said. "The access from below will be blocked, so they will attempt to breach from above. Gather those who can fight and protect the high levels until all are safe."

He tapped the bracelet again, and Heru-pa's face disappeared.

He lifted Wen and put him into Dharr's arms. "Get him to safety."

"My Lord…" Dharr started then staggered and slumped.

Horus caught him before he could fall and grasped Dharr's head between his palms. They stood, frozen, until Dharr's eyes began to clear. Horus spoke to him in the Rathadi tongue. Dharr tensed, his eyes shifting to Alyssa.

"Evacuate to the safe zones," Horus commanded before Dharr had a chance to reply. "Protect her with your life." He sped out of the room.

"Wait!" Alyssa called after him. "Don't leave!"

Dharr stepped in her way. "You will obey his command. We must hurry." He rushed into the corridor.

A second detonation tore through the room, catching her in mid-step. The blast lifted her off her feet and tossed her backward as a wave of heat washed over her.

She tumbled across the floor, stone and fiery debris showering her, cutting and burning flesh. She crabbed back, fleeing the onslaught until her back pressed against the floor-to-ceiling window.

A creaking sound groaned from the ceiling, sending a massive strut at her head. Alyssa's scream mixed with the shriek of bending metal and bursting glass as the strut crashed into a horizontal support beam that wrapped the tower, tearing a gaping hole in the glass wall. Shards of glass sailed skyward amid flames.

In a daze, Alyssa staggered to her feet and stared at the

gaping hole and the steel beam that had saved her life. The wind whipped into her, fueling the fire in the room.

Alyssa lifted an arm to shield her face from the heat and neared the fiery inferno that churned between her and the door. She staggered back, coughing, fumes burning her lungs.

"Dharr!" she called out. "Wen!"

No answer. She had no way of knowing if Dharr and Wen had survived the blast. But either way, there was no getting through. She was cut off.

The smoke was turning thicker by the second as the air flowing through the gash in the tower fueled the blaze. She coughed again, tasting ash and smoke.

Her eyes darted to the shattered window. She inched forward and peeked down. Her stomach clenched. The beams and ledges were wide enough to climb, but she'd never make it all the way down. She was good, but not that good. She looked up. The overhang to the rooftop was less than fifty feet up.

Charred debris swirled in fiery eddies as the wall of fire advanced. She had only two choices, stay and burn or try to make it to the roof. One meant certain death, the other gave her a fighting chance.

She crept out onto the narrow ledge.

———

PAUL AND TASHA rounded the corner into the vast atrium. Crowded with hundreds of Rathadi only an hour ago, it stood completely deserted.

Without warning, Paul's vision dimmed, and his feet gave out from under him.

"Tasha!" he cried, crumbling to the floor.

Tasha glanced over her shoulder.

"Paul!" She doubled back and bent over him.

Paul looked up in a haze. Above Tasha's head, flares sparked on the glass copula. *What are those strange lights?*

The beating of helicopter blades reached him an instant before the dome shattered into a thousand pieces.

A dark flash in his peripheral vision was his only warning as a black-clad body slammed Tasha to the ground and another covered him, protecting them from the glass shards raining down. When the lethal shower ended, the figure pushed him against a marble fountain.

"Stay down!" Paul recognized Tef's voice from behind the visor. A second later, a dozen ropes uncoiled from the sky, followed by figures dressed in tactical gear, rappelling down.

Tef pushed off him and knelt in a shooter's stance. She fired three rounds from her automatic rifle then ducked behind the cover again. One of the intruders slid down the rope and crashed to the ground with a thud.

A moment later, bullets strafed their cover. Paul pressed his body against the cold marble, trying to stave off the panic.

A battery of automatic weapons fired from behind him. Paul panicked, checking his body, but he had all his arms and legs. A moment later several thuds rang through the atrium as more of the attackers fell from the ropes. Paul risked a glance back. A dozen Hybrids fired in formation from behind a short wall. Tasha and the Rathadi who shielded her were retreating for the cover.

Tef grabbed his shoulder and pushed him back. "Stay behind me!" she ordered.

She moved back, shielding him with her body as they fell back. Mid-step, Tef staggered and collapsed.

"Tef!" Paul cried. He summoned his remaining strength and dragged her behind cover again. She lay on the ground, writhing.

He lifted her helmet. Her skin glistened with sweat and blood filled her eyes. She wheezed.

"Tef!" he yelled, grasping her shoulders.

She snapped back at the sound of his voice, seeming to recover for a heartbeat. She reached down and pulled a pen-sized cylinder from a thigh pocket, curled her fist around it, then drove it into her leg.

Her body contorted with another spasm, and she screamed. A moment later, her eyes regained focus.

"What's happening?" he asked.

"Infection," she breathed.

Infection?

He pointed at the cylinder. "Is that a cure?"

"No," she said. "It boosts the immune system, slows it down…" she said between breaths, "and endorphins."

Paul pointed to the attackers. "Are those…?"

"Pureans," Tef hissed. She took another two breaths to recover then pushed to her knees and reached for her helmet.

"Let's move!" she ordered.

They pulled back for the cover once again. Another salvo of shots opened up. Tef jerked as several bullets impacted her body armor. One bullet whizzed by Paul's head and shattered a glass panel a few feet behind him. After what seemed like an eternity in the hailstorm of bullets, they hurdled over the short wall and collapsed behind cover.

Paul's vision blurred. Tef winced. "Paul, your eyes!" she called out.

One of the Rathadi rushed for him as the others continued firing, holding back the Pureans.

"You brought this on us!" Heru-pa screamed and pinned him to the ground. Paul gasped for breath.

"Stop!" Tef yelled. "The enemy is out there, not here!"

"We can't trust them!" Heru-pa fired back. "They brought the disease with them!"

"Let him go!" Tasha pleaded. "He didn't do anything! I think it was me…"

Heru-pa released Paul and pointed his weapon at her. "You?"

"You don't have the symptoms," Tef challenged.

"I… I don't understand it either, but Yuri Korzo, the scientist who works for Nephthys, he injected me—"

Heru-pa rushed Tasha.

Tef stepped into his path. "Enough! We have a job to do. We must hold them off until the civilians evacuate!"

Heru-pa tensed before backing off. He waved over another Rathadi soldier.

"Guard them," he spat.

"But we can help!" Tasha cried.

"Do not let them get away," Heru-pa addressed the soldier, ignoring Tasha. "I will deal with them later." He stormed off.

Tef put a hand on Paul's shoulder and followed Heru-pa.

The Rathadi soldier positioned himself at the wall and eyed them warily as Tasha knelt beside Paul.

"How are you?" she asked.

Paul swallowed, trying to hold back the bile in his throat as he lay on the floor, panting. He shifted his gaze over Tasha's head when a flicker of a movement on the tower above the shattered dome caught his attention. A cold wash swept through him when he recognized the shape clinging to the glass wall. He pulled Tasha closer.

"We're looking for Alyssa, right?" he whispered.

"Yeah?" she replied.

"I just found her."

Tasha followed his eyes. "What...?"

Paul squeezed Tasha's hand. "You have to get up to that tower," Paul said. "I'll never make it—" he glanced at the Rathadi—"but I can help you get there."

Tasha nodded in understanding.

A moment later Paul screamed, thrashing his body.

Tasha recoiled. "Help him!" she yelled to the Rathadi soldier.

The soldier rushed to Paul and sank down next to him. He leaned over. Paul marshalled all the power in his shoulders and heaved himself at the Rathadi, pulling him down into a bear hug.

Tasha lurched up and into the corridor.

The Rathadi freed one of his arms and slammed his elbow into Paul's ribs. What air Paul had left was knocked from him and pain danced in front of his eyes. The Rathadi pivoted and lifted his weapon at Tasha. Paul drove his leg into the back of the soldier's knee. The Rathadi fired, but the shots went high, slamming into the ceiling above Tasha's head. An instant later, she vanished into the stairwell. Paul breathed out, trembling. He glanced up—just in time to see the stock of the soldier's weapon plunge at his face.

———

ANOTHER GUST HAMMERED into Alyssa as she scaled up the wall of glass. She fought to ignore the throbbing in her hands and the cuts from the rough edges of metal protruding from the building. Steel and glass were nothing like any rock she had ever tackled, but the drop beneath her was a strong motivator for learning quickly and for adapting her moves.

Soon, her fingers and feet found useful notches and grooves. She didn't think about each action, she just kept moving. Before long, she was twenty feet above the shattered window. Adrenaline flowed through her veins, and she surged with body heat despite the frigid wind biting at her. She forced herself to keep her eyes above her hands, but the darkness of the glass and multitude of reflections confounded her vision, enveloping her in a vertical glass labyrinth.

Another explosion shook the building. Her right hand slipped, and she lost her grip. She somehow managed to find a ledge with the tips of her fingers. She clung to the wall, too afraid to move or breathe, her heart pounding like a gavel, sending cold shivers to every extremity.

She sucked in air and tried to calm herself, focusing only on her breathing. She erased all other thoughts from her mind and continued the ascent. By the time she reached the overhang for the roof her fingers were raw, her forearms hard as the steel beams she scaled. Breathless and trembling, she appraised the horizontal ledge above her with a pained stare. This part would be hard on a good day, with fresh limbs. She needed a break before challenging it.

She found a wide enough crack between two steel beams

to lock off on her hands. She tried to rest by propping her shoulder against the building and letting each arm hang alternately until she regained some of her strength for the final move. She held on with both hands and swung her feet over her head, locking them into another crack on the overhang. Every fiber of her body screamed as she willed her torso to lift and surge beyond the overhang. She reached for the edge of the roof, adrenaline burning away her pain—and rolled onto the narrow ledge. Relief swept through her, chilling her to the bone like the wind that whipped into her body as she lay exposed on the cold stone, shivering, robbed of all strength.

She lost track of time when a cry of shock followed by a thud echoed from the other side of the short safety barrier that separated her from the roof terrace. She peeked over it just in time to see one of Nephthys's black-clad soldiers crash into the ground lifelessly while another sprawled near the barrier, writhing. Horus covered the distance to a third soldier in a blur, seizing him before he even took a step. His head snapped, and his body collapsed to the rooftop.

The stillness that followed was interrupted by the sound of lazy clapping.

Alyssa froze when she recognized the figure emerging from behind the spire.

"Nephthys," the word left Horus's mouth like a curse.

"Brother." The frost in Nephthys's voice matched the icy glare from her golden eyes.

Horus lunged at her in a blur. Nephthys stepped aside, lightning fast. She drove a fist into his back. He staggered and fell to one knee.

"The millennia have made you nothing if not predictable," Nephthys said.

"Why?" he asked, snarling.

"To repay what Thoth did to my people."

"Your people?" Horus cried. "You are Rathadi! We are your people. You are Thoth's blood!"

"No, Brother. My people are dead. Slaughtered by your hand. And tonight, you shall taste retribution."

Without warning, Nephthys rushed him. The two thin scepters in her hands appeared out of nowhere. A series of rapid strikes and kicks drove him back. She kicked out with her right leg at his head, but he caught it and threw her back. She sailed through the air, flipping. Before she landed, he charged and connected a kick to her torso that sent her flying against the glass spire.

"I will not let you take her!" he growled.

Nephthys lifted her head, a trickle of blood flowing from her lip, but her eyes were victorious. "Her bloodline makes her strong. She will serve her role," she said. "Alyssa will be my vessel."

A bolt of terror passed through Alyssa, pure and undiluted. She rose to her feet behind the barrier, unable to take a breath.

"V-vessel?" she stammered.

Horus's head snapped to her. "You should not be here!"

Nephthys's eyes blazed with triumph. "So, he has not revealed the truth to you?" She rose to her feet.

"The truth?" Alyssa spat. "What do you know of truth?"

"You are the first female offspring in Horus's direct bloodline," Nephthys continued, wiping the blood from her lip.

"Born of a union between your human mother—" she turned to look Horus dead in the eye—"and a Rathadi father."

The words whipped into Alyssa harder than the wind. She staggered. "No…" she murmured, but couldn't put any strength in her words. She reached for Horus. "She's lying. Tell me she's lying. She always lies." A shiver of anger shot through her and her face hardened. "Kade is my father. My mother was a Hybrid!"

Nephthys sneered. "Your mother was human."

Alyssa's eyes seared into Horus. "You… and my mom?"

"He abandoned her when—" Nephthys started.

"Is this true?" Alyssa cried, bile rising up in her throat.

"I was only trying to protect her," Horus uttered, his face caving. "I was—"

The soft metallic clink reached Alyssa's ears an instant before Nephthys hurled one of her silver scepters. The thin rod snapped open, each end splitting into three thin blades. Horus twisted to avoid the lethal projectile. Nephthys closed the distance between them and pressed her other bladed scepter against his throat.

"And so it ends," she whispered. "You shall die knowing that I have taken everything from you. Your Rathadi. Your daughter."

Alyssa's vision blurred, heartbeat pounding in her temples. She spotted the pistol beside Nephthys's slain soldier. She picked it up and lifted it to her own head.

"Stop!" she screamed.

Nephthys turned at her voice. Her eyes widened ever so slightly.

"Call off the attack," Alyssa said.

Two other Purean soldiers rushed onto the roof, their weapons drawn. Nephthys lifted her hand, commanding them to stop.

"Call off the attack, or you can wipe your precious vessel off this roof," Alyssa said, trembling.

Nephthys's lips curved into a smile that iced the blood beneath Alyssa's skin. "We will make a formidable pair," she said, and she pulled the bladed scepter away from Horus's throat.

He moved beside Alyssa.

"You truly are fit to be my vessel," Nephthys said. She spoke a word. Alyssa did not understand it.

Then her body was not her own as she watched herself draw the weapon away from her head and point it at Horus.

She squeezed the trigger.

Again.

And again.

Horus froze. He grimaced, confusion rippling through his face, before he slumped and dropped to the floor. Alyssa pointed the weapon at his head. Everything inside her screamed, yet she stood paralyzed.

"Kill him," Nephthys said.

———

TASHA CRACKED OPEN the door from the stairwell. She moved into the hallway, inside the spire that rose a hundred feet above her head.

The entrance to the roof was blocked by two huge black-clad figures, facing out onto the roof, their backs to her. She swallowed and tightened her fingers around the hilt of the fire axe she borrowed from the emergency box in the stairwell. Not exactly her weapon of choice, but it would suffice. She closed the door behind her silently. She lifted the axe, stalking to the two men. A couple more steps and—

She glimpsed the scene on the roof. Tasha's body went numb, the axe forgotten. Alyssa, moving as if in a trance, stood over Horus at the edge of the roof, pointing a pistol at his head.

"Alyssa!" the scream left Tasha's mouth. The men turned as one and rushed her.

———

THE SCREAM CUT through the trance, filling Alyssa's mind with memories of a past life.

Her eyes found Nephthys, the woman's gaze piercing into her…

…*like the dagger that Nephthys presses against Anja's throat.*

"Give yourself up, Horus," my sister says, "and your lover shall live."

Anja stares at me, her chest rising in shallow, rapid breaths. Gradually, calmness replaces the fear in her eyes.

"No, Horus," she whispers. "Not for me."

Her gaze brushes my soul.

"Take care of our daughter," she says. "Take care of Alyssa."

She wraps her hands around Nephthys's wrist and drives the dagger into her own throat.

"No!" the night fills with…

…Alyssa's scream. She pointed the weapon at Nephthys and fired. The woman's face contorted as the bullet struck her shoulder, spinning her with the impact.

Alyssa aimed again when she spotted the two black-clad figures in the entrance to the roof and—

Tasha?

She didn't have time to think as they lifted their automatic weapons. She dove behind the short wall and pulled Horus's lifeless body beside her an instant before the Purean weapons opened up.

PAUL PRESSED his body against the stone floor, cowering beside the two remaining Rathadi. The smoke churned above his face in the burning air. He covered his mouth and nose with the crook of his elbow to protect his lungs from the searing heat. A racking cough shook through him. He lifted the shirt away from his face. Angry red spots covered the material. He pushed up and leaned against the makeshift barrier, breathing heavily.

He glanced back to the last remaining evacuation pod, waiting to be released and sent down the escape shaft into the underground, joining the others. The Rathadi soldiers slumped inside it, senseless, strapped into their jump seats.

Tef popped up beside him and squeezed off several rounds then crouched down again. The Rathadi had been able to slow the advance of the Pureans, but the illness and number of the intruders were overwhelming them. They had long given up guarding him, needing every weapon to hold off the attack. It was only a question of time before they were overrun. Heru-pa ducked out and fired off several precise shots. For some reason, he and Tasha seemed to be the only ones not affected by the illness.

"We must get to the last pod!" Heru-pa called out.

"Not without Dharr and Wen!" Tef fired back.

"We cannot risk the fate of the others—"

"He will be here!"

Heru-pa lifted his hand to the bracelet. "Two minutes," he said.

Tef nodded then staggered and fell to the ground.

"Tef!" Paul cried out.

He crawled to her and slipped off her helmet. Glossy eyes stared back at him. Whatever last reserve the Rathadi had been riding, it had finally given out.

More shots rang out from the Pureans, muffled cracks in staccato repetition that impacted the wall behind him. Heru-pa ducked out again to shoot, then he froze. Paul followed his eyes to the other side of the atrium.

Dharr staggered into view before collapsing on the ground, a small boy rolling from his arms. The boy clambered up, struggling to pull Dharr behind a tree.

Three Pureans rushed for him.

"Wen!" Heru-pa yelled. "Run!"

The boy lifted his head and scurried toward him on shaky legs.

Heru-pa leaped over the barrier and rushed for him, his armor taking bullets.

A Purean almost made it to Wen. He reached for him when the boy dodged him like a jackrabbit then cut around a second soldier and continued for Heru-pa with faltering steps. The third Purean stretched for the boy when he dropped to the ground, taking a hit from Heru-pa's rifle.

Heru-pa hoisted the boy and shielded him with his body as they retreated to the barrier. He lifted the boy into Paul's arms and spun, rushing back for Dharr.

Paul spotted the little gray canister bouncing in front of the barrier an instant before a deafening blast tore through the atrium. Paul flew back, arms outstretched, showered by a deadly rainfall of concrete, glass, and steel.

He lay on the ground, curled up and unable to move, blind and deaf, save for the banshees shrieking in his ears.

Paul groaned. He twisted his head to the boy and Tef, both sprawled on the ground. He coughed, spitting up blood, his breathing coming in ragged gasps.

He summoned his remaining strength and willed himself across the floor to Tef. He pulled one of the cylinders from her thigh pocket and drove it into his leg, triggering the injection.

The pain in his head and pounding of his heart was instantaneous. He screamed, cold sweat flooding his body, as his heart threatened to pound out of his chest. An instant later it was over. His vision cleared. He felt stronger.

He lifted Wen and staggered to the evacuation pod. He strapped the boy into the seat among the other unconscious Rathadi then shuffled back for Tef and pulled her inside the pod, his strength ebbing with every step. He collapsed on top of her and lifted his hand to the release button.

Paul yelped as he was yanked from the pod by his legs. The huge shape came out of nowhere, barreling into him. On instinct, he swung at the giant's head and connected with his jaw, buying himself a split second. Paul flipped and scrambled on his hands and knees for the escape pod. He almost made it to the hatch when the Purean lunged onto him.

He drove two quick punches into Paul's ribs, knocking the wind out of him, and flipped him onto his back. As Paul gasped for air, he kept trying to use his legs to lift up the attacker's body, but it was like being pinned underneath a truck. Paul stretched his hand desperately into the pod, trying to reach the release lever. The giant threw a punch to Paul's head that rattled his teeth then clamped his huge hands around Paul's throat. Paul twisted and writhed his torso, but he was losing the battle. His vision began to close in.

Paul forced the darkness from the periphery of his vision and reached up to Tef's body inside the pod, desperately fumbling to the pocket on her thigh. He clamped his fist around one of the cylinders. His strength fading, he pulled it out and drove it into the Purean's neck.

The giant froze, then screamed, his body spasming.

Paul stretched his arm as far as he could into the escape pod and flipped the release lever, barely getting his limb back before the metal door slammed down and into the Purean. He gasped for air as he watched the light over the hatch turn green, signaling that the pod had released successfully, then he collapsed.

———

"HOLD YOUR FIRE!" Nephthys bellowed. "I want her alive and undamaged."

The firing stopped.

Alyssa hunkered on the ledge, her back flattened against the short wall. She pressed her hands against Horus's wounds, desperately trying to stem the flow of blood. Pure terror surged through her veins. Her body shook. Her mind refused to believe what had just happened.

What she had just done.

"Where are you going to go, Alyssa?" Nephthys's voice rang out, mocking.

A flame curled in the pit of Alyssa's stomach, rising up to her chest. Her fingers coiled around the pistol as the blood rose to her cheeks.

Alyssa snarled.

She ducked out and fired her weapon, a feral scream escaping her lips. The shots went wild, but Nephthys and her soldiers took cover.

"You are only delaying the inevitable," Nephthys called out.

Alyssa rose from behind the wall and fired, pumping the trigger again and again until the slide locked.

The silence still echoed in her ears when the soldiers cautiously ventured from behind their covers. Nephthys stood at the entrance to the building, a triumphant shine in her eyes despite the crimson stain on her shoulder.

A palm grasped Alyssa's arm. Horus stirred. His eyelid fluttered open.

He's alive!

She fell to her knees beside him. "I'm sorry... I'm so sorry..." she whimpered.

"It was not you," Horus whispered between ragged breaths.

Her eyes stung with tears as the Purean soldiers stalked

toward them. She crumbled beside him, inhaling a trembling breath. She stared at her hands, stained with his blood. The guilt clawed at her chest, wilting the fire inside her to an icy numbness.

A gust of wind whipped away the hair from her face. Darkness swirled, pulling her in. She gazed into the emptiness below. Her jaw tightened, and her breathing grew harder.

I will never be her vessel.

She squeezed Horus's hand.

I'm sorry…

Alyssa closed her eyes and veered to the edge.

Her palm grazed the bracelet on his forearm. Her mind leaped.

The plane!

Alyssa held her breath as she tapped the bracelet. It activated. She pressed the triangular symbol for the plane and the sequence Dharr showed her to summon it. A moment later the twin jet engines spun up on the tower below. She rose to her feet again, facing Nephthys and the Pureans. Nephthys's lips curved into a cold smile.

"You will be a worthy—"

The jet appeared behind Alyssa. The Pureans stopped in mid-stride. Nephthys dashed inside the building an instant before the automatic guns on the jet erupted.

———

HERU-PA WOKE to the heat and the sound of his own coughing. Thick black clouds choked the air, billowing into the high atrium, hungry flames rolling outward. The once majestic space cracked and wilted under the weight of the fire, glass and metal mixing into a fiery inferno.

A stir from his bracelet forced his eyes from the ghastly view. He glanced at the alert. The jet had been launched.

Horus?

A moan rang out beside him.

Dharr!

Memories flooded back as a fresh spat of flames belched out with a growled rush of heat and smoke. Heru-pa's eyes scanned the space, searching for a path through the flames. Any escape route down had been completely blocked off by the debris and flame. He rose to his feet and lifted Dharr then staggered to the stairwell, heading for the roof.

————

THE PLANE HOVERED JUST beyond the rooftop, and the ramp lowered to the ledge as more explosions rattled the building. Alyssa grunted, struggling to help Horus to his feet. She half-dragged, half-carried him into the jet.

They collapsed on the floor as the ramp closed behind them and the jet lifted. She knelt at Horus's side, panting.

"The consciousness..." He swallowed, his face knotting with pain.

"We must find Heru-pa!" Alyssa cried.

His fingers locked around her arm. "There is no time..." He locked his gaze on her.

Alyssa froze, her heart thudding in her throat, as the meaning of the words sank in.

"No!" she cried, her voice cracking. "Heru-pa is your heir! I am... I am nobody!"

"You are my daughter," he whispered. "I should have told you sooner. I... I am sorry... I was trying to protect you." His breathing grew slow and shallow.

"Don't speak," she pleaded.

"Your mother, she wasn't looking for the Hall." His words came out slowly, between labored breaths. "She was looking for me."

"I know... I know that now."

His face twisted again.

"The legacy... it must be preserved."

Alyssa caved. Her tears flowed unchecked down her cheeks and dripped from her chin. She kneeled at his side, still as a statue.

"It is time," Horus said.

He took a slow breath, as if to gather all of his remaining energy. Alyssa willed her muscles to move and helped him to his knees. He placed his palms on Alyssa's head, his thumbs and forefingers forming a triangle.

"I don't know what to do..." she sobbed, his touch waking shivers under her skin.

"Open your mind to me," he whispered. Their gazes locked.

"You are the legacy of Ra," he said, his voice whispering away.

His eye closed.

Alyssa trembled, tears streaming down her cheeks. She focused on her breathing. A memory. Her mother's eyes...

I am Alyssa Morgan.

Daughter of Horus and Anja.

A blaze of light flooded her mind.

I shall know no fear.

Then darkness.

———

THE SMOKE BILLOWED THICKER with every step as Heru-pa clambered up the last few stairs, heaving, clutching Dharr in his arms. Another explosion tore through the building, pushing him onto the roof. He tapped his bracelet. Several long second later the jet appeared and touched down on the landing pad, lowering the ramp.

Heru-pa lumbered inside. He stopped, his mind rejecting the abomination before him.

Horus and Alyssa knelt, facing each other. His father's clothes were stained with blood, his palms on Alyssa's head, locked together in the sacred bond of legacy.

Dharr slipped from his arms and hit the floor, moaning.

Heru-pa roared. He rushed at Alyssa, his hand coiled around the hilt of his knife.

"Stop!" Dharr's voice rang through the cabin. "She is your sister!" Dharr's voice was weak, but the words cut through Heru-pa, freezing him to the floor.

He spun, his eyes burning bright with betrayal. "You lie!" he spat.

"In the name of Ra," Dharr's voice rasped. "I speak true."

Heru-pa dropped the knife and collapsed beside Horus. He placed a hand on his chest, staring at his blood-soaked shirt.

Horus's hands slipped off Alyssa's head and he slumped into Heru-pa's arms.

Alyssa's chest rose and fell.

"Alyssa?" Dharr moaned. He staggered to her.

Her eyelids fluttered.

"Alyssa, are you—?"

The word died in his throat as she opened her eyes, yellow irises staring back at him.

———

NEPHTHYS STOOD on the spired tower and watched the jet take off from the landing pad on the tower across from the shattered dome. The blood pounded in her ears when she faced the girl on the floor. The girl's violet eyes glared at her, defiantly, her back against the wall.

"You have robbed me of my prize." Nephthys's words were barely a whisper through her clenched jaw.

Yuri Korzo shuffled beside Nephthys, clearing his throat. "Her immunity to the ancient bioweapon is a promising development," he offered meekly. "While we could not have predicted it, you have my assurance that we will get to the bottom of it." He drew near the girl, a ghoulish smile on his face. "By the time I am through with you, Miss Renley, I shall know your deepest secrets."

The girl pressed her lips together into a white line.

The door opened, and two other Purean soldiers stepped onto the roof, lugging a body between them. They threw the young man on the floor.

The girl rushed to him. "Paul!"

His eyes fluttered open. "Tasha?" he croaked, his eyes glossy.

Korzo's smile evaporated. He rushed to the girl and yanked her head back.

"Your name is Tasha?" his voice trembled. "Where were you born?"

"St. Petersburg," she said, her lip curling.

His hands shook as he pushed back the sleeve of her right arm. He spotted a small round scar on her upper arm, and he withered. He faced Nephthys with a pained stare.

"It's not the Horus virus to which the girl is immune," he said. "She is immune to smallpox. The Horus virus never had a chance to infect her."

Nephthys pursed her lips. "Yet you claimed vaccinations to smallpox have been discontinued," she said, her voice tight. "That there was no natural immunity to it?"

"The vaccinations continued for much longer in Eastern Europe. I... I thought since she was Renley's daughter—"

"Lord Renley adopted me when I was a child," Tasha interrupted, a smile building as she seemed to sense Yuri Korzo's distress. "My birth name is Natasha Mendeva."

Korzo sank to the floor.

Nephthys inhaled deeply.

"Well, Miss *Mendeva*, it turns out you are not as useful to me as I had hoped." She eyed the trio before them. "However, two of you could still be used as bargaining chips for my vessel. I have no use for the third one."

She motioned two of her men, who seized Korzo's arms and hauled him to the edge of the tower. His eyes bulged as realization struck.

"No, please!" he wailed.

Nephthys gave a small nod. Yuri Korzo's scream rang into

the night as he plummeted through the flames and billowing smoke, fading out long before his body struck the ground.

Nephthys faced the pair as her choppers drew near. "I hope that you are as dear to Alyssa Morgan as I think you are," she whispered, her voice barely audible, "for your sake."

THE CONSTANT HUM of the jet hovered above the silent void inside Alyssa as she stood in the cramped cabin. The sterile metal surfaces added to the chill in her blood, a coldness that brought the synapses in her brain to a standstill.

Dharr lay before her in a narrow cot, the needle in his arm connected to the saline bag above his head. His breathing seemed less labored than it was when she first brought him into the medical bay. She had transfused him some of her blood, hoping to slow the infection. Heru-pa seemed just as unaffected by the disease, at least so far, as she has been. He hadn't moved from Horus's side since he had come on board, completely ignoring Alyssa as he held a silent vigil over his father's body in the aft cabin.

Dharr's eyes fluttered open.

"Where am—?" The rest of the sentence was reduced to a fit of coughing.

Alyssa lifted his head as the spasms seized his body. Dark soot mixed with drops of blood splattered the inside of the oxygen mask on his face. He lifted it over his head and wiped his mouth with his sleeve. Alyssa pulled the mask back down over his mouth and nose.

"You have to keep this on. You inhaled a lot of smoke."

Dharr looked like he was about to argue, but his lips tightened, and he nodded. His wheezing calmed, and he took deep, steady breaths.

"We're on the jet," Alyssa said, "on our way to meet the others." Her throat tightened when the image of Tasha's limp body lying at Nephthys's feet flashed across her mind.

Not all of them...

Alyssa took a steeling breath before asking. "Did Paul make it out?"

"He was with the others during the evacuation. He should be on one of the transports," Dharr replied.

She exhaled, closing her eyes. Tears welled up behind her eyelids when the door opened.

Heru-pa shot her a scathing glance from the doorway. "You have brought this upon us."

Alyssa wanted to argue, to deny it, but she could not find the strength as she stared at the pain hidden beneath the rage in his gaze. Tears threatened again to fill her eyes, but she refused to let them come.

"Can the illness be cured?" Dharr broke the silence.

"I received a message from Bes," Heru-pa replied, his face glum. "They are working on slowing it down, but it continues to mutate." His lips pressed into a tight line. "It will eventually destroy the Rathadi."

Alyssa's stomach roiled at his words. "There must be something we can do!" she cried, her mind racing. "And why are you and I not affected?"

Heru-pa glared at her, unblinking. He showed no flicker of acknowledgement.

Dharr swallowed. "Thoth's weapon can never harm Horus's direct descendants."

"Is that why Nephthys wanted me? Because I'm a direct descendant?"

Heru-pa drew near, his face a handspan from hers. "You may be Horus's bastard child, but you will never be a true Rathadi," he seethed. "You are an abomination." He turned on his heel and left.

Alyssa stood, frozen. A bitter taste choked her mouth.

Dharr touched her hand. "It is his grief speaking."

What if he's right?

"It should have been Heru-pa, not me," she said.

"There was no time," Dharr said. "Heru-pa knows it, even if he cannot admit it to himself." He squeezed her hand. "You preserved the legacy."

Alyssa stood in sullen silence. She swallowed to gain her voice. "I thought I would have his memories," she said finally.

"Your brain would be overwhelmed if it attempted to absorb eons of memories in a single instant," he said. "The memories will reveal themselves to you in time, and with decades of meditation and guidance."

Alyssa nodded slowly.

Dharr's jaw tightened, as if to steady himself before speaking. "Some of the Rathadi may share Heru-pa's reluctance to accept what has occurred, but you shall always have my support."

Alyssa gave him a blank look. "Why would you want to help me?"

"It was Horus's last command that I protect you with my life."

Alyssa stared at the floor, teeth gnawing at her lip. Another long silence stretched, with each lost in their own thoughts, before Dharr finally spoke.

"How did Horus die?"

Alyssa's knees weakened as a cold wash swept through her. She pressed the heels of her hands to her eyes, gathering herself. She raised her head.

"Nephthys killed him," she said, forcing the tremor from her voice.

Dharr studied her for several heartbeats before Alyssa turned, afraid that her face would betray her. She leaned a hand against the wall, her knees trembling.

The memory of the shots echoed like cracks of thunder. With each crack, pain jolted through her, bolts searing one after another through her head, flashing the image before her.

His eye burning through her, wide with shock and betrayal.

The pressure built up in her chest, robbing her breath. The tears welled up from deep inside, cold trails streaming freely down her cheeks.

Forgive me, Father…

END OF BOOK TWO

ACKNOWLEDGMENTS

This book would not have been possible without the unending support of my amazing family who continue to be my first readers, Vera, Sarah, Misha, and Heather. Thank you for always being there for me, no matter the time of day—or night—and for letting me interrupt whatever you might be doing to hear out my excited, "I just thought of something! What if Alyssa/Horus/Paul were to...?" Your honest opinion, support and patience will forever be appreciated.

A special thank you to my daughter, Sarah, for keeping me grounded in the world and mind of a precocious teenager and for (once again) agreeing to write an author's bio for her old man.

A debt of gratitude goes out to my intrepid beta readers: Shohinee Deb, Calais Fitzmaurice, Amber Hodges, Carlos Mock, Matt Paauw, and Mike Snodgrass. Your feedback and insightful comments helped make this a better book. On behalf of all the readers, thank you.

Phil Athans, editor extraordinaire, thank you for continuing to lend your sharp eyes, astute criticism, and sage advice. It is a privilege to work with you.

Igor Reshetnikov, once again, for the beautiful cover art. People say you shouldn't judge a book by its cover. Authors can only hope for that to happen if your work graces their books.

Scott George, Christy Lumm, and Sue Ardelji from Hampton Roads Academy for taking time to discuss the ever-evolving rules of the English language with me.

My wife, Vera, for her infinite and tireless support with every single aspect of this book. You have my love and endless gratitude.

Finally, a thank you to all of you, my readers for allowing me to share my worlds with you. Your enthusiasm and support mean more to me than I can express in words.

As always, any and all errors in this work rest squarely on my own shoulders.

A SIXTEEN-YEAR-OLD'S
OPINIONATED AND UPDATED
BIOGRAPHY ON THE DARK ELF M.
SASINOWSKI

Have my thoughts on my dearest, darling father changed in the past year? I am sixteen now, so do I now realize that it is super-awesome that this is Dad's second book or that he is radically cooler now? Will this bio be different because I, myself, am more mature and can write a far-superior-yet-equally-as-funny author biography?

Umm... no.

To catch y'all up with the times, Dad is now re-married, and he also has a stepson (which means I have a step brother!) Although divorced, he is also best friends with my mom. It may be a weird family, but it is an awesome one and none of us would trade it for anything. It may not be a nuclear family, but we're the bomb!

What else can I say about the old man? He has a broadsword on top of his writing desk, he won a couple of international awards for Heir of Ra, he listens to alternative as well as classic rock... and yet he is still somehow an uber-geek. Honestly, how does he do that? It baffles me.

However, he often surprises me with bits of both nerdiness mixed with actual coolness (please don't tell him I said that...)

I recently discovered that he knows all the words to Madonna's *Like A Prayer* and my life will be forever changed. He also played Dungeons and Dragons as a kid, which we as a family have picked up again. (I get to be the Dungeon Master; he uses his creative juice on the Blood of Ra.) He also has a collection of original Star Wars action figurines that he keeps in a hand-made spaceship in his office.

Bear-looking puppies and Nazgûl on Fell Beasts, foreign movies on Netflix and point-five past light speed, blasters set to stun and the one precious ring, these are a few of his favorite things! (to the tune of that song)

See y'all when Dad finishes his third book! Don't forget to check out our website, Facebook, and Instagram pages for updates!

Sarah

WWW.HEIROFRA.COM

facebook.com/heirofra

instagram.com/heirofra_book

amazon.com/author/msasinowski